"Things are changing, Jonas.

"If you weren't so darned thickheaded, you'd see it."

"But I also know that people have to be fundamentally compatible to make a relationship work."

Whitney glared at him. "Oh, that sounds so rational! What are you going to do, Jonas, make every woman you meet take a psychological profile test? What about feelings? What about chemistry? You talk about letting go of the reins, but that's the one thing you'll never do, not where your emotions are concerned."

"Don't tempt me, Whitney."

"What do you think I've been trying to to do all night?"

His laughter was rich and free and infectious. Before she could decide whether to laugh with him, Whitney found herself pulled against a hard chest. "You want me to cut loose? All right, Whitney, but don't complain if you don't like it...."

ABOUT THE AUTHOR

Jacqueline Diamond is a former news reporter and editor whose career included four years with the Associated Press in L.A. Now a full-time novelist, she continues to write theater stories free-lance for AP and recently interviewed Christopher Reeve, Michael York, Alan Bates and Andrew Stevens. She lives with her husband and son in La Habra, California.

In *Capers and Rainbows* she picks up with Whitney Greystone, who first burst upon the scene in #218 *Unlikely Partners* as a flighty heiress who took over her family-owned Brite Cola company and ran into trouble with its CEO, Jonas Ameling.

Books by Jacqueline Diamond

HARLEQUIN AMERICAN ROMANCE

Don't miss any of our special offers. Write to us at the following address for information on our newest releases.

Harlequin Reader Service
901 Fuhrmann Blvd., P.O. Box 1397, Buffalo, NY 14240
Canadian address: P.O. Box 603,
Fort Erie, Ont. L2A 5X3

Capers and Rainbows
Jacqueline Diamond

Harlequin Books

TORONTO • NEW YORK • LONDON
AMSTERDAM • PARIS • SYDNEY • HAMBURG
STOCKHOLM • ATHENS • TOKYO • MILAN

For Lenore and Arthur

Published November 1988

First printing September 1988

ISBN 0-373-16270-7

Prologue

Mickey Mouse hadn't uttered so much as a squeak this morning.

Whitney Greystone rolled over on her water bed and stared at the Disney clock in disgust. She must have switched the alarm off in her sleep sometime last night.

From the clear September sunshine flooding through the bedroom window of her second-story apartment, Whitney gathered it was already well past eight o'clock. If she didn't hurry, she was going to be late. With a yawn, she threw off the covers and sat up, then groaned as she felt her back muscles stiffen.

Mornings just weren't Whitney's best time. Especially when she could hear the lulling murmur of water lapping at the beach a few hundred feet away. The sound always made her feel like curling under the covers and catching a few more winks.

Well, it was her own fault, she reflected as she pulled on her brightly decorated silk kimono. By mistake, she pushed her hands into the long hanging part of the sleeve, then had to wriggle them free.

Right now, Whitney could be living a life of indolent luxury. After all, most people still thought of her as the madcap heiress who got into one scrape or another on behalf of her latest pet charity or some waif she'd taken under her wing. But that had all come to an end two years ago. Well, at least the lazy part had; somehow Whitney still found herself falling for every hard-luck story that came her way.

Only she didn't have time for that anymore. Not since she'd taken over as chief executive officer of Brite Cola, struggling to save the company her father had founded from the three years of gross mismanagement inflicted on it by her half brother Gavin.

Whitney had been determined to prevent the company's sale to a conglomerate, and slowly she'd seen her efforts pay off. Brite Cola wasn't out of the woods yet, but at least she could see daylight once in a while.

Thinking of daylight made Whitney blink. She really shouldn't have stayed up until two o'clock, but a couple of old friends from the drug rehabilitation clinic where she used to volunteer had dropped by, and she'd felt obligated to dole out Brite Cola and sympathy while they brought her up-to-date on their lives.

Still unsure that she could be counted among the living, Whitney staggered into the tiled bathroom and splashed cold water on her face. Then she examined herself critically in the mirror, trying to see herself as Jonas Ameling would see her at their meeting later this morning. Well, not much later. Nine-thirty, to be precise.

She'd read descriptions of herself in the press often enough to know what adjectives the reporters used. A tawny mane of hair, light green eyes—were they becoming flecked with brown, or were they just bloodshot this morning?—and usually someone managed to mention her long legs. She'd been called the ultimate California girl so often that Whitney wished she'd grown up in Idaho.

And even though she was twenty-eight, she still looked about five years younger, which was just the opposite of what she wanted. Wouldn't you think when a person got to be near thirty that she'd take on a certain patina, an aura of maturity?

As she rinsed out her mouth, Whitney had to admit that age simply wasn't helping. In Jonas's eyes, she was still the same flaky kid he'd known all his life.

Oh, sure, they'd managed to work together on a more or less professional level these past two years since he'd become president of Brite Cola and nominally her boss, although he lived in Northern California at the Ameling Vineyards, which he had inherited and ran superbly. He'd kept his word about not interfering too much with Whitney's ideas, and he'd even offered a few grudging compliments about the way she'd improved staff morale at the plant.

But Jonas was nine years older and not the least bit interested in Whitney romantically. And maybe he was right; after all, they were total opposites in their life-styles and personalities.

Whitney shuffled into the kitchenette and drew back the curtains from the glass doors that opened onto the balcony.

Below, sunlight glinted off the colorful sail of a catamaran skimming across Newport Harbor. The beach here on Balboa Island was serenely empty except for a woman walking a dog. *Thank goodness* school was back in session.

Whitney popped some rye bread into the toaster and stuck a mug of Brite Cola in the microwave oven. Heating it up as a breakfast drink was one of her ideas that hadn't panned out yet, but she was sure its day would come.

When everything was ready, Whitney took a sip and swirled the soft drink around in her mouth, the way she'd seen Jonas do with his best estate cabernet sauvignon. Of course, Brite Cola wasn't in the same class as the products of Ameling Vineyards, but it did have a unique tang of cherry, lime and coconut. It was still made from the original recipe devised by Whitney's grandfather at his drugstore during the Depression.

Whitney took a bite of toast and then nearly knocked over her cola as a tremendous crash shook the apartment. For one disoriented moment she thought Southern California was finally getting its much-heralded earthquake, then realized the noise had come from downstairs.

She would have ignored it, except for the series of girlish shrieks that followed, along with cries of "Oh, no!" and "I was nowhere near it!" and "How are we going to pay for that?"

I've done it again, Whitney thought glumly. I've fallen for another hard-luck story. Will I never learn?

Still carrying her toast, she thrust her feet into a pair of thong sandals and flapped down the exterior wooden staircase, coughing a little in the fresh salt breeze and trying to keep the kimono from flying up above her knees.

Buying this two-story, two-unit building was another one of her ideas that hadn't exactly worked as planned.

It had made good sense at the time. Whitney never liked to buy herself status symbols like expensive cars and beachfront homes, but she *had* been tired of that tacky apartment in a singles complex a few miles inland. So she'd compromised by buying this duplex. The idea was to live in the upstairs apartment herself and use the lower one for visiting VIPs at Brite Cola and for a-week-at-the-beach prizes to outstanding employees.

Only there always seemed to be someone who desperately needed a place to live for a few months.

Last time it had been a mother with three school-age children who claimed they'd been unfairly evicted from their previous home. The second day, the kids had shredded the curtains and broken a window while their mom sat in the bedroom glued to her favorite soap opera. After giving them the first month's rent for another apartment, Whitney had reluctantly sent them packing.

This time it was three ditsy sophomores from the University of California at Irvine who'd begged to rent the place and sworn they just couldn't find one anywhere else close enough to commute to campus by bicycle, since none of them could afford a car.

So Whitney had agreed to let them move in. Just for this school year.

With a sigh she knocked on the door.

One of the girls answered it, a guilty look plastered onto her face. Whitney couldn't remember whether this one was Mindy, Candy or Sarajane. All three girls had light brown hair and dark tans, although Candy was a little blonder than the others.

"What happened?" Whitney asked as she downed the last of her toast.

"Well, we were moving the furniture around and we kind of knocked over a lamp," the girl said.

One of her roommates appeared with the damaged appliance, a mock-Tiffany lamp with "Brite Cola" worked into the stained glass. "Was it real expensive?"

"Maybe we could pay for it on time," said the third girl.

Before answering, Whitney peered past her and saw that the tastefully subdued furnishings—selected by a decorator—had been rearranged so that the sofa was in full sunlight, while everything else was half smothered beneath piles of damp bathing suits and beach towels.

"Put everything back the way it was." The note of authority in Whitney's voice brought immediate nods from the girls. "You're going to ruin that sofa. Don't you know colors fade in sunlight? And hang your damp clothes in the bathroom. Understand?"

There was a round of agreement.

"I'll deduct the lamp from your security deposit," she finished, then remembered she hadn't collected one. "Oh, fudge. Well…never mind. But if you damage anything else, out you go."

Clearly intimidated, the girls chorused their apologies, and Whitney trudged back up the steps.

Somehow the encounter left her feeling off balance, she reflected as she slid back her closet doors to pick an outfit for the day. Maybe it was because seeing those three fluffheads reminded her that she wasn't a kid anymore. Or maybe it reminded her of how far she still had to go.

Take this wardrobe, for instance. Whitney frowned, examining the splashy silk dresses and prewashed designer jeans that suited the extremes of her onetime life-style a lot more than her current role as chief executive officer.

Not that she hadn't picked out a couple of tailored suits, with the help of her best friend, Sarah McCord. But she'd forgotten to retrieve them from the cleaners yesterday.

Finally Whitney settled on a tweed skirt and a tailored blouse. It ought to be restrained enough for Jonas, and that was the goal, wasn't it?

She tossed the clothes onto the bed and was heading for the shower when the phone rang.

It was the organizer of a Halloween charity auction for which Whitney had volunteered to serve as emcee. The woman wanted to be sure Whitney would wear something truly outrageous, which was what people had come to expect of her. "After all, you're our biggest draw," the caller pointed out.

Whitney was beginning to wish she hadn't offered her services, but it was too late to back out now. "I'm going to rent a costume. Maybe a Renaissance gown..."

"You've got to be kidding!" The woman's voice shot up an octave. "Everybody remembers how you showed up a few years ago as a blueberry muffin. And what about the time you dressed as a bag of laundry? You can't disappoint them!"

"How about if I come as a lady executive? That should really shock everybody." Whitney immediately regretted her sarcasm. "Don't worry. Maybe I'll disguise myself as a file cabinet."

It was an off-the-top-of-the-head remark, but the organizer seized on the idea. "Terrific! Can we send some photos to the press ahead of time? The more tickets we sell, the more money for the Save-the-Homeless Foundation."

"Okay." It took a few more minutes to disentangle herself from the conversation, but at last Whitney was on her way to the shower. Her terrifically efficient secretary, Mattie Brown, would be able to find a suitable costume designer, Whitney felt sure. Only how did one dress up as a file cabinet?

The hot water felt wonderful on Whitney's sleep-cramped muscles. She adjusted the shower head to send streams of water pulsating against her back, and closed her eyes to relish the sensation.

It took a moment to realize that the doorbell was ringing. Now what troubles had the terrible trio downstairs managed to get themselves into?

Muttering to herself, Whitney toweled off quickly, jerked off her shower cap, pulled on her kimono and dashed for the door. She yanked it open, poised to deliver a tongue-lashing, and then stopped in dismay.

"Good morning." Jonas managed to infuse the simple words with heavy irony. "Off to a late start, are we?"

"I'm sorry." Whitney always seemed to be apologizing to him, she reflected. But what else could she say? It was obviously way past nine-thirty. He must have come here from her office, figuring he'd waste half the morning if he waited for her to show up.

Besides, the sight of Jonas Ameling standing outside her door was enough to render any woman speechless at this hour of the day. Or any hour.

His three-piece tailored suit only managed to emphasize the lean masculinity of the body inside. And there was something riveting about the way his eyes were boring into Whitney's. As usual, too, she had to resist the impulse to reach up and ruffle that perfectly trimmed reddish-brown hair with the startling streak of salt-and-pepper gray in front.

"I lost track of the time." As she stepped back to let him in, Whitney suddenly remembered what she was wearing. Or rather, wasn't wearing.

She could feel the sea breeze play over the deep V on her breasts left by the half-closed robe, and became aware at the same time that the lower part of the kimono was blowing open at thigh level. And her long blond hair, which she usually tucked into a businesslike twist these days, was falling loose around her shoulders.

"You look like you just got out of the shower." Was that a hint of breathlessness in Jonas's voice?

"I did."

As if by instinct, he reached out to touch a free-floating strand of her hair. A quivering awareness awoke in Whitney, of Jonas as an elemental male. She usually tried hard not to think about him that way, but the unexpectedness of his arrival had stripped away her defenses.

He, too, obviously hadn't been prepared for this intimate an encounter. "You shouldn't open the door that way. A man might get ideas."

"What kind of ideas?" They were so close, Whitney could feel the heat from his body. Jonas was only a few inches taller than her. If she leaned forward, their lips would meet....

He must have been thinking along the same lines, because his jaw tightened and he looked away sharply. "Don't tease me, Whitney. I might do something about it."

And she wanted him to, had wanted him to for years. But she knew only too well that it wouldn't lead anywhere. Instead, it would probably destroy the delicate accord they'd managed to establish.

"Someday I may take you up on that." Whitney tried to keep her tone light as she moved away toward the bedroom. "Just a minute and I'll make myself presentable."

Without waiting for a response, she hurried in and closed the door. Her fingers were numb as she pulled on a slip and the skirt and blouse, and it took quite a struggle to work her legs into the panty hose. Whitney's whole body felt as if it were on fire. *We could be in here together....*

But now that she was calming down, she really couldn't imagine Jonas doing anything like that. No doubt he would come to his senses in a few minutes, and they'd both be horribly embarrassed.

Deciding there wasn't time to curl her hair, Whitney fastened it back with a clip, slipped on her shoes and went to join Jonas.

He'd fixed a cup of instant coffee and was gazing out the window.

"Can we start over?" Whitney asked, pausing a few feet away.

Jonas half turned and took in her conservative outfit. "I think we'd better." He gestured toward the window. "Who are those girls down there?"

"My new tenants." Whitney shrugged. "You know me. I can't resist a sob story."

"There are worse faults." Jonas sat at the kitchen table and pulled a notebook from his inside coat pocket. "Such as being late for an appointment. Not to mention that you left me alone with those gung ho public relations types yesterday afternoon after I flew in from Sonoma."

"I'm sorry." There, she was saying it again. Whitney groaned inwardly as she pulled up a chair and joined him at the table.

She'd been scheduled to join Jonas at Brite Cola's PR firm in Los Angeles that previous afternoon, but had had to cancel when there was a report of an explosion in her garage. She'd rushed home to find that some fireworks she'd stored in July and forgotten about had ignited spontaneously. "At least there wasn't much damage."

"So Mattie informed me." Jonas got along quite well with Whitney's secretary. It was a good thing Mattie was over fifty, or Whitney might have been jealous. "Shall we get down to business?" At least he refrained from making any further sarcastic comments, which under the circumstances was showing a lot of restraint, Whitney had to admit.

"Let's hear it," she said.

"Well, they agree that Brite Cola would benefit from a major promotion, as you suggested." Jonas was focusing on his notes. "And they liked the idea of a contest."

Whitney felt a little better. When it came to her company, she was at least marginally competent, maybe even a touch gifted. Although it was difficult buckling down to routine matters, she knew she had a flair for dealing with employees and with the public.

"What did they come up with?" She wished more than ever that she'd been at that meeting yesterday, to hear everything firsthand.

"They've been playing with the idea of identifying Brite Cola with California—youth and beaches, that sort of thing." Jonas glanced at his notes. "They suggested a sweepstakes—first prize would be a trip to California and a motorcycle and a lifetime supply of swimwear."

"A motorcycle?" Whitney demanded. "Those things are dangerous."

"We could make it a motor home." Jonas didn't sound very enthusiastic.

"It's a boring idea." Whitney stared out the window, wondering if any contest could capture the wild, free feeling that living at the beach gave her.

"I agree." Jonas's ready concurrence came as something of a surprise.

"You have another idea?" she ventured.

"As a matter of fact . . ." His mouth curved into a rare grin. In that moment, when his eyes sparkled and his jaw muscles relaxed, he looked young and touchable and almost irresistible. Almost. "I figure we're promoting the California dream, something bubbly and fresh. A suitable prize might be, say, a lifetime membership to a health spa, plus installation of a whirlpool bath in the winner's home."

Whitney sighed. She'd hoped Jonas would come up with something she could agree to wholeheartedly. "But don't you see—I want to capture the public's attention, not just get them to fill out an entry blank!"

His eyes regained their customary wariness. "I was suggesting what I'd like myself, if I were an average hardworking citizen."

"As opposed to a lazy good-for-nothing?" Whitney teased. "You work harder than anyone I know."

"I'd like to hear your idea. I assume you have one." He obviously wasn't in a mood to joke around. But then, Jonas rarely was.

"Well, yes . . ." Whitney's mind had just gone blank. "It came to me a couple of nights ago as I was falling asleep. Now wait a minute. I know I wrote it down somewhere."

Cursing her own lack of preparation, she darted into her bedroom and sorted through the stray papers and writing supplies on her Regency desk. The problem was that she had a habit of writing memos to herself on small white pads and then tossing them onto any available surface so that they all ended up in a jumble.

Irritated at the careless habits she'd developed over the years, Whitney brushed aside slip after slip of paper. There were notes about new stores she'd seen advertised, a reminder to clean the summer's gunk from her barbecue grill, and a list of odds and ends she needed to purchase for the apartment.

Finally she found the right note. Relieved, Whitney went back to join Jonas. "Look, I'm sorry about the delay and the disorganization. I meant to get up early but I must have turned off the alarm in my sleep."

He refrained from commenting. "And your suggestion?"

Whitney peered down at the words she'd scrawled while half awake. At the time, the idea had been crystal-clear, but now she couldn't quite remember what it had been. "Let's see—housewife. Essay. Glamour."

"That's it?"

"Wait a minute." Whitney closed her eyes against the distracting sight of Jonas's disapproval, and mercifully the concept came back to her. "Now I remember!" Her eyes flew open. "It's not a sweepstakes, it's an essay contest called 'Rise to Your Brite Dream.'"

So far, Jonas didn't look impressed.

"It's for housewives, and I guess you'd have to include house husbands so you wouldn't be accused of sexism," Whitney pressed on. "They'd write an essay about why they need a break from their routine, and the best sob story—and believe me, I'm an expert in picking them—wins a dream vacation to Hollywood. Without their family! You know, an appearance on a TV show, a new wardrobe, champagne and lobster dinners, a beauty make-over—everything women dream about while they're ironing shirts and changing diapers!"

There was no immediate response. But then, Jonas had never been known for going off half-cocked. Instead, he frowned to himself, then nodded slowly. "It's a good gimmick. But I don't like the part about separating the winner from her—or his—family."

"Why not?" Whitney demanded.

"You're tempting fate. What if the woman decides she doesn't want to go back?"

"She'll go back." Whitney didn't know why, but she felt absolutely certain of that. "She'll be horribly homesick after a week or two. Trust me."

"Then why would she want a prize like that in the first place?" Jonas was watching her closely. "Whitney, just because you live like a playgirl doesn't mean other women want that kind of life. Most of them have different values."

"Then why do they watch soap operas all the time?" she flared.

"It's escapism. That doesn't mean they want to live that way."

"Of course they don't! We're just offering an escape for two weeks." Whitney didn't want to get into an argument, but his references to her life-style rankled. "And what do you mean, I live like a playgirl? I work hard—just ask Mattie! And I have pretty conventional values myself in a lot of ways."

"I don't suppose it's any of my concern." The stiffness in Jonas's response only infuriated Whitney further.

"Oh, yes it is, because you're my oldest friend. Can't you see I've changed? Jonas, I'm not a kid anymore." Whitney glanced around urgently, looking for some tangible sign she could point to, even something as simple as her new and tasteful decor.

Unfortunately, her submission to an interior designer hadn't entirely squelched Whitney's impulsiveness. The simplicity of her oak sideboard, for example, was marred by a truly kitschy statuette she'd picked up at a garage sale, of an Italian winegrower holding a bunch of purple grapes. For some reason it had reminded her of Sonoma and Jonas.

"I'm not here to pass judgment on the way you live." Jonas's eyes had followed her gaze and he couldn't hide a wince at the ugliness of the statuette. "It's a good idea, Whitney, and I have no doubt you can promote it better than anyone. And maybe you're right. People always seem fascinated by your shenanigans, so I suppose a lot of women probably do dream about acting like you."

But I'm tired of my shenanigans! I want to be elegant and refined, the kind of woman you'd fall for. Whitney bit her lip. Why did she keep thinking crazy things like that? She and Jonas would never be compatible, no matter how much she changed. "Okay. I'll call the PR firm today and tell them what we've decided. I want to get the ball rolling."

"Fine." As Jonas stood up, he paused for a moment to look at Whitney. She could feel the sunshine from the window playing across her shoulders. A photographer had taken a picture of her backlighted like this once, and her hair had glowed like a halo. Was that what Jonas was seeing now?

He reached out and traced the outline of her temple and cheekbone with his thumb. "You know," he murmured, "if you ever do grow up, you're going to be something special."

"I am grown-up, Jonas." Whitney took a deep breath. "You just haven't noticed."

"I've noticed." His gaze swept across her body, and Whitney felt her skin tingle beneath his inspection. Then, abruptly, he was all business. "You'd better get to the office before Mattie wonders if you've dropped off the face of the earth." He strode out of the apartment without so much as a goodbye.

The combination of anger and regret that surged through Whitney was all too familiar. Encounters with Jonas had a way of arousing these particular emotions.

Clearing away the breakfast dishes, she paused to look out the window. One of the girls from downstairs, wearing a miniscule string bikini, was standing on the oceanfront sidewalk chatting with a blond surfer.

A playgirl life-style, that was what Jonas had called it. Maybe he was right, Whitney admitted silently. In a lot of ways, she had what many women probably fantasized about—wealth and freedom and glamour. Then why did it feel so empty?

Tearing her thoughts away, Whitney picked up the slip of paper with the notes about the contest. She had her work cut out for her these next few months, and the future of Brite Cola would depend to a large extent on the success of this promotion. Whatever Jonas might think, Whitney took her responsibilities seriously.

She pushed her restlessness to the back of her mind, picked up her purse and set out for the office.

Chapter One

"Listen to this one." Whitney pulled a sheet of lined paper out of the stack of essays piled on her living-room floor. "'I can take my husband, and my kids aren't too bad. It's the dog I've got to get away from.' Now there's a unique approach."

"I don't see how you and Mattie managed to whittle these down in the first place. Out of all those thousands!" said her best friend, Sarah, who was sitting cross-legged in front of the sofa. There was nothing showy about Sarah's short brown hair or her soft-spoken manner, and yet she always managed to look sexy in a healthy, natural way.

Maybe it was happiness that did it. Having a loving husband and a one-year-old son had given Sarah a glow that Whitney couldn't help envying.

By contrast, Whitney felt practically haggard. The past months had been exciting but draining, too. The contest had caught the imagination of the press and the public, and brought in more than twenty thousand entries. It had taken Mattie and her weeks to narrow the choice to a stack of one hundred, which Sarah was now helping her evaluate.

Evidence of the winter's hard work was everywhere. Most prominent was the row of framed magazine covers with pictures of Whitney that hung along one wall of the living room. A couple of them dated back two and a half years to when she'd first taken control of Brite Cola, but most of them were new. One featured Whitney with her hair pulled back, wearing a tailored suit, while in another picture her hair blew free and the top button of her lacy blouse fell open.

Well, it was all in the interest of Brite Cola, wasn't it? At least the stories focused on the promotion, although most of them took a sly poke at the contrast between Whitney and the mythical frazzled housewife she was trying to find.

"Here's a lady with twelve kids and she's sick of doing dishes and changing diapers." Sarah shook her head in disbelief as she examined the sheet of paper with its jam and butter stains. "I can't imagine having twelve children. Sometimes Kip drives me crazy, and he's just one little baby."

"I don't know." Whitney arched her back and repressed the rebellious thought that today was, after all, Saturday, the weather was exceptionally nice for February, and the beach was waiting for her right at the bottom of the stairs. "I can sympathize but, after all, who twisted her arm and forced her to have twelve kids? I don't want somebody people will feel sorry for. I want someone that women will identify with."

"But don't you wish you could help them all?"

Whitney sighed. "Of course. But I wouldn't mind trading places with some of them, either. Some of those husbands sound terrific."

"Brooding over Jonas again?" Sarah took a sip of herb tea and regarded Whitney sympathetically.

"No. I'm almost over him. I mean, look at how cold he's been these past few months. He practically glowers every time I go on another TV talk show." Whitney tucked an errant strand of hair behind her ear.

"He's jealous," Sarah pronounced. "You *do* get a lot of masculine attention, you know. Didn't you tell me the producer of one of the shows took you out a few times?"

"It didn't mean anything." Whitney stared glumly at the carpet. "Besides, what about what's-her-name, that lady lawyer he's dating in San Francisco?"

"Cynthia McCambridge?" Sarah shrugged. "Michael and I met her the last time we were up there. Don't wince that way, Whitney. She's a block of ice."

"Just Jonas's type." Whitney wished her chest didn't contract so painfully at the thought of Jonas with another woman.

"Maybe that's what he thinks, but he's wrong." Sarah clasped her hands around her knees. "Why don't the two of you quit fighting and let nature take its course?"

The topic was getting too heavy for Whitney to handle in her present mood. "Maybe we'd better get on with picking a winner." Downstairs, someone put on the latest Tina Turner disc, and the walls began to shake. "Only a few more months till school's out," Whitney muttered.

Fortunately the stereo was quickly cut off and, after the sound of brief argument, one of the girls began picking out songs from *The King and I* on a keyboard. The music provided a pleasant background as the two women discussed the merits of each of the hundred entries. At last they settled on three finalists.

One had six children and a husband who traveled for a living. She would certainly arouse a lot of sympathy, and her letter was well written, but it lacked any hint of humor.

Then there was Sarah's first choice, a house husband who wrote amusingly of the tribulations of his chosen work and the reactions of his friends.

"I like him too," Whitney admitted, "but if I were a housewife who didn't have his options, I'd resent seeing him win."

"I suppose so, but he really is clever," Sarah said.

And then there was Whitney's choice, a thirty-nine-year-old mother of two from Houston who was a onetime aspiring singer and second runner-up for Miss Texas. She declared quite frankly that she was twenty pounds overweight but dieting like mad in hopes of winning and being transformed by the beauty make-over.

But what really won Whitney's interest was the woman's descriptions of her teenage children and her husband.

"Ben is the salt of the earth but I could do with a pinch more sugar," the woman had written. "When he isn't working, he's planted in front of the TV watching a game. I can gauge the passing of the seasons by whether it's football, basketball or baseball.

"My son, Jimmy, is a girl-crazy seventeen. He thinks moms are good for picking up clothes, cooking and loaning the car keys. I've got to shake him up before he gets married and turns some unsuspecting young woman into a drudge.

"And then there's Gini. She's fifteen and likes her hair color to match her eye shadow, which changes every week. I don't mind that; I like pastels. But she's the original rebel without a cause. Last week, as a joke, I told her I liked Michael Jackson, and she immediately dumped all his records into the back of her closet. Nothing I do is enough, and anything I ask is too much. My only hope is that she'll marry someone like her brother and find out what real suffering is."

"I like her," Whitney said. "And she's probably pretty enough to blossom like Cinderella after she had her makeover. The press will love that."

"Maybe you'd better talk to Jonas before you make the final decision," Sarah warned.

Whitney reluctantly agreed. "He'll pick the lady with six children. But you're right. I'd better consult him."

Sarah checked her watch. "I've got to get home and take Kip off Michael's hands—he's playing tennis this afternoon with one of his editors." Michael headed a magazine publishing company, while Sarah, a former librarian, now wrote a book review column for the *Orange County Regis-*

ter. "And I've got to get to work on this week's column. Let me know what you decide."

"Thanks, Sarah. You've been a terrific help." Whitney saw her friend to the door, then dialed Jonas's number in Sonoma.

The housekeeper, Lupe, told her somewhat hesitantly that Jonas was spending the weekend in Lake Tahoe. "At the Brite Cola cabin."

Now, why would Jonas have gone there by himself? Whitney wondered as she hung up. Or maybe he wasn't by himself.

Well, she *did* know the phone number. She'd stayed at the cabin often enough when it belonged exclusively to her family, and since then she'd loaned it to employees as a reward in various in-house promotions.

She didn't want to wait until Monday to get the contest resolved. Besides, if Jonas had taken his lawyer friend away for the weekend, what concern was that of Whitney's?

Trying to pretend her heart wasn't beating in her throat and her hands hadn't turned clammy, she dialed the number.

And got a busy signal.

Well, at least they weren't out skiing and unreachable for the day. On the other hand, people sometimes took the phone off the hook while . . . Squelching the thought, Whitney stepped out the door to take a short walk on the beach and calm her nerves before she tried again.

IT WAS ALMOST ONE O'CLOCK and breakfast was still sitting untouched on the rustic dining table, getting cold. In fact, Jonas realized as he stared at the lumpy scrambled eggs, he was going to have to throw them out and start over.

Cynthia had been on the phone for the better part of the past three hours.

"I want to go over that deposition again," she was saying into the mouthpiece as she adjusted the phone against her shoulder. "We'll just have to ask for another postponement. There's something that bothers me and I can't quite put my finger on it."

Standing up from the sofa, Jonas crossed to the table and scraped the eggs into the trash. Well, so much for the romantic breakfast à deux that he'd planned. Even the spray of red roses looked a trifle weary in their white florist's vase.

Finally he heard the click of the phone settling into its cradle. "Jonas, I'm sorry." But Cynthia didn't sound particularly distressed. "You know what my work is like."

He took a deep breath to stifle his annoyance. "I suppose I do. I just didn't realize it would follow you to Tahoe."

"I'll make the eggs." With her customary efficiency, Cynthia moved into the kitchen and wrapped an apron around her designer slacks and sweater. She'd descended this morning already bandbox perfect. For once, even Jonas, cooking breakfast in his bathrobe and feeling rumpled after a night on the aging mattress in the second bedroom, had found himself at a disadvantage.

He'd had plenty of time to dress and shave since then. Still, there was no point in letting his irritation spoil their weekend, even though the whole idea had been to wrest Cynthia away from her work so they could really get to know each other. Although they'd been dating for several months, they always seemed to be rushing to one business-related function or another that was followed by a brief good-night kiss at Cynthia's door.

Just now, she was regarding him sympathetically as she pulled the egg carton from the refrigerator. The morning light brought out the creamy clearness of her skin, so pale against the deep auburn hair. As always, Jonas regarded her beauty with a cool aesthetic appreciation and wondered why he couldn't summon up a corresponding passion.

He'd hoped this weekend would change all that, but so far it wasn't working.

"Is it too late to go skiing today?" Cynthia asked as she cracked the eggs into a bowl. "I suppose the lifts will be jammed."

"Probably. The snowpack's perfect." Glancing past her out the window at the white-draped world, Jonas had a sudden mental image of Whitney flashing down a slope in a burst of color. Of course, that had been years ago, when their families used to meet up here. "Never mind. We can ski tomorrow."

"You're always such a good sport." Cynthia measured out the milk before pouring it on the eggs, then added a precise quarter teaspoon of salt. "You're the first man I've gone out with who didn't howl about my long hours."

"I suppose it's because I know what it's like." Actually, Jonas had to admit, Cynthia's frequent unavailability had been convenient, since he often had to fly down to Newport Beach on Brite Cola business or was tied up for long stretches at the winery. The strange part was that, even though Cynthia was exactly the sort of woman he'd been looking for, he never missed her when they were apart. "But I wanted this weekend to be different."

"It will be. Starting now." Cynthia flashed him an orthodontist's dream of a smile that was cut off as she searched through the drawers and emerged with a whisk, bypassing the simple fork that Jonas had used to stir the first batch of eggs.

"Right." Impulsively, he strode into the living room and put an album on the stereo. Soon a romantic song filled the air.

The only problem was that this was Whitney's album. Jonas remembered when she'd bought it—they'd been hurrying down a street in San Francisco last year, late for a meeting at the beverage association convention, and she'd darted away without warning into a record shop. She'd bounced out a few minutes later clutching the album and waving aside Jonas's bad temper at the delay. *I just had to have it! We can listen to it tonight, okay?* And she'd skipped ahead like a child, then turned to grin at him in a way that made him want to forget about the meeting, the album and everything except those merry eyes and tantalizing lips....

Jonas jerked his thoughts back to the present. There was no point in giving in to adolescent fantasies about Whitney. He'd learned that a long time ago. They were cut from far different cloth, and usually at each other's throats within minutes of finding themselves in the same room.

So why was he wasting time thinking about her when he finally had Cynthia to himself?

"Jonas? Don't you want your eggs?"

He looked up guiltily, realizing Cynthia must have been calling him to the table. "Sorry. I was listening to the music."

"I hope they're done the way you like them." She slid onto the redwood bench at the table and tucked a napkin neatly across her lap.

"Perfect." Jonas sat down across from her and forced himself to look pleased, even though the eggs were too well scrambled, which made them bland.

"And I made fresh coffee." Cynthia gestured to his cup.

That, at least, tasted fine, and Jonas began to relax. Well, here they were. Now, what should they talk about? "Would you like to visit the casinos this afternoon?"

"The casinos? I'm not much of a gambler." Cynthia sounded distracted. "I suppose it's the wrong time of year to go for a sail? Frankly, it's been years since I had any leisure time. I've forgotten how to be lazy."

"Well, skiing and gambling are the main attractions around here in February. Maybe we could take in a show tonight." *Something sexy,* Jonas resolved as he reached for the newspaper he'd picked up at the airport when they arrived late last night. He flipped to the entertainment section, searching for something to put them in the mood for a mutual seduction.

"You pick whatever you like." Cynthia poured herself a second cup of coffee. "I did bring a few papers along to read when I get a chance"—she must have noticed his frown, because she added quickly—"but it isn't urgent."

Jonas nibbled at a cold slice of bacon while he riffled through the paper. A singer known for his ballads was appearing at one of the clubs, but Whitney had once described the man as sounding like a calf in search of an udder, and the singer had never been able to inspire a romantic mood in Jonas since then.

The phone rang.

"Sorry." Cynthia shot him an apologetic look as she laid aside her fork and went to answer it. "Oh, yes, he is." She held out the receiver. "It's for you."

Puzzled, Jonas went to take it. He hadn't told anyone except Lupe where he was going.

"Am I interrupting something?" It was Whitney.

"Is something wrong?" At the possibility that she might be in serious trouble, adrenaline jolted through Jonas's system. "You haven't had an accident?"

"No, of course not." There was a tautness to her voice that didn't sound like the Whitney he knew. Could that be because Cynthia had answered the phone? *No, he must be imagining things.* Whitney was always the center of plenty of male interest, so why should she care if he took a woman to Tahoe for the weekend?

"Then would you mind telling me what this is about?"

"The contest. Sarah and I have whittled it down to three finalists and I want to call the winner today. We did promise to notify the lucky lady by the middle of February, you know, and besides, there are a lot of arrangements to be made. She's supposed to appear on *The Karl Kauer Show* and it goes on hiatus the end of March, so..."

"Slow down." Jonas tried to gather his thoughts. Across the room, Cynthia was studying him thoughtfully. "You want me to pick the winner?"

"Well...I just thought I'd better call. To touch bases. But if you're busy..." Whitney had obviously already decided who she wanted, and she didn't think he'd approve.

"Fill me in."

She outlined the three finalists quickly. There was no question in Jonas's mind who should win. "The woman with six kids has it hands down."

"Now wait a minute." Paper rustled. "Listen to this." Whitney read a passage about a selfish son and a rebellious daughter, which was amusing, Jonas had to admit. "Her name's Carol Truax and I like her. I mean, I think I would like her if I met her."

"And you don't like the other lady? What's that supposed to mean? This is a contest to promote Brite Cola, not make friends for Whitney Greystone."

"I'm looking for pizzazz!" Whitney's outrage vibrated in his ear. "Excitement! That special something that will make the press sit up and take notice. Someone who'll capture the public's imagination."

In all fairness, Jonas had to concede that Whitney had a flair for knowing what would appeal to the press. On the other hand... "I don't like what she said about shaking up her son. Remember, she's coming out here alone. Suppose she decides to do something shocking?"

"All the better!" Whitney was rolling full tilt now. "I *want* somebody with a mind of her own. Otherwise this whole promotion is going to fizzle out. We've built up to a climax, and now we have to provide it."

"I don't like it," Jonas said.

"Your instincts are always so conservative. Jonas, you can't bore the public into buying Brite Cola. You have to get them stirred up!"

"Yes, but when you're around, things have a way of getting out of hand." As usual, Whitney had managed to bring out his fighting spirit. "Remember the way you got Brite Cola away from Gavin? Threatening to publish the secret formula in the newspaper? You could have ruined the company, yourself and a lot of other people."

"But it worked out all right in the end, didn't it?" Whitney's tone softened slightly. "Thanks to you, arranging for us to buy up the rest of the stock. Look, I know I'm kind of flighty. You're the stable one. I won't pick Carol as the winner without your approval. Please say yes, Jonas!"

He exhaled deeply. Now that the decision was up to him, he could see Whitney's point. Carol *did* sound like a public relations dream. "All right. But we'll keep close tabs on her and make sure she doesn't go off the deep end. All right?"

"You're wonderful." Whitney hesitated. "Jonas, this friend of yours—Cynthia?—she must be someone special. I—I hope you're both very happy."

Damn it, why did she have to make it sound as if he were getting married? He and Cynthia hadn't even gone to bed together. "We're—" he cleared his throat "—having a good time, thank you. I'll see you in a couple of weeks."

"Bye." She clicked off.

"Business." Jonas returned to the table. He'd told Cynthia about the Brite Cola promotion long ago.

"Is that all?" Her gray eyes regarded him piercingly.

"Meaning what?"

"Meaning you were more animated during that telephone conversation than I've ever seen you." Cynthia stacked her dishes neatly. "Just what *is* going on between you and Whitney Greystone?"

That was the one question Jonas didn't know how to answer. "Well, we have sort of a brother-sister relationship."

"Maybe that's what you think." Cynthia folded her hands in front of her, looking intimidatingly lawyerlike. "I'm pretty good at reading people, Jonas. I agree, from what you've said, that it sounds like you and Whitney are about as incompatible as two people can be. And that you and I ought to go together like peaches and cream. But it still doesn't add up."

"And what would you recommend, counselor?" Jonas could feel his attempt at a joke fall flat even as he spoke the words.

Cynthia's perfectly sculpted mouth twisted ruefully. "I hate to say this, but I think you need to confront whatever's going on between you and Whitney. Because until you get it resolved one way or the other, your love life is going nowhere."

Every rational bone in Jonas's body urged him to argue, but his emotions told him she was right. "Damn it—I wouldn't even know where to start. The idea is preposterous."

"But I'm right?"

"I suppose so." Jonas toyed with the remainder of his eggs, which were looking less appetizing by the minute. "I'll have to think about it."

"For my own selfish sake, I hope you can get her out of your system." Cynthia folded her napkin and set it aside. "Do you suppose we could get in a little skiing today after all? That snow really is tempting."

"We can give it a try." They might as well, Jonas reflected as he swung to his feet. It was the most physical thing they were likely to do this weekend.

Besides, he needed some time to be alone with his thoughts. Because he still didn't know what he was going to do about Whitney.

Chapter Two

Whitney sat staring at the phone for a long time after hanging up.

She ought to have been prepared for this. Why did it come as such a shock, then, that Jonas had taken Cynthia away for the weekend? Why did Whitney's heart ache at the thought of the two of them curled up together in that cozy cabin? Why did tears prick at her eyes and the skin pull taut across her cheekbones as if she were going to cry?

Okay, so I'm in love with him, and it's hopeless. That's nothing new.

Whitney took a couple of deep breaths and tried to remember how to meditate. She hadn't had time for her yoga since taking over at Brite Cola, and suddenly it seemed like an exercise in futility.

Now, wait a minute. She wasn't going to let this get her down, was she? Maybe she ought to be grateful, Whitney told herself as she gulped in some more air. Once Jonas was married off to his lady lawyer, Whitney would be free to fall in love with someone else.

It didn't help to remind herself that she'd tried that once. After a whirlwind shipboard romance, she'd gotten herself engaged to Michael McCord years ago, before he met Sarah. Fortunately, she and Michael had both realized the truth in time, and parted as friends.

But maybe things would be different now. After all, Jonas had still been unattached then. But if he were married, maybe she'd finally be able to get him out of her system.

Like hell she would.

The knock at the door came as a welcome relief, and Whitney hurried to open it.

"Can you spare some teriyaki sauce?" It was her next-door neighbor, Larry Toland, who drew a syndicated cartoon under the pen name Lars. Instinctively, Whitney assessed his attractions, which wasn't hard to do. Larry was tall and easygoing, with shaggy light brown hair and piercing blue eyes. And a muscular body that was displayed to advantage by his skimpy swim trunks. Now, why couldn't she fall for someone like him, who enjoyed living at the beach and taking life as it came?

"Sure." Whitney stepped back to let him in. "Trying another new stir-fry dish?"

Larry grinned ruefully. "Actually I'm doing some urgent improvisation. My brother and his wife are coming for dinner tonight, and I bought a new kind of Szechuan sauce. Well, I just sampled it and it's hot as fire. I need some teriyaki to cut it down to size."

"Follow me." Whitney strode through the apartment into the kitchen and began poking through the disorganized pantry. "Let's see. I've got a lot of take-out packets of soy sauce—and mustard—ketchup—oh, wait a minute. No, that's Worcestershire sauce. Oh, here it is." She handed the bottle of teriyaki sauce to Larry.

"Great. Want to join us? They're coming over at four to get in some sunbathing."

It was the perfect invitation from an eligible, attractive man, but suddenly Whitney knew she couldn't handle it. Not right now, not while she was still hurting at the thought of Jonas making love to another woman. "Maybe another time. But thanks."

"Sure." Larry didn't look particularly perturbed at her refusal. "You'll have your teriyaki back tomorrow, if that's soon enough."

"Are you kidding? I haven't touched that stuff in months." Whitney usually settled for take-out food or frozen dinners.

She waved goodbye and stood at the top of the steps watching Larry go down, the sunshine highlighting his broad shoulders. As he reached the bottom, one of the college girls—Whitney thought it was Mindy, but it might have been Sarajane—tossed a beach ball at him and giggled outrageously when he batted it back.

Guys like Larry didn't go begging. So why had she turned him down?

Whitney headed back into the room and picked up Carol Truax's essay. Well, here at least was a project that would take her full concentration for the next month or so. Maybe by then the ache of missing Jonas would have faded.

Without giving herself time to think further, Whitney dialed the number listed at the top of the entry.

"Yeah, hi, this is Gini." The girl at the other end of the line sounded as if she were chewing gum.

"Could I speak to Carol, please?"

"Oh." The phone was thumped down and the girl called, "Hey, Mom, it's for you! Can you hurry it up? I'm expecting an important call!"

In the distance, Whitney heard the hum of a dishwasher and a strained voice responding, "I'll be right there."

Whitney tried to picture a typical suburban house filled with the people Carol had described, and immediately found herself caught up in the drama of what was about to happen when Carol found out she'd won the contest.

"Hello? This is Carol." The voice was soft, with a pleasant Southern accent.

"Hi, Carol. This is Whitney Greystone." She paused for a moment to let realization dawn. "I'm calling to tell you that you've won the Rise-to-Your-Brite-Dream contest."

"I'm sorry, I don't understand. Are you selling something?" the woman asked.

"Let me start over. I'm Whitney Greystone of the Brite Cola company. Remember that essay you wrote, about why you'd like to take a trip to Hollywood by yourself?"

"Oh—oh, yes." Carol sounded as if she were having trouble breathing. "Did you say I won something?"

"You're it, lady. You get the trip, the appearance on *The Karl Kauer Show*, the whole banana. Is next month all right? I can have my secretary call you Monday to finalize the arrangements."

"I won? This isn't some kind of a joke, is it?" Exultation warred with suspicion. "Who is this? Mary Jean? Sue Anne? Come on, don't *do* this to me!"

"I'll tell you what," Whitney said. "Would you like me to give you my number here in California, and you can call me back collect?"

"You don't sound like anybody I know," Carol admitted. "Is this really Whitney Greystone? How come you're calling me on a Saturday?"

"Because I just finished sorting through the finalists and picked you, and I didn't see any point in waiting." Whitney found herself liking Carol more and more by the minute. *She's as goofy as I am.* "Honest, this isn't a joke. I'm sitting here in my apartment on Balboa Island looking out at the beach, and in a few weeks you're going to be sitting on a beach yourself."

"I'd rather sit on Karl Kauer," Carol responded promptly. "He's my favorite singer and he's gorgeous."

"Maybe that can be arranged." Whitney chuckled. "Any other special requests?"

"I want to see King Kong—you know, at that studio tour—and I want my picture taken with Mickey Mouse, and

I want to meet some rock star so my kids will be impressed. And maybe get a basketball autographed by the Lakers, so my husband will notice I've been gone. How's that sound?"

"My secretary will see to everything," Whitney promised. "Give it some thought tomorrow and she'll go over it all with you on Monday, okay?"

"You aren't kidding?" Carol probed. "This is really on the level? I'm almost afraid to tell anybody, in case I dreamed it."

"Don't worry. Hey, I nearly forgot." Whitney glanced down at the entry again. "You used to be a singer, didn't you? Maybe we can fix it so you and Karl sing a duet together."

"I'd love you forever, honey," Carol said.

After they hung up, Whitney found her gloominess had vanished, at least for the moment. It was wonderful to be able to bring someone else so much happiness.

It had been just plain stuffiness on Jonas's part to worry about how Carol would act when she got out here. This lady had her feet on the ground, even if her head was way up in the air, Whitney felt sure.

She picked up the phone again to call Sarah and tell her the latest developments.

BUSY WAS AN INADEQUATE WORD to describe the next six weeks in Whitney's life. Her secretary might handle such arrangements as hotel and airplane bookings, but it took Whitney to answer questions from the press, make sure the producer of *The Karl Kauer Show* had a duet written into the script and generally add flourishes to the trip.

Jonas flew down to be among the greeting party for Carol. Whitney found herself unusually constrained in his presence, afraid to be alone with him in case he wanted to tell her that he and Cynthia were getting married. But he didn't mention the subject, a fact that gave her only a small amount of hope.

At least Carol, when she arrived, turned out to be everything they'd hoped for.

Lively and outspoken, she clearly enjoyed every minute of her arrival at Los Angeles International Airport and bantered easily with the reporters. Her diet had been a success, and her make-over the next day at a Beverly Hills salon indeed transformed the Houston housewife into a mature version of Cinderella at the ball. A television magazine show covered every minute of it in delirious detail.

The whole two weeks of the visit, Carol and Whitney were in demand for print interviews and television appearances. And, after some initial hesitation on both sides—Carol wasn't used to being around well-known heiresses, and Whitney was impressed by anyone who could handle two teenagers and a husband and retain her sense of humor—the two women became fast friends.

In fact, things were going so well that Whitney felt a touch apprehensive. Once upon a time, she had taken it for granted that her life would fall into place naturally, but these last few years she'd developed a vague suspicion of too much good luck.

"What have I overlooked?" she asked Jonas the night before Carol's return home. They were sitting in the television studio where *The Karl Kauer Show* was taped in front of an audience, waiting for the second performance. The half-hour program, after a week's rehearsal, was performed twice before two different audiences, and the laughter and applause were combined before the show was televised.

Jonas turned to Whitney with a puzzled, distracted air. "Overlooked?"

"I keep feeling as if there ought to be at least a few snags." Wearily, Whitney brushed her hair off her forehead. It had been a long day, most of it spent here at the studio sitting around watching Carol have a good time, and Whitney would much rather be home in bed.

Except that then she wouldn't be with Jonas. And she couldn't help wishing today would stretch on and on, because tomorrow he too would be flying home. Back to Cynthia.

"I owe you an apology." Jonas touched Whitney's shoulder lightly, but it was enough to envelope them both in shared warmth. "I really didn't think you could pull things off this smoothly, but you've done a terrific job."

Being complimented on her efficiency wasn't exactly what Whitney wanted to hear. On the other hand, at least she and Jonas weren't fighting, for a change. "Mattie did most of it."

"I don't think so. You're the one with the good ideas, and you're the one who picked Carol." Faint lines around his eyes showed that Jonas, too, was tired, but at least he seemed relaxed. "And these past two and half years, you've worked hard, Whitney. I think Brite Cola is finally getting on a firm footing."

A knot tied itself deep within Whitney's stomach. "You mean you're—ready to give up being president?" It was true that Jonas had promised long ago to turn everything over to Whitney when she proved she could handle it, even though he owned as much stock as she did. But then they'd never see each other.

"Maybe after we see the results of this promotion," he agreed.

Down on the stage, a thin young man with an animated face had begun telling jokes to warm up the audience, but Whitney couldn't concentrate on his antics.

She couldn't bear the suspense any longer. "Jonas, is—is there anything you want to tell me?"

His gaze flickered warily. "What do you mean?"

"About—oh, women or anything." Whitney took a deep breath. "You know. Cynthia."

"She thinks you and I have some unfinished business to take care of," he muttered.

That was the last thing Whitney had expected to hear. "Cynthia said that? Why? When?"

"That weekend when nothing happened." Jonas was frowning down at the stage. "At Tahoe."

Nothing happened. A tuneless song wove its way through Whitney's brain and she felt ten pounds lighter. *Nothing happened!* "But why would she say a thing like that? I've never even met Cynthia."

"It must have been something about our telephone conversation." Jonas grimaced. "I can't imagine what put that idea into her head. Can you?"

"Oh, Jonas, you big ox, why do you have to be so stuffy?" *Oops.* Whitney hadn't meant to speak those words aloud, but it was too late to take them back.

"I beg your pardon?" Despite the day's exhaustion, the light of battle was dawning in his eyes. "What do you mean, stuffy? Damn it, I thought you were finally growing up, but just now you sounded about twelve years old."

Before Whitney could formulate a reply, the warm-up man was introducing the show's stars. Enthusiastic applause greeted Karl Kauer, and the audience cheered loudly when Carol appeared.

She's already practically famous. How will she ever settle down again in Houston?

Right now, there wasn't much of the housewife left in the sparkling woman on stage, with her stylishly cut honey-colored hair and slender figure. Carol looked so alive and buoyant that Whitney half expected her to fly right off the set.

Some of Whitney's uneasiness returned. She'd been able to hear both sides of the conversation a few days ago, when Carol called home using the speakerphone in the Brite Cola office.

Ben Truax had groused about eating TV dinners and complained that the laundry wasn't ironing his shirts properly. Jimmy had informed his mother that he'd seen her on television and found her antics absolutely embarrassing. And Gini had whined at her mother for tying up the phone when she was expecting a call from her boyfriend.

It had been almost enough to make Whitney conclude that the single life wasn't so bad, after all.

And now, well, it was obvious that Carol loved performing. Especially with Karl Kauer.

There was no mistaking the chemistry between them. The scriptwriters had devised a plot in which Karl, who played a bachelor country singer coping with life in Los Angeles, reencountered his childhood sweetheart but finally lost her to her fiancé. With Carol's Southern accent, she was perfect for the part. And by the time they sang their duet, the good vibrations were unmistakable.

Carol's sweet soprano might not be as strong as a professional singer's, but it blended harmoniously with Karl's rich baritone. And Whitney wasn't sure all those intimate glances had been ordered by the director.

By the time the show was over and the audience departing, Whitney was glad tonight was Carol's swan song. They might have to rope and tie her to get her on the plane tomorrow as it was.

"That went well." Jonas took Whitney's arm to help her down the aisle.

"You think so?" Maybe she was wrong about the sparks between Carol and Karl. "Let's collect Waking Beauty and take her back to her hotel."

Several reporters were waiting a few minutes later as Carol emerged from the stage door in street makeup and one of the figure-hugging dresses that had been part of her prize wardrobe. There was no hint of weariness about the lady from Houston as she cheerfully answered questions, and it was another fifteen minutes before the reporters finally left.

"Ready to hit the hay?" Whitney asked.

"Are you kidding?" Carol pulled a compact from her new designer purse and studied her reflection in the mirror.

"Honey, you may live this way all the time, but tonight's my last taste of life in the fast lane."

Whitney groaned inwardly. "I guess you'd like to go out somewhere?"

Carol regarded her and Jonas. "You folks look tired. I'll tell you what. Karl offered to take me to some of those nightclubs in Hollywood I've heard about. Why don't you two get some rest, and I'll see you in the morning?"

Whitney's instincts screamed a warning. "I don't know. I should be getting my second wind soon."

"It's not like I need a chaperone," Carol teased.

Jonas caught Whitney's elbow. "The lady's right. You're worn out and so am I, and we'd just put a damper on Carol's last night on the town."

As he spoke, Karl Kauer strode toward them. Despite his darkly handsome face, there was an open honesty to his expression that made Whitney want to trust him. On the other hand, he was regarding Carol as if she were made of Godiva chocolates.

"It's just that I feel responsible," Whitney said weakly.

"This is a fine time to turn into a den mother." Jonas steered her away impatiently. "Carol, we'll pick you up at seven, okay?"

Carol pretended to pout, an expression that made her appear more like nineteen than thirty-nine. "That's awfully early, but otherwise I guess I'd miss the plane. Whitney, you look just plain wiped out. Get some sleep."

"'Night." Whitney gave Carol a quick hug and then stumbled away on Jonas's arm.

Neither of them said much on the hour-long drive back to Balboa Island. Jonas was staying at the nearby Marriott Hotel, and Whitney half expected him to just drop her off, but he escorted her upstairs.

In fact, he looked less tired than he had an hour ago as he waited for Whitney to unlock the door, and she had to admit the fresh sea breeze was invigorating.

"How about a glass of wine?" She left the lights off so they could enjoy the lights of the harbor.

"Sounds good." He took a seat on the sofa as Whitney bumbled her way into the kitchen.

From her selection of Ameling wines, Whitney picked a white zinfandel that was already open, and poured it into two crystal glasses, squinting to see in the dim glow from the refrigerator.

She'd been trying to figure out on the drive home how Cynthia could have been so perceptive. Maybe the lady lawyer wasn't such a washout after all. In fact, she sounded pretty sharp.

And generous. Or maybe just plain crazy. Because she'd had Jonas all to herself for a weekend and apparently hadn't done her utmost to win him over.

In fact, by the time she handed Jonas his glass, Whitney had almost persuaded himself that Cynthia really wasn't all that interested in him.

"So what are you going to do?" she asked, debating whether to sit next to him and finally flopping onto the carpet instead.

"About what?"

"About you and me. Or is that a dead issue?"

In the moonlight, the planes of Jonas's face stood out harshly. He was a handsome man, but he needed softening. "I've been trying to look at this thing logically. I don't suppose there's any use denying that we're attracted to each other."

"You might say that." Whitney averted her face and took a sip of wine.

"On the other hand, I've never met anyone as opposite to me in every way." Jonas was staring out at the harbor when she dared to peek up at him. "Maybe you can tell me—how do we break this off once and for all, and get on with our lives?"

"Maybe we should make love." The words slipped out of Whitney unbidden.

"You're joking, right?"

"Am I?"

They looked at each other, really looked for the first time since leaving the television studio. "I don't think that's a very good idea," Jonas said.

"I guess I don't either," Whitney admitted. She turned to set aside her empty glass and winced. "Ouch."

"What's the matter?"

She arched her back. "I've been so tense all day, afraid something would go wrong, and now I've got a cramp between my shoulder blades. I guess I'd better take some aspirin."

"Lie down." Jonas reached for her arm. "Here, on the couch. I'll give you a massage."

"As Carol would say, I'll love you forever." Years ago, after Whitney's mother had died of cancer while Whitney was a teenager, it had been Jonas who comforted her in his own quiet way. She could still remember one night when she'd felt as stiff as a board, and he'd given her an extended back rub that had finally enabled her to get some much-needed sleep. Feeling herself relax already, Whitney stretched out beside him.

She heard the clink of Jonas's glass as he set it on an end table, and felt her hair lifted off her neck. Then strong, sure hands began kneading the muscles from neck to waist, probing each knot and crevice in turn.

Was she reading in too much, or did he really express more with his hands than he ever had with words? How familiar his touch seemed, and how loving, as if he cherished each stroke as much as she did.

Slowly the tautness eased from Whitney's body, to be replaced by a different kind of tension, a humming awareness of the man who sat beside her. She had a sense of stars peering in from the night sky, of an intimacy that had been building for years, of a banked fire beginning to glow.

The pace of the massage slowed, then speeded up again. In the semidarkness, she heard Jonas's breath come more quickly.

Without pausing to reflect, Whitney rolled over. For an instant, before he realized what she'd done, his hands cupped her breasts, sending warmth surging all the way down to her ankles.

With a groan, Jonas bent over her and his breath sighed across her throat. Then their lips met, softly at first, and Whitney felt herself open to him. This moment had been destined all their lives. There was no stopping this rhythm in the blood, this soul-weaving that bound them together....

The telephone rang.

"Forget it." Whitney wrapped her arms around Jonas's neck, but already she felt him slipping away from her, returning to his customary distance.

"What if it's Carol?" His voice was slightly hoarse. "What if she's run into some kind of problem?"

"Damn it." Annoyed, Whitney sat up. "I hate responsibility." She flung herself across the room and jerked the phone from its cradle. "Hello?"

The masculine voice at the other end had a faintly nasal edge to its Southern accent. "Is this Whitney Greystone?"

"It had better be, at this hour," she snapped.

"This is Ben Truax. I just tried to call Carol, but she's not at the hotel."

Oh, great. Whitney tried to make her tone more placating. "I know. She was all keyed up after the taping so she went out with...some friends."

"No, you don't understand." Ben sounded worried. "She's checked out of the hotel."

"Checked out?" Whitney repeated. "I don't think so. They must have made a mistake."

"That's what I said, so I talked with the assistant manager. He said she was just there half an hour ago and she signed out. He said..." There was the sound of a throat being cleared. "He said he recognized the man with her as Karl Kauer."

Whitney's head felt light, as if she'd drunk too much wine. "I'm sure there's a logical explanation for all this. Let me check it out and get back to you."

"I'd appreciate that."

Quickly, she told Jonas what Ben had said, then called Carol's hotel. *Yes,* the clerk said, Mrs. Truax had checked out.

Whitney stalked across to her bedroom and, turning on the light, pawed through her phone index until she found the number for Karl's manager, Bob Abernathy.

"I don't believe this is happening." Jonas was shaking his head as Whitney dialed. "It doesn't make sense. You don't suppose she decided to take an earlier flight and surprise her family?"

"Are you kidding?" When Bob answered, Whitney related the situation to him. He promised to call her right back, and she hung up. "He's going to try Karl's house in Malibu."

"You were right. We should have stayed with her." Jonas paced across the living room. "Damn it."

"I suppose you could point out that you had your doubts about Carol from the beginning." Whitney still hadn't given up hope that the situation was all a mistake, but she was feeling increasingly dubious.

Jonas turned toward her, looking almost angry. "You really don't know me very well, do you?"

"What do you mean?"

"Sometimes I get the impression you think I'm a rigid, self-righteous ass. Do you think I'm going to blame you for this?" He pulled the curtains shut, as if to shield them from the once-romantic night. "Whitney, I went along with your choice; in fact, until just now, I thought you'd made a brilliant decision. Whatever happens next, we're in this together."

Suddenly Whitney didn't feel quite so bad. Jonas was right; she *had* misjudged him. And his last words made her feel better than she had in a long time.

And after all, Carol might be a little wild, but she wasn't going to run out on her family. There was a plausible explanation for all this.

The phone rang again, and Whitney snatched it up. "Hello?"

It was Bob Abernathy. "The housekeeper says he just left. He called her from the studio and told her to pack a suitcase, then he picked it up and drove away like the hounds of hell were after him."

"What about Carol?"

"She was with him. Whitney, I have no idea where they're going, but I'll do my best to find out."

"Thanks." Slowly, Whitney hung up and turned to Jonas.

"How bad is it?" he said.

"They're gone."

It took him a minute to digest the news. Then he said, "Carol's our responsibility. We're going to have to find her."

Whitney nodded slowly. As Jonas had said, they were in this together.

Chapter Three

Dealing with Ben Truax under these circumstances was the last thing Whitney wanted to do, but she had no choice. She'd learned over the past couple of years that certain chores, like firing an incompetent plant manager, couldn't be delegated. And neither could telling a husband that his wife, whom Brite Cola had so obligingly spirited away to a life of hedonism, had just abandoned ship.

He picked up the phone before the first ring was completed. "Hello?"

"It's Whitney." She took a deep breath. "You were right. Carol's checked out. We're trying to find out where she's gone."

"Was that Kauer person with her?"

There was no avoiding a direct question like that. "I'm afraid so."

The voice on the other end of the line rose by an octave. "This is your fault, you realize that? I'm holding you personally responsible...."

In the background, Whitney heard a girl's sleepy voice say, "What's going on, Dad?"

"Never mind." Ben's voice came back more strongly as he said, "Well? What are you planning to do about this mess?"

What Whitney wanted to do was hang up and cry, but she couldn't. "Mr. Truax, I'm sure this is all a misunderstanding. In the meantime, Brite Cola will be happy to fly you and your children to Los Angeles for a vacation of your own, and to be at hand to advise us while we locate your wife."

"I don't see what good it's going to do for us to visit California, of all places," Ben grumbled. "I warned her. Bunch of maniacs live out there. Jogging around on their surfboards, eating that yogurt junk."

"California?" shrieked a girl's voice, close enough to the receiver to hurt Whitney's eardrum. "They're offering to fly us out to California and you're turning it down? You stay home if you want to, but Jimmy and I are going! Right, Jimmy?"

"What's this all about, Dad?" came a boy's voice.

"I'll call you back," Ben said into the phone, and hung up.

Whitney groaned inwardly and turned to Jonas. Only then did she remember what Ben Truax's initial call had interrupted. *Darn it,* she and Jonas had been on the verge of... of making what might be the biggest mistake of their lives.

At least, that's what she tried to tell herself. But her body still tingled at the memory of his hands on her skin.

Ruthlessly Whitney shoved the thought aside. "Now what?" she asked. "I guess we might as well give up on getting any sleep tonight."

Jonas was sitting on the sofa, tapping his fingers on the coffee table. "Where would they go? Why would they do this? I don't believe it."

"Maybe it's a joke," Whitney offered weakly. "Want some coffee?"

"Strong," Jonas said.

By the time she got back with two overfilled mugs, Jonas was making notes on one of her stray pads. "We've got to be very careful how we handle this."

"I just hope Ben Truax doesn't pack a lawyer in his suitcase." Whitney handed him one of the cups.

"We'll leave the issue of legal liability until later." Jonas frowned. "I don't suppose we can be held accountable for a wife's disloyalty, but you never know. However, my main concern right now is the future of Brite Cola."

And just like that, he made everything seem a hundred times worse.

Until this moment Whitney hadn't given any thought to what the backfiring of her promotion might mean. But now that he'd pointed it out, she could see endless trouble ahead. Sneering jokes by TV comics, critical editorials by the same newspapers that had been so eager to jump on the bandwagon, smirks over office watercoolers across the country. Punch lines about Brite Cola's effect on the libido, to the point where no one would buy it except as a joke.

It wasn't fair. Burying her face in her hands, Whitney thought back over the last couple of years. She hadn't worked so hard just for the money. Or even to save the jobs of all those loyal workers, although that had been important.

Her main concern had been her father. He might be dead, but in her heart he was still watching over things. Building up Brite Cola had been his labor of love, his life's task. It had sickened her when Gavin nearly destroyed the company through his carelessness. Restoring and strengthening the business was something Whitney had done for her father.

And she'd failed.

"We have to keep this out of the press," Jonas said.

"What?" Dazed, she looked over at him. Did he really think it was possible to hush this thing up?

Misunderstanding, he snapped, "Well I certainly hope you weren't planning to send out a news release!"

"Of course not!" Whitney straightened. "I'm not a fool, Jonas. But what about the airport tomorrow? A lot of reporters were planning to see Carol off."

"Oh." Jonas thought for a minute. "What's that local wire service, the one the news media use for tips?"

"City News," Whitney said. "Right. I'll call and tell them Carol went home early—no, that won't work. What about the reporters in Houston?"

"Say she and her family have gone on another two weeks' vacation to an undisclosed site, courtesy of Brite Cola." Jonas paced across the carpet. "Sort of a chance to get reacquainted, and reward her family for their patience."

"Do you think Ben Truax will sit still for that?"

"I expect he'd rather the newspapers didn't print that his wife had run off with another man," Jonas pointed out.

"Oh. Right." Despite the weariness that was invading her bones, Whitney could see her job was just beginning. "I guess he'd hardly want all his friends to know."

The next few hours were spent on the telephone. Whitney had to leave messages at most of the Houston media, and make notes to have her secretary call the others in the morning, but at least she managed to get the word out across Southern California.

Ben Truax called back. He wasn't crazy about having his kids miss school, but under these upsetting circumstances he doubted they'd learn much anyway. Besides, Whitney gathered, he wasn't up to coping with his wife's disappearance and his daughter's nagging at the same time. He'd need today to pack and make arrangements, and would fly out on Sunday.

Jonas slept on the sofa, or at least he tossed and turned on the sofa while Whitney huddled miserably in her bed, dozing intermittently. In the morning, they gulped down some microwave bacon and eggs along with a stiff dose of black coffee, and got back to work.

By Saturday night, the Truaxes had a plane reservation, the rest of the news media had been more or less fended off, and Bob Abernathy had alerted everyone he could think of who might be contacted by the runaway couple. Whitney spent another restless night, but as Sunday dragged on there was still no word of Carol.

"You've been a real trouper about this," Jonas said that evening as they downed hamburgers at the airport, waiting for the disgruntled Houstonians to arrive.

"Keeping busy takes my mind off how rotten I feel," Whitney admitted. "Do you realize Carol and Karl have been together for two nights? By now, they must have . . ."

"I don't believe it." Jonas signaled the waitress for the check.

"You didn't pick up the sparks between the two of them?"

"I didn't mean that." Jonas pointed toward the doorway. "That's what I don't believe."

Two men dressed as Roman centurions were striding into the restaurant.

"Someone must be shooting a movie around here." Then Whitney remembered they were in the airport. "Maybe it's science fiction."

"And maybe we've fallen down the rabbit hole," Jonas muttered. "I always seem to feel that way when I'm around you, anyway."

For once, Whitney didn't have the heart to argue. Instead, she watched as the two men ordered pitchers of beer. "Isn't there something called the Society for Creative Anachronism? Maybe they're members."

"Maybe they're just nuts," Jonas said.

The costumes didn't look terribly real up close, Whitney observed. The helmets were clearly made of plastic and their sandals were vinyl.

She stood up and walked over. "Hi," she said.

"Greetings." One of the men held out his hand, palm up.

"Are you actors or something?"

"No. We're promoting Roman Medallion potato chips."
He turned so she could read the slogan across the back of his
tunic.

"I never heard of them," Whitney said.

"You have now."

"So I have." She returned to her table. Jonas had undoubtedly seen the slogan. "Some promoters have really
dumb ideas. And some of us have good ideas that end up
dumb."

"Whitney." He leaned across the table and caught her
hands. His palms felt slightly rough; that came from taking
a personal interest in the business of growing and processing grapes, Whitney reflected irrelevantly. "You have to
learn to believe in yourself."

"How can I do that when I keep lousing things up?
And," she pointed out, "when I have you around to keep
reminding me of that fact?"

"I'm not blaming you this time." He didn't rise to the
bait. "This isn't your fault, Whitney. You've done a su-
perb job with Brite Cola. Surprised the hell out of me, I
have to admit."

"Well, gee, thanks."

"And a lot of other people." He kept a tight grip on her
hands, and Whitney found herself wishing he'd never let go.
Maybe the Truaxes' plane would get sidetracked to Minne-
sota or somewhere, and they'd take days to get here. . . .
"You have a lot of talent and a lot of spunk. If you could
just get organized, you'd knock 'em dead."

Would I knock you dead? she wondered, but didn't dare
ask. "I'll try to remember that."

Jonas released her and checked his watch. "Their plane's
due in five minutes."

"I haven't heard an announcement."

"They don't announce flights in here."

"Oh." Whitney stood up and grabbed the check before Jonas could get it. "Brite Cola is paying. We're here on business."

"I have a Brite Cola credit card, too," he said, and took the bill away.

As they walked to the arrival gate, Whitney had to stifle a series of yawns. The sunlight coming through the windows had a thin, stretched-out quality, and her eyes itched.

She wondered how much sleep Carol had gotten the last two nights.

What was that woman up to, anyway? She wouldn't really abandon her family, no matter how crotchety they acted, would she? And Karl Kauer might be a hunk, but he was a performer, and if he had to make a choice, his career would always come first.

Whitney wished she had Carol in front of her, just for five minutes. Just long enough to tell her that Hollywood love affairs hardly ever lasted, and that being single wasn't all it was cracked up to be. Neither were glamour or money. They weren't exactly chicken feed, but they could still leave you with a hollow feeling in the morning.

I never told her how much I admired her, and envied her having a family like that. She must have gotten the idea I'm just delirious with joy all the time, living the high life. That idiot.

Whitney took a deep breath as several businessmen strode down the ramp from the airplane. She would need all her wits about her.

The Truax family bulged out in the middle of the long stream of arriving passengers. It was obvious they didn't trust the baggage handling system. Ben Truax was carrying a hefty clothes bag and the largest suitcase that would fit under an airplane seat. Gini Truax, who had a still-unfocused version of her mother's sweet features oddly framed by bleached-white hair with a green stripe down one side, was wearing what looked like three layers of clothing.

Jimmy, dark like his father but with about a pound of mousse in his hair, carried a mismatched trio of tote bags. No doubt Carol had taken the best luggage with her.

"Hi." Whitney waved them over. "Need some help?"

"We can manage," Ben Truax snapped, but Jonas had already relieved Gini of an oversize canvas bag and taken two of the totes from Jimmy. "Who's this?"

She tried not to react to the suspicious hostility in his tone. "This is Jonas Ameling, president of Brite Cola."

Ben barely nodded to acknowledge the introduction. "Anything new?"

"Not so far." They were striding toward the escalator. "We've booked rooms for you at the Marriott Hotel in Newport Beach. It's not far from the ocean, and it's near where I live."

"When are we gonna see Disneyland?" Gini demanded. "And I wanna go to some rock concerts. Can I get Madonna's autograph? And I need a new swimsuit. Mine is positively antique."

"Oh, stuff it, wouldja?" Jimmy looked uncomfortable at his sister's self-centered chatter. "I want to know where Mom is. She wouldn't really leave us. I know she wouldn't."

"That's what I think, too." Whitney resisted the urge to put an arm around his shoulder, knowing he'd shrug it off.

"We're in contact with Kauer's manager. He doesn't know any more about this than we do, or so he says." Jonas led them past the baggage room, in which the Truaxes showed not the least interest. "There's always the possibility that this is Karl's idea of a publicity stunt."

"Carol should have better sense than to fall for something like that." But Ben looked slightly relieved, Whitney thought. She was grateful to Jonas for coming up with the suggestion. She only hoped it was true.

Jonas drove them from the airport on the hour's journey to Newport Beach. He didn't bother to indicate points of interest on the way, because there weren't any. The freeway cut between industrial and commercial buildings, and Whitney had to admit the flat sweep of land didn't look particularly inviting, even with the sun setting rosily behind palm trees.

"Where's the ocean?" Gini said. Whitney pointed. "How come you can't see it?"

"Because it's too far away," Jimmy snapped. "Wise up, wouldja?"

"That's enough out of you both." Ben twisted around in the front seat to glare at them. Whitney, who was wedged between the two teenagers, wondered if she was going to get caught in the middle if the two started poking each other.

How does Carol stand it?

Immediately she gave herself a silent scolding. *If they were my kids, I'd think they were wonderful.*

Maybe.

Once they left the freeway, the scenery began to improve. Cresting a coastal bluff, they caught a splendid view of the darkening ocean below them.

"Where's the surfers?" Gini said.

"Out there." Whitney pointed at some faint dots on the horizon, and wished she were sitting on the beach watching them. Right now, she couldn't figure out why she'd ever wanted to be an executive or do anything other than indulge herself. You stuck your neck out, and look what happened.

On the other hand, she wouldn't want to go through life as a selfish adolescent like Gini.

"Well, this is nice enough," Ben conceded as they pulled to a halt in front of the hotel.

"I'll get a porter." Jonas started out of the car.

"No need for that." Ben jumped out and headed for the trunk. "We can carry our own luggage."

Ignoring him, Jonas waved for a porter and helped him unload the suitcases. Inside, the teenagers unwillingly looked impressed by the plant-draped courtyard in the center of the hotel.

"This is like something out of the movies," Jimmy said. "People waiting on you—and all those restaurants. You could eat anything you want."

"Everybody's too old," Gini grumbled. "I mean, honestly, I didn't come to California to hang around with people my parents' age! Where's the action?"

"Just a minute." Ben stopped Jonas, who had finished checking them in. "I need a TV guide."

"There's one in your room, sir," the clerk said.

"If there's anything else you need, I'll have my secretary pick it up," Whitney added. She handed Ben some brochures she'd scooped up from the reception desk, and followed the porter toward the elevators. "Here are some of the tours available. And here's an entertainment guide. We can line up tickets for any performances you want."

Gini snatched the brochures as they filed into the elevator. "Lemme see."

The three Truaxes grumbled at each other all the way up to their floor. Ben wanted to take in a basketball game; Jimmy was disappointed to learn he was too young to visit a topless nightclub; and Gini was torn between cramming in half a dozen rock concerts and trying to con Whitney into a spending spree on Rodeo Drive. "I mean, you owe us that, at least!"

Once again Jimmy looked uncomfortable. "You make it sound like they could pay us off for Mom. It's not like she's for sale, meat brain."

"Oh, don't be an airhead."

The elevator doors opened, not a minute too soon. For the first time in her life, Whitney understood why people suffered from claustrophobia.

Her sympathy for Carol was growing by the minute.

She wondered if all teenagers acted like this. If so, she might rethink her desire to have children. Or maybe plan to take a five-year vacation after they turned thirteen.

"Well." Ben looked slightly placated as they were ushered into a suite. "This is all right." The view over the ocean was stunning, and even Gini stopped chattering for a minute.

"I thought you might want to relax tonight." Whitney took advantage of the pause. "There's a variety of restaurants here at the hotel, and you can charge the bill to your room. Brite Cola will take care of it."

"Room service, too?" Jimmy asked, and grinned when she nodded.

"My secretary will be in touch with you in the morning to make any arrangements you want," Whitney added as Jonas tipped the porter and dismissed him. "She's lined up a rental car, too. And we'll keep you updated about Carol."

"I hope she learns her lesson." Ben sounded annoyed, but not bitter. Apparently, like Whitney, he couldn't believe his wife was really having an affair. "Meanwhile, I don't see any reason why the kids and I shouldn't enjoy ourselves. We've put up with enough inconvenience the past couple of weeks. Frankly, my wife's been selfish, leaving us alone that way, and I think she'll come to see that."

Whitney resisted the temptation to point out that Lincoln had freed the slaves more than a hundred years ago. She suspected Carol had made that same observation at least once.

It was a relief to get back into the elevator with Jonas. "Are they really awful, or is it just my imagination?"

"Don't forget they're under a lot of stress," he said. "But I have to admit, I can't quite picture Carol as a domestic drudge."

Whitney summoned up an image of the sparkling, lively woman she'd come to know during the past few weeks. "I can't either."

"Let's grab a bite to eat and then check in with Bob Abernathy."

They stopped nearby for tacos. "I keep wondering if I was like Gini when I was a teenager," Whitney admitted as they ate.

"Well, you had your obnoxious moments." Jonas quirked an eyebrow, and Whitney was relieved to see that he was kidding. "Actually, you weren't nearly as whiny. Gini seems to expect other people to meet her needs. You, on the other hand, thought you were perfectly capable of doing anything you wanted."

"Hotheaded?" Whitney grimaced. "I was, wasn't I. And kind of spoiled."

"In a way." Jonas sipped his cola through a straw. Right now, he reminded Whitney more of the gangly young man she'd grown up with than of the reserved sophisticate he'd become. "You were always an easy touch for anyone with a sob story. You cared about other people. Yes, you were spoiled in the sense that you didn't have a lot of responsibilities and you always had plenty of money, but you were never self-centered or insensitive."

"That's nice to know." She would have liked a less backhanded compliment, but from Jonas she would take what she could get. "Well, I guess we've ingested enough heartburn for one evening. Shall we go call Bob?"

"I guess we'd better."

As they drove to Balboa Island, it occurred to Whitney that she and Jonas hadn't quarreled all day. In this adventure, they were both on the same side for once.

She almost hoped Carol would stay lost a little while longer.

The red light was glowing on Whitney's message machine when they arrived, and she played back the tape. Several reporters had phoned to request interviews. Whitney made a mental note to call Mattie in the morning and ask her to stall them.

And Bob Abernathy had left a message. "I may have something for you," his voice said. "You can reach me at home."

Whitney dialed his number. "It's me. What've you got?"

"A tip from one of Karl's backup musicians." Bob sounded as tired as Whitney felt. "He just got a call to be at a studio in Nashville for a late-night recording session tomorrow night. The producer didn't say who was going to be singing, but it might be Karl."

"Yeah; why else would they schedule a session at the last minute?" Whitney tugged at an earring that was pinching. "Do you think he and Carol are going to cut a record?"

"I don't know if she's part of it or not." A TV set was blaring in the background. "But if I were you, I'd be there."

"Wait." Jonas grabbed the phone before Whitney could hang up. "We're going to Nashville, right?" She nodded, and he spoke into the receiver. "Bob, I don't want us checking into a hotel. Someone might see us and put two and two together."

The men talked for a minute before hanging up. "Bob's associate in Nashville is on vacation right now and might be willing to lend us his house." Sure enough, the phone rang a minute later, and Jonas conducted a brief conversation. "It's all set," he told Whitney when he was finished. "I'll make the plane reservations. Then I'd better go back to the hotel and pack."

"And try to get some sleep," Whitney said.

Jonas finished his arrangements quickly and efficiently, and then left.

Which was probably the way the whole search would go, Whitney reflected ruefully as she heated up a mug of Brite Cola. She sat drinking it on the balcony, gazing over the dark harbor at the lighted houses on the peninsula and listening to the soft slap of waves on the beach.

Something had nearly happened between her and Jonas on Friday night, before Ben called. What would it have meant, if they had made love?

That's easy. He would have felt guilty and responsible and angry at himself, and we'd have ended up being politely distant, not even friends anymore.

But it would also have meant he would have stayed with Whitney these past two nights, instead of going back to the hotel. Maybe a few nights of love with Jonas weren't enough for a lifetime, but they would be better than never having him at all.

Resolutely she stood up and went back into the apartment. She had a long day ahead of her tomorrow.

Chapter Four

It was an even longer day than Whitney had anticipated. Jonas called to wake her up at 4 a.m., explaining that he had plane reservations for 7 a.m.

"You've got to be kidding," she muttered into the phone. "What are you, some kind of maniac?"

"It's the only direct nonstop flight I could find." Jonas sounded disgustingly wide-awake for such an early hour. "Remember, there's a two-hour time difference, and we need to get settled in and find the studio."

Whitney closed her eyes and leaned back against the pillow. Except for the small circle of light from her bedside lamp, the world was dark. She felt like a child, wanting to burrow back under the covers and ignore the need to get up and go to school. Only she wasn't a child and she couldn't play hooky. "Okay, okay."

"I'll pick you up in an hour."

There wasn't much traffic on the freeway yet, and they arrived at Los Angeles International in plenty of time. Whitney had hoped to catch a nap on the plane, but the flight attendants bustled about serving breakfast as soon as the seat belt light went out.

Five hours later, they were descending toward a rich green patchwork of farms and suburbs when Whitney began to come out of her grumpy daze. "It's too bad we won't have time to see the sights." She handed her empty coffee cup to the steward. "I've never been to Nashville before."

"I hear they've had a building boom these past few years." Jonas, who had taken the window seat at Whitney's insistence, was gazing out with a thoughtful expression.

"I guess I've always thought of Nashville as sort of a cow town," she admitted. "What else is there, besides country music?"

"Oh, hotels and restaurants," Jonas said. "Along with Vanderbilt University, Fisk University, the biggest religious publishing industry in the country, churches, stores, banks...."

"I get the picture." Whitney hated feeling ignorant, but she'd gotten used to the sensation when she was around Jonas. "What did you do, spend the night boning up?"

"I've been here before." The seat belt sign came on, and the captain's voice over the intercom informed them that the temperature was a pleasant seventy-six degrees and they would be deplaning through the forward exit.

Nashville's airport was a lot larger than Whitney had expected, and a poster apologizing for the dust explained that it was still undergoing expansion. The people surging around her looked smartly dressed and the only cowboy hat she spotted was on a man whose T-shirt said Native New Yorker.

"I guess I don't need to worry that we're sleeping in a log cabin, huh?" she asked as they claimed their suitcases.

Jonas was in no mood for joking. "Stay here with the bags while I pick up our car."

A few minutes later, Whitney found herself trying to navigate from a map provided by the car rental agency. On paper, she discovered, Nashville looked like a huge spiderweb. "How come all the streets stick out of one place like spokes on a wheel?" she demanded irritably. "Take one wrong turn and you end up in Memphis."

"Would you quit grousing and direct me toward Harding Place?" Jonas steered out of the airport onto a busy road.

"Well, slow down! I haven't even found the airport yet."

They snapped at each other as they drove along the twisting, unpredictable streets until they finally came to a halt on the graveled driveway of a two-story white brick house. "This is it?" Whitney asked. "Do they serve mint juleps?"

"That's Kentucky." Jonas swung out of the car and opened the trunk.

"Who cares?" Hands on hips, Whitney glared at him.

"Now look here—"

"What happened to your sense of humor, Jonas? Leave it in L.A.?"

He lifted the suitcases and set them on the gravel. "I don't enjoy wild-goose chases, Whitney, and I've been on two too many in my life."

"Oh." Whitney felt the self-righteousness whoosh out of her. She'd forgotten the way she'd inconvenienced Jonas when she and Gavin were fighting it out for control of Brite Cola and she'd done a disappearing act with the secret formula. "I was just trying to make the best of things."

Jonas's grim expression softened. "You're right. Now let's see if we can scare up something to drink, mint julep or not."

As they hauled their bags up the steps, the double doors were opened by a woman in a white apron. "You must be the folks from Brite Cola." She stepped aside to let them in. "I usually only come in on Wednesdays and Fridays, but they asked me to give you a key and make sure you got settled."

"I'm sorry if we inconvenienced you," Whitney said.

"That's all right." The woman waved her hand airily as she escorted them up a broad, curving staircase.

As they walked along the hallway, Whitney glanced into the high-ceilinged rooms, taking in the antique furniture and paintings of hunting scenes that could have come from an English manor. The master bedroom, which Jonas insisted that Whitney take, was flooded with afternoon light through the gauzy curtains.

"There's food in the refrigerator, so you folks help yourselves," the housekeeper said. "You going to be here Wednesday? I can do your laundry then."

Whitney smiled at the woman's refreshingly down-home accent. "I don't think so, but we're not sure."

"Well, just make yourselves at home. If you need anything, here's my name and number." She handed Whitney a slip of paper. "I'm going now."

As soon as they heard the back door close behind her, Whitney said, "This is some place."

"Beats a hotel any day." Jonas carried his suitcase into a bedroom across the hall. "We'll need to restock the refrigerator before we leave, and I've arranged for a case of our reserve wines to be sent to our hosts."

"I'll send them a couple of cases of Brite Cola, too." Whitney wished she'd thought of it first.

She felt awkward, making room in someone else's closet for her clothes, but after a while she began to relax. It had been a long time since she'd stayed in a real, solid house instead of an apartment, and she was surprised to discover she relished the sense of stability.

Stability? That had been the last thing she'd ever expected to want, Whitney reflected as she fixed ham and cheese sandwiches for a late lunch and Jonas dished out some potato salad.

After they ate, Whitney seized the opportunity to take a nap. Exhausted, she fell asleep almost instantly.

The room was in darkness when she awoke. From the other end of the house, she could hear the faint strumming of a guitar and a deep masculine voice singing softly.

Had their hosts come home unexpectedly?

Flicking on a light, Whitney brushed her hair and put on a flowing cotton dress. Then she padded downstairs to see what was going on.

She made her way through the kitchen and paused in the doorway to the den. Paneled in gleaming oak, the room was lined with shelves of records and compact discs, and on the far wall towered an array of high tech stereo equipment.

Seated on the edge of a couch, Jonas was leaning over a guitar, picking out a tune.

"I didn't know you sang." Whitney was sorry when the notes ceased abruptly.

"I don't." Jonas set the guitar aside.

"Yes, you do. I heard you." She stepped into the room. "You were good."

"Not good enough." There was an unfamiliar tinge of sadness in Jonas's voice.

"Not good enough for what?" Whitney sank onto the carpet at his feet, leaning her head against the sofa. She wished this were their home, that she and Jonas lived here together.

"For Nashville," Jonas said.

Whitney twisted around to look at him. "You wanted to be a singer? I never knew that!" Then she remembered seeing a guitar in the den of his house in Sonoma. She'd assumed it was merely part of the Spanish-style decor.

"It was a long time ago." Jonas ran his hand over the curving wood of the instrument. "Eighteen years ago, to be precise. I was in college, and you were ten years old."

"Born too late," Whitney muttered.

He smiled. "Hardly. Anyway, I was always bucking the tide. Country music wasn't very popular back then; that was the era of acid rock and the Beatles. But I liked country songs. I even wrote a few, and I guess I thought they were pretty good."

"I'd like to hear them," she said.

He shook his head. "I've forgotten them by now. So one summer while I was in college, I came out here to Nashville to try my luck. I sang at a few restaurants and at a concert in the park—it was amateur night—and tried to peddle my songs along Music Row. I won't say it was a waste of time. After all, I had the privilege of hearing some of the greats at the Grand Ole Opryhouse—the original one, the Ryman Auditorium, not the new one at Opryland."

"But?" Whitney prompted.

"I was working as a waiter; I didn't want to take my parents' money when I was trying to prove myself. And gradually I came to realize that Nashville was full of young people like me, who had pleasant singing voices and could write a passable tune. But it wasn't the same as having real talent. So I went home and learned the wine business."

"Play something for me," Whitney said.

Jonas hesitated, then picked up the guitar again. "Maybe I do remember something." His fingers strummed across the strings, and he began to sing.

Whitney relaxed into the flow of his voice, her body vibrating with the resonant timbre. Time stood still as he sang, segueing into another song, about a young man seeing an old girlfriend through fresh eyes.

I wish he'd see me that way. I wish he'd write a song for me.

The last notes drifted away and Jonas set the guitar down with a hollow thump. "We'd better go eat. It's almost eight, and the recording session starts at ten."

"They must work all night." Reluctantly, Whitney stood up.

"Till 1 a.m.," Bob said. "It's a three-hour session."

Slowly the romantic, melancholy mood slipped away, leaving her feeling as if she'd glimpsed the dark side of the moon. How could she have known Jonas all her life and not known about this part of him?

Well, he's known me all my life, and there's plenty he doesn't know about me, either.

They ate Cajun food at Crawdaddy's, an offbeat restaurant built to resemble a 1920s fish camp. Located in downtown Nashville, it overlooked the Cumberland River.

"This area was really run-down that summer I spent here," Jonas noted as he finished his spicy shrimp. "They're redeveloping the riverfront, and it's a vast improvement."

Whitney had to admit that so far she was finding the city charming. Although she'd traveled through Europe, she hadn't seen much of the United States before. "I guess we Californians tend to think we're the center of the universe," she admitted. "This would be a nice city to live in."

"If you can take the humidity." Jonas signaled for the check. "It's not bad right now, but in another month or so you can take a bath just walking down the street."

"Every place has its drawbacks, I guess." Gazing at him with her chin resting in her palm, Whitney wasn't interested in talking about the weather. She was struggling against the urge to reach out and run her hand across Jonas's taut jawline. She didn't want to go to a recording studio and look for Carol; she wanted to go back to the house and make love to Jonas.

As she tagged along at Jonas's heels on their way to the car, Whitney reflected ruefully that if she'd been any other woman, he probably would have taken her arm.

They drove down Broad Street in silence, past the red brick buildings of Vanderbilt University, then turned left. "It's right around here," Jonas said. "I'm going to see if I can find it by memory."

"Suits me." Whitney wouldn't be able to see the map in the dark, anyway.

"Damn," Jonas said a few minutes later as they wound through streets lined with old houses converted into a variety of shops and offices. "They've changed everything. This street used to go through, I could swear."

Whitney peered at her watch in the dark. The luminous dial said it was a quarter to ten. "Maybe it's a good thing if we're late. They'll be so busy singing they might not notice us." Another thought occurred to her. "Is it going to be hard getting into the building? What if they have guards?"

Jonas made a sound somewhere between a click and a growl. "I sure hope things haven't changed *that* much."

"There!" Whitney pointed to a low, modern structure. "That says Country Music Hall of Fame."

"At last." They passed an odd mixture of structures, tall modern buildings scattered between remodeled brick houses. Most of them had something to do with the music industry, Whitney noted from the signs, but here and there she spotted a real estate office or a hair salon.

"It's not like L.A." She pictured the Capital Records tower in Hollywood, wedged between bustling city streets.

"And I hope it never is." Jonas steered around a corner and into a small parking lot behind another row of buildings. "It's changed more than I'd like already. That place right on the corner that's some kind of museum used to be the RCA studio. Now it's just another tourist trap."

He cut the engine and Whitney started to get out of the car, but Jonas caught her arm. "Wait a minute. I think the studio is right through there." He indicated a door in the back of the building. "We don't want Carol and Karl to see us before we see them."

"If they're here." Whitney certainly hoped this whole trip hadn't been in vain.

They sat for what felt like an eternity, until the rhythmic bounce of music poured out through the door. A shiver of excitement went up Whitney's back. She wished she didn't have to worry about catching the runaways. All she wanted to do right now was watch and listen and enjoy.

"Okay. Let's go in." Jonas slid out of the car, and Whitney joined him. At the back door, a woman wearing blue jeans and smoking a cigarette regarded them quizzically.

"We're friends of Carol's," Whitney said, and hoped they wouldn't draw a blank stare.

Instead, the woman nodded in acknowledgement. "You'll have to be real quiet. Just slip through there. There's some chairs in the back of the control room."

The studio was a huge rectangular room, nearly dark except for small colored lights overhead. Whitney could make out the shapes of the musicians and of a couple wearing earphones, who stood facing the lighted control booth. The woman was about Carol's size, and the man, judging from his wide shoulders and low-hipped stance, was definitely Karl Kauer.

Whitney squelched the impulse to dash across the floor and grab her quarry. After all, it wasn't as if she had any legal right to seize Carol. And she suspected that if she interrupted this session, she and Jonas would find themselves tossed into the alley outside.

"How come it's so dark?" she whispered as Jonas paused to get his bearings. "It's not like a TV studio at all."

"It helps the musicians concentrate," he murmured back, his breath warm against Whitney's ear.

She fell silent as the music stopped and a man in the control room said something into a microphone. The singers nodded.

The music started again, and she followed Jonas into the control booth. The two men sitting at the vast console appeared to take no notice, and she gathered it wasn't unusual to have visitors drop in. In fact, the whole atmosphere was a lot more casual than she'd expected.

From here, Whitney had a good view of Carol's and Karl's faces. Both were concentrating on their song, a catchy tune about a girl from Texas and a boy from Nashville, that had obviously been tailored to the occasion.

They gave no sign of noticing Whitney and Jonas in the back of the control room. She wasn't sure whether they were even visible, although the booth was better lighted than the rest of the studio.

As the musicians and singers repeated the song over and over, pausing occasionally to listen to the playback on an overhead speaker, Jonas quietly explained the setup to Whitney.

The console with its hundreds of levers, he said, controlled something in the neighborhood of two dozen different tracks. Each instrument and singer had at least one track, and others could be dubbed in later. At some point after the session, the producer would come back and mix the tracks until he was satisfied with the total effect.

With Jonas's help, Whitney identified the instruments: mostly a range of guitars, along with a keyboard and synthesizer. The drums were isolated in a structure that looked like a little hut, to keep their noise from leaking onto the other tracks.

"It must cost a fortune to have a session like this," Whitney muttered.

"The studio alone probably costs around $150 an hour," Jonas said. "They can cut two or three songs in a three-hour session, but that doesn't include the overdubbing and mixing later. Or what they have to pay the musicians."

They paused as Carol began experimenting with a new harmony line. The keyboard player picked it up and echoed her, creating a rich effect.

Caught up in the experience, Whitney almost forgot why she was here. *Thank goodness;* Carol and Karl apparently hadn't noticed them.

"When do we make our move?" she whispered as the singers took a short break and then returned to work on a second song.

"I think we can wait till it's over." Jonas frowned, scrutinizing Carol's face as if trying to read her motives. "We don't want to make a nuisance of ourselves."

So far, the relationship between Carol and Karl looked all business, Whitney noted with relief. There was an obvious comradeship between them, but she hadn't seen any smooching or cuddling. On the other hand, maybe they were just being discreet because so many people were present.

She wouldn't really leave her family. Maybe she just wanted to have this recording session. After all, she did want to be a singer when she was young.

Whitney hoped that was all there was to the escapade. Perhaps Carol hadn't wanted to contend with her family's objections to launching a career. But the least she could have done was to let Whitney in on her plans.

As the evening wore on, Karl didn't seem affected by the strain of continuous singing, but Carol's voice was wearing thin. She had a lovely tone, but, Whitney suspected, sturdiness was one of the marks of a professional. She hoped Carol wouldn't be too disappointed if her career turned out to be a limited one.

It was after midnight when the producer called for another five-minute break. Carol look relieved.

As the singers strolled outside, chatting with the musicians and sipping coffees from paper cups, Whitney and Jonas ducked down, pretending to search for something they'd dropped on the floor. The engineer began playing back the second song so loudly that Whitney was almost deafened.

Faintly she thought she heard a car start. She glanced over at Jonas and saw a look of alarm cross his face.

"Come on!" He hauled her out of the control booth and they raced for the door.

"They wouldn't just—"

They dashed into the parking lot, in time to see a white van pulling away with Karl at the wheel and Carol beside him.

"Damn!" Jonas and Whitney scrambled into their car, but by the time they reached the street, the van had disappeared.

"Maybe we could go back and ask the producer," Whitney suggested.

"Are you kidding? Who do you think tipped them off?" Jonas paused at a signal light. "Hell. This whole trip was for nothing."

"I was hoping maybe Carol just ran away for this recording session," Whitney admitted. "I guess not, huh?"

"It doesn't look that way."

They crisscrossed the streets around Music Row, but there was no sign of the van. "Doesn't Karl have a house in Nashville?" she asked.

"Yes, but Bob's had it checked, and they're not staying there. Karl has a lot of friends." Jonas looked grim. "I'm afraid we've wasted our time."

No, we haven't. I've learned some things about you I didn't know before. But Whitney kept her thoughts to herself.

Glumly they drove back to their quarters. Whitney found herself increasingly resenting Carol's selfishness. "It might have occurred to her that she was going to inconvenience a lot of innocent people," she grumbled as Jonas turned the key in the front door lock and they stepped inside.

He didn't say anything, but he didn't need to. Hearing her own words spoken aloud, Whitney remembered what she'd put Jonas through, and Michael and Sarah, two and half years ago.

Darn it, why did everything seem to reinforce Jonas's view of her as a scatterbrained child? She'd hoped that by spending time with her, he would begin to see how much she'd changed, but so far it didn't seem to be working out that way.

Jonas said a brief good-night outside his bedroom and closed the door behind him. Whitney's emotions were jumbled as she retreated to change for bed.

Earlier this evening, during the intimate mood created when Jonas was singing to her, it had occurred to Whitney that later tonight they might wind up in each other's arms. Wherever it led—and it would most likely not lead anywhere in particular—at least she'd know what it was like to be Jonas's lover.

Well, no chance of that now. Not with Carol and Karl souring everything with their disappearing act.

Tomorrow, Whitney reflected as she brushed her teeth, she and Jonas would have to endure another flight and a disgruntled reception by the Truax family. Just imagining Ben's reaction was enough to make her want to give Carol a good spanking.

"THERE'S ONE GOOD THING about all this," Jonas said the next day as they drove to the airport.

"Don't keep me in suspense." Whitney hugged her knees, wishing the bright late-March sunshine would give way to some more appropriate gray skies.

"So far, we've managed to keep this whole escapade confidential." Jonas maneuvered through a crowded intersection. "Brite Cola's reputation is still safe."

"And so is Carol's." Whitney was beginning to wish she'd eaten breakfast. She hadn't felt hungry all morning, but they were driving past a coffee shop and suddenly her stomach was demanding to be filled. "Do we have time to get something to eat?"

Jonas checked his watch. "Sure." They swung into the parking lot. "I'm working up an appetite, too."

The polished interior of the restaurant and its hamburgers-and-chili menu would have fitted in almost anywhere—Southern California, Nashville, or, Whitney imagined, Toledo or Miami—except for the fact that the breakfasts featured grits instead of potatoes. "Maybe I'll have an omelet," she said. "I want to find out what grits taste like."

"They taste like cream of wheat." Jonas ordered a cheeseburger. "But suit yourself."

He was right about the grits. "They're not bad." Whitney picked up a strip of bacon with her finger and nibbled on it. "Want some?"

Jonas shook his head. "Don't wave that in my face, Whitney."

"I wasn't—" She bit her lip. *Darn it,* he always managed to make her feel like a child. "Okay, you tell me. How do sophisticated people behave at the breakfast table?"

His mouth twisted ruefully. "Sometimes they never get to the breakfast table."

"What does that mean?"

"I was just remembering—never mind."

Who had he eaten breakfast with? Cynthia, of course. "You can't stop now."

"All right. At Tahoe. Cynthia was on the phone most of the time when we were in the cabin."

What a relief. Whitney had been afraid there might be some more romantic reason for not getting to the breakfast table, even though Jonas *had* said nothing happened that weekend. "That's what lawyers are like, is it?"

"Are you finished?" He checked his watch again. "I don't want to cut this too close."

Whitney stuffed the last strip of bacon into her mouth. "All done."

Outside in the parking lot, a trucker's radio was blaring the news. As Whitney opened her car door, she heard the announcer say, "And here's an interesting item. Singer Karl Kauer was spotted partying at Tootsie's Orchid Lounge last night with—get this—Carol Truax, the Brite Cola girl. Wonder what happened to Carol's husband?"

"Oh, no." Whitney slumped onto the seat. "I can't believe it. How could they do this to us?"

"I doubt if Carol is concerned about what happens to Brite Cola." Jonas's mouth set into a harsh line as he started the car.

Chapter Five

"It's not like Carol to run off that way," Ben Truax insisted. "You must have frightened her."

"All we did was show up." Whitney tried not to let exasperation get the better of her, but it wasn't easy.

She and Jonas had arrived at the hotel suite only a quarter of an hour before, coming directly from the airport, and had filled in the Truaxes on their frustrating trip.

Ben's response had been to repeat, in one way or another, that Whitney and Jonas must be at fault. It was hard to rein in her impatience, especially when she longed to go home, take a hot bath and forget she'd ever heard of Carol Truax.

"Why would she just run off like that?" Jimmy was pacing around the sofa, talking more to himself than to the others. "I mean, that doesn't sound like Mom, but obviously, she did it."

"There's something funny going on here." Ben ignored his son's remark. "Something mighty funny."

Whitney, on the verge of snapping back out of sheer exhaustion, reminded herself that Ben was under a lot of stress, too. It was understandable that he would blame his problems on others rather than admit there was something fundamentally wrong between his wife and himself.

"This may just be her way of establishing herself as a singer," she said placatingly. "She probably feels insecure about facing up to you until she's proved herself."

"Gimme a break." Gini, slouched on the sofa, was wearing a new pair of tight jeans and a stylishly ragged overblouse. Mattie, whom Whitney had telephoned from the airport, had reported that the Truaxes had already spent a small fortune, eating at the best restaurants and shopping at the stores in Fashion Island near their hotel. "Mom doesn't want to admit she's getting old. So she's running around trying to act like a kid, only she's making a fool of herself."

"Don't be an idiot." Jimmy glared at his sister. "You aren't even trying to understand."

"Can it, fat face!"

"Quiet, both of you." Ben turned toward Whitney and opened his mouth, but before he could say anything, the phone rang.

"I'll get it!" Gini leaped for the phone. "I think it's for me. Hello?" Then she made a face. "It's Mom."

Ben snatched the receiver out of her hand. "What the hell is going on, Carol?" His bluster died away as he listened.

Whitney waited anxiously. Was Carol calling to ask for a divorce? She didn't doubt that the Truax family would be devastated—or that they'd find some grounds to sue Brite Cola for alienation of affection.

But Ben was nodding thoughtfully. "I see. All right. Fine. I'll tell them." And he hung up.

"Where is she? We need to talk to her." Jonas reached toward the phone. "I'll call her back."

"She's in Nashville, but they're leaving. She didn't say where they're going." To Whitney's eye, Ben looked somewhat relieved, "Now if you folks would excuse us, I'd like to have a little chat with my children."

"Oh, Dad!" Gini whined. "I need to phone Huey. It's been two days and he promised to call every day, and he'd better have a good excuse or I'll—"

"Be quiet." Ben regarded Whitney and Jonas levelly. "Now, if you don't mind?"

"We'll be in touch." Jonas, like Whitney, had obviously gotten the point that Carol's message was private.

They speculated about what she'd said while driving to Whitney's apartment, but all it added up to was a big question mark.

"Her husband didn't seem angry," Jonas pointed out. "I guess she doesn't want a divorce after all."

"I just hope she shows up soon so I can wring her neck." Relentlessly, Whitney flipped the dials on the radio.

She stopped abruptly at a disc jockey's patter. "Have you heard the latest about Brite Cola? It seems some scientists have discovered it boosts the sex drive. Hey, I'm gonna buy a case of that stuff!"

Jonas inhaled sharply. "If Carol *doesn't* turn up soon, you'll have to stand in line to murder her."

"It's not fair." Tears stung at Whitney's eyes. "We've worked so hard to save Brite Cola!"

"Don't let it get to you. Things aren't that bad—yet."

He dropped her off at the apartment. "I'm going back to the hotel and get some sleep. I'd suggest you do the same. I'll see you at your office in the morning."

"What do we do next?" Whitney asked as she picked up her small suitcase from the back seat. "About Carol, I mean?"

Jonas shrugged. "Not much we can do for the moment. I'll talk to Bob Abernathy tomorrow."

As he drove off, Whitney felt the weight of the past few days descend on her shoulders. How could so much go wrong in such a short time?

Although Jonas hadn't rubbed it in, she couldn't help feeling that this trouble was all a result of her own impetuousness. She'd trusted her instincts over his more cautious judgment in establishing this contest, and then in picking Carol.

Would she ever learn to think things through, to look before she leaped? It might be too late to convince Jonas that she had matured, but maybe it was time to start curbing her impulsive nature, for her own sake.

Clumping up the staircase to her apartment, Whitney frowned as she heard a rumble of music from the ground-floor unit. If she hadn't been such a patsy and rented it out, it would have been available for Jonas to use. Then he would have been close at hand instead of a mile or so away at the hotel.

She wasn't going to be such an easy touch any more. From now on, Whitney Greystone was going to act like a grown-up.

If she could just figure out how.

JONAS ARRIVED at the Brite Cola offices at 9 a.m., which he estimated was at least an hour before he could expect to see Whitney.

He needed to be in a business environment, to focus his thoughts on income and cost containment, marketing strategies and shipping rates. Dry, practical things that he was good at.

Because, Jonas reflected ruefully as he took the elevator to the third floor, he wasn't very good at the subject that had been occupying his thoughts for the past few days.

The subject was Whitney.

He didn't like to admit it, but she *was* growing up. Her vivid blue eyes were taking on more depth, her coltish movements were mellowing into a mature sensuality, and yet she had lost none of her appealing freshness.

He liked the way she'd handled Ben Truax, keeping her temper in spite of severe provocation and using a bit of gentle psychology to avoid fireworks. And, unlike so many people he knew, Whitney hadn't lost her ability to care deeply about things. Her tears at the prospect of losing Brite Cola had touched him, because he knew Whitney had been thinking of her father. He also knew how much labor and love she'd put into the company these past few years.

The elevator doors opened and Jonas stepped out. The Brite Cola offices had been modernized about a year ago, with lights recessed in the ceiling and a streamlined, low-key decor. The gray carpeting hushed his footsteps.

"Oh, hello, Mr. Ameling." The receptionist smiled at him brightly. "I don't believe Miss Greystone is in yet."

"I'd be very surprised if she was." He walked back to his office, which was down the hall next to Whitney's. The room was impersonal, the desk cleared of papers, the wastebasket pristinely empty, the walls adorned only with decorator-selected Currier & Ives prints.

It was obvious no one worked here regularly. Jonas had thought, when he and Whitney took over the company, that he would have to spend a lot of time keeping tabs on her, but that hadn't turned out to be the case.

She'd done a good job. *Damn it,* she wasn't a little girl any more. But the thought of what she'd become, and how he was beginning to feel about her, was downright terrifying.

I don't want to fall in love with Whitney.

Maybe it was already too late. Why else had he dreamed about her last night, and the night before? Why else had he come so close to making love with her on Friday night? It had been apparent even to Cynthia that there was something going on between him and the girl he'd known since childhood.

Jonas sat down behind the desk, wishing he'd brought some papers to keep his mind occupied. He needed to stay busy. What he ought to do, he decided, was to review Brite Cola's operations to make sure he'd made the right decision to give up his post as president and hand everything over to Whitney.

If, of course, there was anything left to hand over after the jokesters got finished with Brite Cola. But that was an issue outside his sphere of influence, and he couldn't allow it to disrupt his calculations.

More than anything, Jonas liked to feel that things were under control. He needed his work and his life to be orderly and well regulated.

Which was exactly why he could never allow himself to fall in love with Whitney. She was the opposite of him, a dangerously unpredictable figure who subscribed to no conventions and questioned everything. Every time he was near her, she managed to turn Jonas's world upside down.

At one time, he had thought that when she grew up, she would become settled and systematical, as he was. Now he could see that that wasn't true. Nor should it be. Whitney would die of boredom if she had to live the way Jonas did. She was exciting, unique, adventurous, and he would never want to stuff her into a box.

They were, he concluded for the umpteenth time, simply incompatible.

"Mr. Ameling?" Mattie, Whitney's secretary, appeared in the doorway. "Sorry, I was down running off some photocopies. I didn't realize you'd come in."

"No problem." Jonas relaxed. He always felt comfortable with Mattie, who was motherly, well organized and utterly dependable. "I know it's a tall order, but I'd like to review all the operations here, the way Whitney's running everything."

Mattie shot him a knowing look. "She won't like it."

"Don't get me wrong. It's not that I don't trust her." There was no reason not to confide in Mattie. "I'm thinking of giving up my position. I promised in the beginning that I'd hand Whitney the reins when she'd proved she was ready. Well, I think the time has come."

"Even after this Carol Truax thing?" Mattie knew him and Whitney well enough to be blunt.

"What do you think?" Jonas leaned forward. "You work with her every day. I know she has terrific ideas, and the employees seem to like her. Is she organized enough?"

"Is a hurricane organized?" Mattie chuckled. "No, I take that back. Keeping things in order is my job. I think Whitney's terrific. I don't believe she'd fly off into orbit without you to steady her, but I'm not responsible for the well-being of this company. So I think I'd better take the Fifth Amendment."

"Touché." Jonas stood up. "We might as well get started. I've got a lot of work ahead of me."

He felt better already. Account books and productivity reports reduced the world to neat, ordered columns. And he felt comfortable with those.

IT WAS ALMOST TEN-THIRTY when Whitney whirled into the office. She'd managed to shut off her alarm clock in her sleep again, and she was feeling grumpy and annoyed that already she was failing to live up to last night's resolution.

It didn't make her feel any better to find Jonas closeted with her secretary, going over sales figures and distribution arrangements.

"Is something wrong?" she asked.

"Nothing so far." His voice sounded distant, and there was no hint in his eyes of the closeness they'd shared during the past few days. "I thought, as long as I'm here, I might as well do a thorough review of the company's operations."

"Maybe you'd like me to hire an auditor." She had meant the remark to be sarcastic, but he took her seriously.

"That won't be necessary. I have our last annual report."

Whitney bit back an irritable retort. *Darn it,* she didn't want to act petulant. If Jonas felt it was necessary to check on her work, *well, let him find out for himself* that he was wasting his time.

Back in her own office, she began returning phone calls that had accumulated during the past five days. The hardest ones to deal with were from the press.

They'd all heard the stories of Carol and Karl showing up in Nashville. Whitney had to improvise fast.

"They're cutting a record together." No point in keeping that a secret, was there? "I'm not authorized to reveal any further details about it," she told a columnist from a country music magazine. "Yes, her family knows all about it. As a matter of fact, they're getting their turn at a California vacation, courtesy of Brite Cola."

Some of the reporters seemed to take her word for it, but others tried to dig deeper. Why hadn't the record been announced in advance? Why wasn't Carol's husband in Nashville? Why the false story about the family taking a secret vacation with Carol?

Whitney did her best, and by the time the last call had been returned, she sensed that the worst could be staved off for a few days. If they could just get Carol back...

What had she said to her husband last night, anyway? Hoping to find out, Whitney put in a call to Ben Truax, and let the phone ring ten times in the hotel suite before giving up. She checked with Mattie, and learned that the Truaxes had gone on the Universal Studios tour and wouldn't be back until late evening.

It was almost one o'clock. From her office, Whitney could hear Jonas on the telephone, talking to someone at the plant about earthquake preparedness. Her frustration bubbled up to near the boiling point. She didn't need Jonas's display of mistrust on top of her worries about Carol!

The best thing would be to avoid a confrontation by avoiding Jonas. Grimly, Whitney punched out a familiar telephone number and was relieved when Sarah answered.

No, she hadn't eaten lunch yet, and *yes,* she'd be delighted to meet Whitney. Kip was on an outing with his grandparents, so they could talk undisturbed.

They met at a wood-paneled pizza parlor that specialized in all-natural ingredients. Maybe there was something inherently contradictory about insisting on real cheese with your junk food, but Whitney didn't care. She didn't have to be anything but herself with her best friend.

They ordered a medium pizza with spiced beef and onions, then took a booth that was hidden behind a trailing plant. It was after one o'clock by now and the lunch crowd was thinning.

"No luck with Carol, I take it?" Sarah asked.

Whitney shook her head. "You've heard the jokes?"

"Oh, one or two." Sarah's mouth twisted in sympathy. "It'll die out quick enough."

"I'm not so sure." Whitney rested her elbows on the table. "It could really hurt us. I must look like such a fool."

"Not necessarily." Sarah, as usual, was taking an optimistic view of things. "For one thing, people aren't sure yet that this isn't another one of your stunts."

"They think I set it up?" That was a consoling thought.

"I suspect so. Besides, think of all the free publicity you're getting. I'll bet—"

Someone called out their number, and Whitney hurried to the counter to pick up their pizza. She was starving.

"Hey, wow, aren't you Whitney Houston?" asked a teenage boy with spiky hair.

"Greystone." She handed over her claim number and retrieved the pizza.

"Yeah, but I mean, you're famous, right? Maybe I ought to ask for your autograph?"

"I'm not that famous." Whitney ducked back into the privacy of their booth. "Did you see that kid?"

Sarah smiled. "From the way he was checking you out, I figured he was going to ask you for a date."

"He wanted to know if I was Whitney Houston." The pizza was too hot to eat. She pulled a slice onto a paper napkin to let it cool. "I can't sing."

"Can Carol?"

"She's got a decent voice, but nothing great. I hope she's not planning to throw over her family for a show biz career." Whitney picked off a piece of spicy beef and chewed on it thoughtfully. "It just doesn't make sense. She seemed so down-to-earth."

"Don't torture yourself." Sarah took a sip of her Brite Cola. "Nobody blames you, and nobody could have foreseen this. And it may all work out okay."

"I have to admit, Jonas has been a good sport." Too hungry to wait any longer, Whitney attacked her slice of pizza. Coming up for air a few minutes later, she added, "But he's back to normal today. Going over all our records, as if he doesn't think I can run the company."

"That's probably just his way of dealing with a crisis." Sarah finished off her first piece and reached for another. "When trouble hits, some people cope by keeping busy. I remember when my mother had surgery a few years ago, my father could hardly sit still—"

They both looked up, startled, as the plant's tendrils were pushed aside and the teenage boy poked his head into view. "Hey, my girlfriend says she saw your picture in *People* magazine. Is that right?"

"Well, yes, I did have my picture in...."

"Can I have your autograph?" He thrust out a paper napkin and a Bic pen. "Make it to Stella. That's my girlfriend."

"Okay." As Whitney wrote, she heard other noises. When she looked up, half a dozen youthful faces were peering at her. "There must be a high school near here."

"Across the street," the boy agreed solemnly.

A dark-haired girl thrust three napkins at Whitney. "Could you write those to Maria, Joe and Pete? They'll be real excited."

"Who is she?" someone demanded from the rear of the small crowd.

"Whitney Houston," somebody else answered.

"No, I'm not. I'm—"

"Oh, the singer?" Excited voices began to jabber.

"Hey, who's got a pen?"

"I'm gonna go out and buy all her records."

"Quit pushing! I was here first."

Sarah began to laugh. Whitney shot her a quelling look. "You'd think they'd notice I don't look much like Whitney Houston."

"Just enjoy the attention."

Whitney signed her name at least a dozen times, mostly for friends of friends who, she felt sure, would simply throw the napkins away. But it was easier than trying to correct the false impression.

"This is ridiculous," she muttered when the crowd finally dispersed. "And the pizza's getting cold."

"We were talking about Jonas." Sarah, who had been munching quietly throughout the interruption, sat back and regarded Whitney knowingly. "It was obvious when I first met you that you and Jonas were crazy about each other."

"Me about him, maybe," Whitney conceded. "But I'm not his type."

"That's what you think, and probably what he thinks." Sarah finished the last of her cola. "But I don't agree, and neither does Michael. You two could bring out the best in each other if you'd give it a chance."

"I'm ready and willing." Whitney debated whether to eat a fourth slice. "But Jonas—"

"Just needs softening up," Sarah finished for her.

Whitney groaned. "That's like saying the Pacific Ocean needs a little less salt."

"What's it worth to you?" Sarah's expression was serious.

"Worth?"

"How much of an effort are you willing to make? It sounds to me like you've just written him off."

While she thought over Sarah's question, Whitney decided against the fourth piece. Her waistband was already feeling a bit snug. Until the past couple of years, she'd been able to eat anything she wanted and never worry about gaining weight, but her body was changing. That, she supposed, was the price of maturity.

"I'm not going to chase Jonas and tie him up," she said finally. "But I'd meet him halfway."

"That's the funny thing about you," Sarah said. "You hang on like a bulldog for most things you want, but you give up so easily where Jonas is concerned. Meeting him halfway isn't good enough, and you know it. Somebody's got to open that man's eyes to the truth."

Sarah was right, Whitney realized. When she'd wanted control of Brite Cola, she'd flung herself into the contest heart and soul, doing the most outrageous things she could think of. But when it came to Jonas, the prospect of being rejected hurt too much.

"I suppose so," she said. "He does need a nudge in the right direction. Or maybe a good strong push."

A flicker of alarm crossed Sarah's face. "I wasn't suggesting you do anything drastic. I mean, just—well, create a romantic mood. Help his emotions to triumph over his intellect."

Whitney sighed. "What did you think I was going to do, kidnap him?"

"With you, I never know."

"Neither do I," she admitted. "Oh, Sarah, I want a man I can be myself with. Jonas has to accept me as I am."

"But first he has to see you as you are—a twenty-eight-year-old executive who's also a beautiful, strong-willed woman," Sarah said. "Not the kid he used to know."

"Any suggestions?"

"The best way I know to get a man alone in your apartment is to offer him a home-cooked meal. It's amazing how good that sounds to a bachelor."

"Not Jonas. He has a housekeeper, remember? All his meals are home-cooked." But Whitney was beginning to feel better. "On the other hand, he's been eating at restaurants the past few weeks. You might be right."

"I'm glad we agree." Sarah stood up, then paused. "Uh—Whitney, do you know how to cook? I mean, anything fancier than a grilled cheese sandwich?"

"I can wing it," Whitney insisted.

"Good luck," Sarah said. "I'd offer to help you shop, but my parents are due back with Kip in half an hour."

"Oh, I can handle it," Whitney declared.

She stopped at the office and gave the receptionist a memo for Jonas, saying he was expected for dinner at six-thirty. Then she sneaked out before he could read it.

As Sarah had said, sometimes Jonas needed a shove in the right direction.

Chapter Six

"Dear Jonas. Expect you for dinner, 6:30 p.m., my place. Be there. Love, Whitney."

Jonas reread the memo in exasperation, not sure whether to accept or not. It was by no means the first such commanding note he'd received from Whitney over the years, and he thought it was time she learned the rudiments of etiquette.

Writing notes to him had started as a shared joke, when she was about ten years old and feeling frustrated at the slowness with which adolescence was dawning. It had given her a feeling of power to send orders to her "big brother," and he'd found it amusing to humor her.

But she wasn't a kid now, and he didn't feel like her big brother, either. In fact, the last thing he needed was to be alone with Whitney at her apartment.

On the other hand, he wasn't thrilled about eating another dinner at the hotel, or about the possibility of running into the Truaxes, who were staying only two floors below him. He was just too tired to deal with them.

"Had enough for one day?" Mattie began stacking the papers on Jonas's desk.

"I guess I have," he admitted. "Is Whitney around?"

"She played hooky this afternoon." Mattie scooped up a wad of paper that had missed the wastebasket. "I suppose she's out trying to do something about this mess with Carol."

"Let me ask you something as a member of the public, so to speak." Jonas swiveled around in his chair. "What's your impression of all this? Do you think it's Brite Cola's fault, separating her from her family?"

"Oh, pooh." Mattie sniffed. "She's not a teenager, you know. She's old enough to make up her own mind. I think she's mixed-up and self-centered, to tell you the truth, although I have to admit that wasn't my impression when I met her."

"Let's hope other people see it the same way." Jonas unfolded himself from behind the desk, stretching his cramped legs and wincing. He wasn't used to sitting in an office all day; at the vineyard he was constantly on the move, checking on the processing or conferring with his foreman. There was paperwork too, of course, but he had an assistant to handle that.

"Will you be needing to see anything else tomorrow?" Mattie paused in the doorway.

"I don't think so. We did a pretty thorough job today. Thanks, Mattie."

Jonas walked somewhat stiffly to the elevator and then out to his car. As he started the motor, he realized that of course he was going to Whitney's for dinner. He'd never disobeyed one of her summonses before, *so why start now?*

There was a florist's shop on the way, and he stopped there on impulse. Roses seemed too formal and chrysanthemums too old-fashioned, so he settled instead on a bright burst of spring flowers, daisies and multicolored frilly things that Jonas didn't know the name of.

At Balboa Island, he parked on a dead end and walked along the beachfront sidewalk to Whitney's place. Some college-age girls in bikinis were playing volleyball in the twilight under the amorous gazes of several surfers. They made him feel old and out of place, exactly the way he usually felt around Whitney.

But when she opened the door and flashed him a delighted grin, Jonas found himself regarding Whitney with new eyes. After all, he'd been reviewing her rather impressive work as Brite Cola's chief executive officer all day, and besides, she did look mature and self-possessed compared to those girls on the beach.

Mature and self-possessed and golden and glowing, and infinitely sexy.

Jonas whipped the bouquet out from behind his back. "Flowers for my lady."

Whitney gathered them into her arms and inhaled deeply. "They smell wonderful."

"Speaking of smells." Jonas moved past her and sniffed. "Don't tell me you're actually cooking."

"What did you expect?"

"Take-out Chinese food, as usual." He strode into the kitchen. Sure enough, water was bubbling in a pot and hamburger sizzled in a frying pan. On a sideboard lay a loaf of French bread, sliced lengthwise and spread with butter and—so his nose informed him—garlic. "I'm honored."

"Don't jump to any conclusions. I'm kind of experimenting." Whitney tucked the flowers into a blue and white vase and set them on the table. "I hope it turns out to be edible."

"We can always send out for pizza."

"Oh, no. I had that for lunch." She tugged her apron into place. "I've got stuff in the freezer, don't worry."

He leaned against the counter, watching as Whitney drained the hamburger and stirred in a couple of cans of tomato sauce, followed by a can of mushrooms, a dash of sherry and an array of spices.

"I call this hit-or-miss spaghetti." She looked appealingly artless, pushing back a strand of blond hair as she cooked. She was wearing a blue velour jogging suit that would have appeared baggy on anyone else, but only managed to emphasize the firm shape of Whitney's body, while the color brought out the azure of her eyes. *Damn,* but she was a stunning woman.

"To what do I owe this honor?" he asked.

"Remember what we were talking about Friday night, before we were so rudely interrupted?"

"Frankly, no."

Whitney wrinkled her nose at him. "You're going to make me repeat all this, aren't you? To refresh your memory, we were discussing our relationship—which Cynthia, as you'll recall, suggested we needed to work out."

"Go on. It's beginning to come back to me."

"I had lunch with Sarah today and she suggested I take the initiative." Whitney stuck a handful of spaghetti into the boiling water and began to stir it into submission.

"Whoa." Jonas wasn't sure he was following her. "Are you telling me you've planned a seduction?"

From the way she ducked her head, he realized that he'd embarrassed her. *Incredible. Whitney Greystone, embarrassed?*

"Why don't you pick out a bottle of wine from the refrigerator?" she said. "You're the expert."

"Trying to get me drunk?" He opened the heavy door and selected a bottle of Ameling Reserve Cabernet Sauvignon. "You have good taste in wine."

"You sent me a case of it at Christmas, remember?" Whitney retrieved a colander from the cabinet and set it in the sink.

"So I did."

An inner voice of common sense was telling Jonas he ought to put an end to this romantic dinner right now. The whole idea was ridiculous. Whitney was practically his kid sister, for heaven's sake. And even if they did make love, that wouldn't resolve the vast abyss between their personal styles.

But for once, his body was issuing commands of its own. Telling the voice of reason to shut up. Telling his brain that Whitney would feel soft and eager in his arms, that her lips were full, that there was no sense in a man and a woman torturing themselves when they both wanted the same thing.

Maybe it was time they made love. It would clear the air. Maybe becoming another in Whitney's no doubt long line of lovers was actually the sensible thing to do.

"After you ply me with wine, what are you planning to do?" Jonas decanted the red liquid into two cut crystal glasses.

"Would you quit making fun of me?" Whitney glared at him.

"I wasn't, actually."

"You're making this whole thing sound like another one of my zany escapades. Well, it isn't."

"I've never been seduced before." Jonas handed her a glass of wine. "I think I might enjoy it."

"Really?"

"Really."

Whitney turned her head away as she stirred the spaghetti sauce. "You'll have to help."

"I was planning to." Was there another woman in the world who would talk to a man this way? The mixture of childish naiveté and womanly sensuality was almost overwhelming. "I might even teach you a few things."

She lifted the heavy pot and poured the spaghetti into the colander. "I wouldn't be surprised."

The spaghetti, served with a tossed salad and the garlic bread, was delicious, but Jonas's body was throbbing in intimate places. He wanted this meal to be over with. He wanted to get on with the business of devouring Whitney.

There was an unfamiliar shyness about her, in the way she bit her lip and averted her eyes as she ate. As if she were nervous.

Well, there was a first time for everything.

Finally they were finished. Jonas helped her clear the dishes away. Once Whitney brushed against him by accident and he was surprised at the fire that rippled through him at the contact.

"Maybe I'd better take the phone off the hook," she said. At his nod, she crossed and lifted the receiver. A puzzled look crossed Whitney's face and she said, "Hello?"

Damn it, there was somebody on the line. *Please let it be a wrong number.*

But he could tell from her frown that it wasn't.

"You've got to be kidding," she was saying. "Bob, I don't believe it. What are they trying to do, ruin us? They might as well take out an ad in the L.A. *Times*."

Jonas's mellow mood vanished. "It's Abernathy? What's going on?"

Whitney waved him into silence. "Well, which one? Reno or Tahoe or Vegas? And which casino? Can't you pin it down a little better?"

This was sounding worse and worse.

Finally Whitney hung up. "Bob heard a rumor through the same musician that Carol and Karl are planning to turn up at a casino lounge and sing their duet. Only he's not sure which city, just that it's in Nevada."

"Well, great." Jonas could see her wince at the sarcasm in his voice. "Now we're chasing not one but three wild geese. Or is that gooses?"

"Whichever it is, ours is cooked." Whitney slumped onto the couch. "It's a lost cause, Jonas."

"Call him back." The musician had been right about Nashville, after all. "Tell Bob he's got to find out more. He can't expect us to run from one city to another."

"It's tomorrow night." Whitney shrugged resignedly. "He already did his best. Things will just have to work themselves out."

Even though he knew rationally that this new turn of events wasn't Whitney's fault, Jonas's irritation found a target in her outrageously laissez-faire attitude. "So you think we should just wait and see? And I was beginning to think you were a competent businesswoman."

"I am!"

"If those two go onstage and sing together, heaven knows what they'll say. Maybe they'll announce their engagement, for pity's sake. Destroy everything we've been building up these past two and a half years." At the back of his mind, Jonas remembered what Mattie had said, that the public would hold Carol responsible for her own actions. But his temper was well and truly lost, and he couldn't seem to stop the angry words.

"Hey, look." Whitney stood up and faced him, hands on hips. "You can't control everything in the world, Jonas Ameling. There comes a time when you just have to look at things philosophically. I used to study Eastern religions, remember? Maybe all this was written out long before we were born. Maybe—"

"Don't pull that garbage on me!"

"'We'll get a sign." This was the pseudomystical adolescent Whitney he knew all too well from years past. "If we're supposed to catch them, something will tell us which city to go to. But not if we're too busy shouting at each other to pay attention."

"Pay attention to what? Tea leaves? Octopus innards?" Jonas clenched his hands and stalked away, forcing himself to regain control. Whitney had the uncanny ability to provoke him into a rage, something no one else had succeeded in doing since Jonas was a child.

Watching him, Whitney felt a sense of loss ripple through her. Why couldn't Jonas relax a little and let life happen? Some things were simply beyond human control. Now he'd ruined this precious mood between them. *Darn it,* just because she didn't always view life the way he did, that didn't mean she was an idiot.

The phone rang again.

"That had better be Abernathy." Jonas snatched up the receiver. "Bob? Oh. Hello, Lina. Yes, she's right here."

Lina?

Numbly, Whitney reached for the phone.

She hadn't heard from Lina Greystone since they'd bought out Lina's and Gavin's Brite Cola stock two and a half years ago. And although Whitney couldn't avoid noting Lina's comings and goings occasionally in the society pages, she'd never expected to have any further contact with her father's first wife.

Lina had been The Enemy as long as Whitney could remember. Even though her divorce had happened several years before Whitney's parents met, Lina had bitterly resented her ex-husband's remarriage, and particularly his daughter. After all, Lina had expected her son Gavin to inherit everything. The last thing he'd needed was a half-sister to compete with.

Their enmity had come into the open when three years after her father died and left his son to run Brite Cola, it became all too clear that Gavin had mismanaged the company until it was almost worthless.

Lina and Gavin had decided to sell out to a conglomerate, which would no doubt have gutted the company and destroyed its identity. Whitney's tactic in threatening to publish the secret formula had infuriated them, but it had achieved its purpose: Lina and Gavin had finally agreed to sell their shares to Jonas, Michael and her.

She hadn't heard a word from Lina since. Why was the woman calling now? Planning to rub it in about the Brite Cola jokes, perhaps?

"Hello, Lina." Whitney gritted her teeth.

"Hello, darling. How's everything? Just wonderful, I hope! It's been so long. I've been telling myself, I've simply *got* to give Whitney a call." The false gaiety in Lina's voice was the tone she reserved for people from whom she wanted something.

But what could she want from Whitney? According to the society columnists, Lina was practically engaged to Anston Arkady, a millionaire pharmaceuticals exporter. Surely she could wheedle anything she needed from him. "Something wrong, Lina?"

"Wrong?"

"You didn't call me just to shoot the breeze."

"Oh, darling, you haven't changed a bit! Still the same old shoot-from-the-hip Whitney. Why, do you know, I've seen your picture practically everywhere! Magazine covers, newspapers. I don't know where you find the time! Arkady and I—you know Arkady, don't you?—we've been so busy organizing the All-Charity Ball. That's this weekend, and positively everybody is coming. But then, I don't have to tell you that, do I? I'm sure you've heard all about it."

As Lina spoke, Whitney summoned up an image of the regal woman with her classic profile and taut, ungenerous mouth. There would be a cigarette in one hand, no doubt, and probably some assistant fussing in the background, fixing Lina's dramatic sweep of gray and black hair or laying out her clothes. Lina never did anything for herself that could be done by others. "I'm glad to hear you're raising money for charity."

"Well, you know, poor people have to live, too, although God knows why they don't just get a job." That was definitely the smack of lips on a cigarette.

"Lina, if you don't mind, Jonas is here and we were having a—business discussion. If there's something you need, please come out with it." Whitney couldn't seem to help bordering on rudeness where her father's first wife was concerned. Using tact with Lina was like trying to stop a forest fire with a watering can.

"Actually, I just had a call from your brother." Lina paused. Whitney imagined her posing melodramatically, eyes widened, demanding a response just as if Whitney were there in person.

"Half brother."

"He *is* the only family you've got left, but that's neither here nor there." Impatience roughened Lina's voice. "He's about to do something simply awful, and this is the worst possible timing. I can't just run off and leave all the arrangements for the ball up in the air. What would Arkady think? Everyone's depending on me!"

And we wouldn't want to risk losing a millionaire, even if your son's in trouble. "What simply awful thing is Gavin up to now?" It was hard to imagine anything worse than the heavy drinking and womanizing Gavin had been doing for years, with no objections from his mother.

"He's getting married!"

With difficulty, Whitney stifled the impulse to laugh. "That doesn't sound so bad."

"Yes, but it's who he's marrying!" Outrage bristled in the voice at the other end of the telephone line. "A Las Vegas show girl! Can you believe that? How would I explain it to Arkady?"

"Maybe he's in love." Whitney shrugged, for Jonas's benefit. Fortunately, he knew Lina well enough to understand that disentangling oneself from a conversation with her was no simple matter.

"Love? Don't be ridiculous! She's a scheming little gold digger and she knows a good thing when she sees it."

Then why would she want to marry Gavin? "I don't see what I can do about it."

"You could talk some sense to him! I know the two of you have never been close, but you are his sister and frankly, Whitney, you do have class. Seeing you might bring him to his senses, especially in contrast to that cheap little tart he's running around with! You can make him understand that she simply wouldn't fit in."

"Lina, I've got other things to worry about right now." It was time to wrap this thing up. "Gavin's a grown man, and anyway, I'm the last person he'd listen to."

"You've got to go!" Could that be desperation? Obviously it wasn't bad enough for Lina to risk losing Arkady, but still... As she pointed out, Gavin *was* all the family Whitney had left. "At least talk to him. She's probably been slipping drugs into his drink. Some women will stop at nothing! My poor little boy; it just breaks my heart."

Whitney sighed. Rationally, she knew that Lina was motivated entirely by selfishness, and that Gavin was lucky to find any woman at all willing to marry him. But although she'd vowed to start turning her back on hard-luck stories, Whitney was finding it more difficult than she'd imagined.

Jonas was signaling to her to hurry it up. Suddenly, another thought occurred to her. "Okay, Lina," she said. "I'll go. Where's he staying?"

With a sigh of relief, Lina gave her a phone number in Las Vegas. "I can't tell you how much I appreciate this." She provided Whitney with her own telephone number for a follow-up. "It would be so humiliating to have trash like that in the family."

"I'll let you know what happens." Whitney dropped the receiver onto the cradle.

"Well?" Jonas was pacing restlessly. "What have you gotten yourself in for now?"

"We're going to Las Vegas to meet Gavin's fiancée. She's a show girl and Lina wants me to scare her off, but I'm reserving judgment." Whitney picked up the phone again.

"What are you doing?"

"Making reservations."

Jonas snatched the phone out of her hand. "In case you've forgotten, Miss Greystone, we have more important things to worry about. Like the future of Brite Cola."

"It's just like I told you." Whitney grinned, enjoying the infuriating effect on Jonas.

"Like you told me what?"

"I said we'd get a sign. About which city in Nevada we should go to. Las Vegas it is."

He stared at her, his expression mutating from confusion to annoyance to amusement. A deep baritone chuckle rumbled through the room, and Whitney found herself laughing, too.

"This is crazy." Jonas shook his head. "You're the most illogical person I've ever met, Whitney, but you know, they say even a stopped clock is right twice a day."

"Gee, thanks."

"Besides, I'm curious to meet this show girl friend of Gavin's."

"Me, too."

To her surprise, Jonas came and put his arms around Whitney. "I'm sorry I was so hard on you, about your philosophy of life. I tend to mistrust anything that isn't orderly and logical."

"But life isn't orderly and logical." Leaning her head against his shoulder, she drank in the strength of his arms, the tenderness of his embrace.

"Exactly." He sounded wistful. "I miss out on so many things, Whitney. While you do things backward and sideways and upside down, and yet they still work out." He drew back then. "I'd better go."

Suddenly she couldn't bear to be separated from him. Maybe it was Lina's reminder that Whitney was more or less alone in the world, or maybe it was the warm, gentle feeling he'd stirred these last few minutes. "Don't leave."

"We've got to be sensible."

"Why?"

Jonas smiled. "Why, indeed? Because ... Whitney, what happens afterward? You're my closest friend."

"And you don't want to ruin a beautiful friendship by making love?" *Don't be so damn sensible!* she wanted to cry, but then, his logic was one of the things she loved about Jonas. "Then sleep on the sofa. Or you take the bed and I'll take the sofa. Just stay."

He reached out and stroked her hair. "Only until you've made the reservations and gotten settled. Talking to Lina always upsets you. You'll snap out of it."

"Maybe." At least she'd bought a few minutes. Maybe in that time she could think of some other way to hold him. Because if he left now, something inside Whitney would strain as tightly as a rubber band, and sometime in the night it might break entirely.

It took only a moment to arrange a flight to Las Vegas the next morning. They could leave from nearby John Wayne Airport instead of driving all the way to LAX. "I've left you time to stop by your hotel and pack tomorrow," she said pointedly after hanging up.

"Whitney, I can't stay."

"Remember what Cynthia said? We need to get this out of our system."

"I'll never get you out of my system." Jonas stopped abruptly, as if shocked by his own words.

Whitney sensed instinctively that if she didn't take immediate action, Jonas's mind was going to gear up into a potentially fatal attack of common sense. On the other hand, he was clearly feeling uncomfortable about being alone with her in the apartment. "Let's go for a walk."

He opened his mouth as if to object, and then hesitated. "All right. I could use the fresh air."

A few minutes later, wearing a thick hand-knitted Scandinavian sweater, Whitney was strolling alongside Jonas through a night crisp with early spring and thick with stars.

"You might have wondered what I was doing today, reviewing the company's records," he said.

It was far from a romantic opening, but yes, Whitney had to admit, she *was* curious. "Just doing your job, right?"

"Making a decision." Her eyes hadn't grown accustomed enough to the darkness yet to read the expression on his face. "Remember, I said I was planning to hand over the reins to you? Well, I think it's time."

"No." Whitney stopped, ignoring the lap of icy water dangerously near her tennis shoes.

"I thought that was what you wanted." His body sheltered her from the breeze.

"Yes, but—" There was no discreet way to put this.

"Then I'll never see you. There'll be no reason for you to fly down from Sonoma."

"Whitney." His hands were gentle on her shoulders. "We've been friends a long time."

"Things are changing, Jonas." She stared up at him, her vision blurring beneath the tears. Damn it, he wasn't going to bend. "If you weren't so darned thickheaded, you'd see it."

"See what? That you're a grown woman? I know that, Whitney. But I also know that people have to be fundamentally compatible to make a relationship work."

She pulled away and glared at him. "Oh, that sounds so rational! What are you going to do, Jonas, make every woman you meet take a psychological profile test? What about feelings? What about chemistry? You talk about letting go of the reins, but that's the one thing you'll never do, not where your emotions are concerned. You might as well climb into a coffin right now and nail down the lid."

He caught her wrists with a grip so tight that it was almost painful. "Don't tempt me, Whitney."

"What the hell do you think I've been trying to do all night?"

His laughter, when it came, was rich and free and infectious. Before she could decide whether to laugh along with him or knock him onto the sand and pound him into silence, Whitney found herself pulled against a hard chest, and his mouth closed over hers with a ferocity she'd never felt from Jonas before.

Under the onslaught, her lips opened instinctively, and the night and the sea whirled away. There was only the warmth of Jonas, an island in the cold darkness.

Just as suddenly, he lifted his head. "You want me to cut loose? All right, Whitney, but don't complain if you don't like it."

Before she could catch her breath, Jonas hoisted her over his shoulder and strode across the beach to her apartment. *Thank goodness* no one was watching; the curtains were drawn on the downstairs unit—although at this point, Whitney wasn't sure she cared who saw them.

Then they were inside, and she forgot that anyone else existed in the world. Jonas carried her directly into the bedroom and, without a word, pulled her down beside him.

Hungrily his lips explored the crevices of her throat, the pulse points of her wrist, the welcome of her mouth. This was more than warmth; it was fire, and longing, and a great burst of sparks turning the darkness into a conflagration.

Wriggling out of her sweater, Whitney was surprised at how good it felt to be undressing with Jonas. Her body responded naturally to every stroke, every movement.

The fire raging between them burned away the past: the awkwardness of her adolescence, the brother-sister-like quarrels, the unfulfilled longings. There was only one course for them now, and whatever might happen afterward, Whitney knew she would never regret it.

Jonas was a surprisingly sensitive lover, his demands tempered by gentleness, his hands knowing and expert. She couldn't resent the other lovers who must have helped shape him. All these years, he had only been in training for this moment.

When they were united, Whitney was stunned by the sensations that rocketed through her body. She had never known such raw desire, such delirious joy. It felt wanton, almost shocking, and yet from Jonas's response she knew that it was right; this was natural, this was love.

There was a moment of pain, then only pleasure, a pure and rhythmic joining that carried them through the chill of the night into a dawn of the heart, a flaming sunrise that was gradually transformed into softness and satisfaction.

They lay together, Jonas's arms wrapped tightly around Whitney. Only then did self-awareness return to them.

"Whitney?" he murmured.

"Mmm?"

"Were you—did I imagine?" He cleared his throat, so close to her ear that Whitney felt rather than heard the sound. "This couldn't have been your first time."

"Oh, that." She sighed. "Actually, yes. You don't mind, do you?"

He propped himself on his elbow. "But I thought—you always seemed so wild, and I know you dated a lot."

Beside Whitney, the old familiar Mickey Mouse clock was ticking away. The room was the same one she'd slept in for the past two years. And yet everything had changed. "I just never could go through with it. It was never the right moment. Or the right man, I guess."

"You waited for me?" Jonas sat up. "Whitney—"

"Now, don't go making a big deal out of it." She poked him in the thigh. "It simply worked out that way. I didn't plan it."

Slowly Jonas slid under the covers again. "We should have used some protection. I wasn't thinking."

"Wrong time of the month," Whitney said. "I'm not stupid, you know."

"Still, basically nothing has changed." He was talking more to himself than to her. "We're still as different as we ever were. Whitney, I care about you, more than I can say, but—"

"If you utter one more word, I'll cram this alarm clock down your throat." Whitney nestled into her pillow. "I'd like to get some sleep, if you don't mind."

He didn't answer, and a few minutes later she heard his deep, even breathing.

Not long after that, she drifted off, too.

Chapter Seven

The flight to Las Vegas didn't take nearly long enough. Whitney felt as if not only her bags but her mind had been packed hastily, and that key items had probably been left back in her apartment.

Jonas, as usual, looked perfectly groomed as he sat beside her on the plane though she suspected his thoughts were as unsettled as her own.

Just what the hell did happen between us last night, anyway?

Not that she had any questions about the physical side of it. They'd made love well and thoroughly, and it had been even better than Whitney had imagined. In fact, if she'd known it felt this good, she wasn't sure she would have waited so long. On the other hand, with any other man, it would likely have been a grave disappointment.

It simply wasn't fair. Jonas had her hooked. He always had. And yet...

Sometimes, Whitney knew, love wasn't enough. She'd seen couples who adored each other and yet fought viciously and ended up divorcing. You have to be able to live together day in and day out, one friend had told her when announcing that she and her husband were separating. *It's the little things that tear you apart.*

And if there was one thing worse than not marrying Jonas, it would be marrying him and ending up divorced.

Whitney groaned and sank back in her seat.

"Are you feeling all right?" He looked up from reading the business section of the *Los Angeles Times*.

"A little tired." Whitney tried to interest herself in the View section, but her eyes refused to focus.

The future stretched ahead of her like the bank of clouds outside the airplane window, vast and impossible to see through. She knew she would try her best, if Jonas would meet her halfway, but he could be so damn infuriating at times.

Maybe she should just enjoy what they had, for however long it lasted.

Her thoughts turned to Gavin, and she wondered about his relationship with this show girl. Her half-brother was notorious for drinking and having affairs with every attractive woman he could lure into bed. She'd always expected that, if he ever settled down, it would be with someone extremely wealthy. Not for love, but for money.

Then the plane began its descent into Las Vegas, and Whitney had to put her speculation on the back burner.

They had arranged to stay at the casino where the show girl—her name was Maria, Whitney remembered—worked. Once they'd checked in, she dialed the number Lina had given her for Gavin's apartment, while Jonas studied a local entertainment guide to see what country music stars might be in town to play host for Karl and Carol. Assuming, of course, they weren't in Reno or Tahoe.

Gavin's phone rang four times before he answered.

"It's me." Whitney knew her brother would recognize her voice. "Jonas and I just happened to be in town and we'd like to take you and your fiancée to dinner." *Darn it,* why couldn't she have approached the subject in a more roundabout way, she chided herself as soon as the words were out.

"Lina sent you, didn't she?" Gavin's voice had the familiar whiny edge, although at least his words weren't slurred. "You didn't 'just happen' to be in town, Whitney."

"Yes and no." There was no point in lying. Actually, hearing Gavin's voice reminded her of how much she hadn't missed her brother. Maybe it wouldn't be such a bad thing if he refused to see them—but she *was* curious about Maria. "We're here on business, and furthermore, I have no intention of interfering in your life. But when we heard you were engaged, well, it seemed like a good opportunity to meet your future wife."

"She's a show girl." Gavin sounded defiant. "I suppose Mother told you."

"Yes, but she's also going to be my sister-in-law, so I want to meet her," Whitney said. "And so does Jonas."

"What's going on with Brite Cola, anyway? I've been hearing jokes on the radio, something about that woman who won the contest." At least Gavin didn't jump right in and attack her for mishandling the company's publicity, as she had half expected.

"That's why we're here." Whitney decided to tease him along. "And if you'll let us take you to dinner, I'll tell you all about it."

There was a disgruntled silence, at least, knowing Gavin as well as she did, she assumed it was disgruntled. Finally he said, "Well, all right. We'd planned on eating out tonight, anyway, and you can foot the bill, if you like." He named a restaurant in one of the hotels.

"My pleasure," Whitney said.

The dinner was to be an early one, before Maria's first show. "She won't be able to eat much, but she'll have a snack later." Gavin's tone had softened considerably. "Tonight's her last night on the job. I'm taking her away from all this."

"I can't wait to meet her." Whitney said goodbye and turned to find Jonas shaking his head over the entertainment listings.

"There are three country music shows tonight," he grumbled. "Can you believe it? Even if we split up, we can only cover two."

"Besides which, we won't be able to do anything until *after* their appearance," Whitney pointed out. "You weren't planning to run up onstage and grab Carol, were you?"

Jonas tossed the paper onto the carpet in disgust. "Fill me in on the dinner plans."

They had several hours before them, so Jonas spent the time making phone calls around town to try to locate Karl and Carol, without success. Whitney fell asleep by the swimming pool, and was saved from a bad burn only by an alert pool attendant who shaded her with an umbrella.

Trudging stiffly back to the room, she reflected that usually she had a golden tan even this early in the year. But the past few months she'd been too busy for sunbathing.

For once, she looked as if she *had* grown up in Idaho.

Whitney and Jonas had taken a room together, but she found herself dressing for dinner in the privacy of the large bathroom. For some reason, she still felt self-conscious around Jonas. And it wasn't because she lacked a tan, either, Whitney admitted ruefully.

She chose her most sophisticated outfit, a hand-dyed long skirt and shell top in a lavender tone. A hand-painted spray of gold, turquoise and coral enlivened one shoulder of the soft matching jacket, and she wore golden shoes and earrings.

Jonas's eyes widened as she emerged from the bathroom. "You look striking."

"So do you." He was wearing a dark suit that emphasized his broad shoulders and brought out the rich reddish-brown of his eyes. The salt-and-pepper streak in his hair added a formal touch.

"Men aren't supposed to look striking." But he was smiling as he offered his arm. "Shall we?"

They drove their rental car down the Strip between flashing neon signs. The glitter of Las Vegas, concentrated in the midst of the desert, struck Whitney as frenetic, almost desperate. She was glad their visit wouldn't be a long one.

The restaurant Gavin had chosen was plush and sprawling. Looking around, Whitney couldn't get a fix on the exact shape of the room, perhaps because there was a wall of mirrors. Then she spotted her half-brother.

"Hi!" She waved and moved forward. Gavin turned and nodded, his expression guarded.

"He's lost weight," Jonas said.

Whitney studied her brother surreptitiously. "And his face doesn't look so puffy any more."

"Maria's in the ladies' room," Gavin said a moment later as he shook hands with Jonas. "She'll be right out."

"When's the wedding?" Whitney asked.

"Tomorrow."

"You're kidding!" Lina hadn't mentioned it, so she probably hadn't known. "You didn't tell your mother?"

"I left a message on her machine an hour ago." Gavin's jaw tightened, and Whitney was surprised to notice the aristocratic line of his throat, like Lina's. Now that he'd lost weight, her half brother was more attractive than she'd given him credit for. "She has time to get here, if she wants to, but of course she won't. And I didn't want to give her long enough to pull some other trick."

At the word "other," Whitney bristled. "We're not a trick of Lina's, Gavin. I don't even get along with her, as you perfectly well know."

Then she stopped as her brother's eyes softened and his mouth pursed in a mock whistle.

Following his gaze, Whitney spied a tall, slender woman striding toward them. Her well-shaped body was encased in a shimmering sequined gown, and her blond hair was piled regally high atop her head.

As the woman drew closer, the paleness of her hair struck Whitney as unnatural against her olive skin, but she was impressed anyway. Bleached hair or not, Maria had a natural dignity and authority that, Whitney suspected, could stand up even to Lina's haughtiest manner.

Gavin slipped an arm around his fiancée's waist. "Maria, this is my sister Whitney—and an old family friend, Jonas Ameling."

Greetings were exchanged, and the foursome was soon seated at a secluded table.

"I've seen your picture in the magazines." Maria studied Whitney frankly over her menu. "You could have been a show girl, if you'd wanted to."

Lina might have snickered at the suggestion, but Whitney was touched. "That's quite a compliment. But Gavin tells me you're giving up your job."

"Oh, I don't mind." Maria's smile was bright and unaffected. "I wouldn't have stuck it out this long if it weren't for my little boy."

It was obvious that Lina didn't know about this angle. "What's his name?" Whitney asked.

"Bryan. He's six." Maria paused while the waiter took their orders, then added cautiously, "I was never married, you see, and his father wouldn't take responsibility, so it was all up to me."

From the way Gavin's eyes narrowed, Whitney could see he was bracing for a snub. But she felt only respect for Maria's strength. "I'm glad he's going to have a father now."

Gavin smiled for the first time that evening. "He's a cute little guy. He calls me Daddy already."

"Where are you planning to live?" Jonas finally joined in the conversation.

"The L.A. area." Maria took a sip of her wine. Gavin was sticking to soda water, Whitney noticed approvingly. "I don't like New York, and you're the only other family Gavin has. My mother's dead and I don't know where my father is these days, so it will be nice for Bryan to be near his aunt. I grew up there, in east L.A., and I like the climate.''

Whitney was enjoying Maria's openness, and she didn't mind at all the prospect of becoming an aunt. "I never thought I'd have a nephew. I can't wait."

They chatted some more about the wedding arrangements, and then Jonas filled Gavin in on Carol's shenanigans.

"Joe Blazer," Maria said at once. At Whitney's questioning look, she added, "He's playing one of the smaller lounges. I saw in the paper where he was a semiregular on *The Karl Kauer Show*."

"I didn't even notice he was here," Jonas admitted. "Thanks, Maria."

As they finished eating, Maria said, "Whitney, if I'd known you were coming, I'd have arranged for you to be in the wedding. We could still..."

"It's okay." Whitney downed her last mouthful of pecan pie. "I'm just happy we can be there."

"So am I." Maria squeezed her arm before slipping away. "See you tomorrow."

Gavin lingered over coffee, discussing odds and ends from the day's news. Finally he said, "You know, I've never put much value on having a family, but now that I'm going to be a father, I can see that Bryan needs a framework, for holidays and just plain stability. Aunts, maybe even a grandmother, although I have my doubts about how well that'll work out."

"How did the two of you meet?" Jonas asked.

Gavin ducked his head for a moment before answering. "To tell you the truth, I got really drunk one night at a casino. Maria was getting off work and she saw me staggering toward my car and demanded that I let her drive me to my place. She even made sure I got inside okay. I was angry at first, but then I noticed how beautiful she was, and I persuaded her to give me her phone number. In the beginning, I was just planning on a little fun, but she kind of took me in hand. I feel as if I've finally come into the clear after walking through a fog these past few years."

"She's wonderful for you." Whitney placed a hand on her brother's arm. "Gavin, I'm so pleased."

He took a deep breath. "Now that I'm beginning to see things clearly, I guess I owe you an apology. I behaved pretty miserably to you over the years, Whitney. To me, you were nothing but a pest and a usurper. Now I'm glad I have a sister."

"And I a brother." Whitney promised to take her nephew to Disneyland as soon as the mess with Carol was cleared up. And she was pleased to learn that the new family would be honeymooning in Laguna Beach, not far from Newport. "If you need anything, just give me a call."

"We'll keep in touch," Gavin promised as they parted company.

After he left, Jonas said, "I'm still not sure I believe the change in him. I gather he and Maria haven't known each other very long. I hope it lasts."

"So do I."

Slowly, Whitney's thoughts turned to the evening ahead of them. Las Vegas wasn't her idea of a romantic spot, but being with Jonas was enough to turn neon into stardust. Maybe they could have a leisurely soak in the hotel's whirlpool bath, followed by nightcaps à deux in their room, and then . . .

Her reverie was shattered by Jonas's next words, as he rose from the table. "We'd better catch Joe Blazer's act and hope Maria was right."

Oh, yes. Inwardly, Whitney uttered a series of dire threats to Carol for intruding on this precious night. But she had to admit that she and Jonas would never have been spending so much time together in the first place if it hadn't been for their wayward charge.

Luckily, the first show hadn't yet begun when they claimed a small table near the back of the lounge. After ordering an Irish coffee, Whitney gazed around the dimly lit room, hoping against hope that she'd spot Carol or Karl while there was still time to prevent their performance.

Not that the public didn't already have an idea of what was going on, but it might still be possible to smooth things over. If they stood up there and announced that they'd fallen in love, or some such thing, the cat would be out of the bag irrevocably.

There was no sign of the runaways, but Whitney noticed professional-looking cameras on some of the tables. And several of the audience members were holding notepads and pushing buttons on briefcases that probably concealed tape recorders.

She nudged Jonas. "I think somebody alerted the press. At least this must be the right place."

He followed her gaze. "Damn it. Why are they doing this to us?"

"Maybe it was Joe Blazer who called the papers." For some reason, Whitney found herself suddenly wanting to give Carol the benefit of the doubt. "I still can't believe she'd deliberately hurt her family this way."

"Your qualifications as a judge of character are pretty much shot," Jonas muttered.

About to argue back, Whitney checked herself. "I guess I did screw up, didn't I?" A bright side occurred to her. "You're probably having second thoughts about handing over control of the company, then, aren't you?"

"Your weakness for sob stories isn't likely to get Brite Cola into any further trouble," he pointed out calmly. "You've done a good job in every other department. We just won't run any more contests."

"Jonas—" She didn't really want to bring up an intimate subject here and now, but controlling impulses had never been Whitney's strong point. "About last night. You aren't just going to go back to Sonoma when this is over, are you?"

"Why ask me?" He shot her an unexpected, quirky grin. "I feel like I've been flattened by a runaway train these past few weeks, Whitney. For once in my life, I have no idea what I'm going to do. I'm not even sure what I *want* to do."

Before she had time to digest this bit of information, the house lights dimmed and applause greeted a stocky young man who strolled out carrying a guitar. *Come to think of it,* he did look familiar. Whitney wasn't exactly a devoted fan of *The Karl Kauer Show,* but she had caught it from time to time. Joe Blazer, she recalled now, played a cousin of Karl's who hailed from the Ozarks.

"Hi, y'all. Glad you could come down and join us." Joe included his small backup band in the "us." But Whitney felt sure that Carol and Karl were waiting backstage. A shiver of nervous excitement turned her skin prickly and her hands cold. What *were* she and Jonas going to do, anyway?

Joe launched into a twangy, toe-tapping song that concluded to generous applause. He tried out a couple of jokes, which were only mildly amusing, and then sang an old-fashioned ballad about lost love.

Afterward, he acknowledged the applause with a bow, then said, "I thought you folks might enjoy a special treat. I've got two friends of mine here tonight." Whitney's hands clenched of their own accord. "They've just recorded a song in Nashville, and while it won't be out for a coupla months, I thought you might enjoy a little preview. Here to sing 'Texas Girl' are Karl Kauer and Carol Truax."

Clapping and good-natured shouts greeted the couple as they stepped out into the spotlight. Whitney winced as the flashbulbs went off, and she heard Jonas cursing quietly.

The band struck up the intro that Whitney had heard in Nashville, and Karl and Carol began singing.

Close up, she noted, Carol looked a bit tired. Was it the strain of traveling, or had she begun to miss her family? What exactly *had* Carol said to Ben on the phone the other night?

On the other hand, Karl radiated confidence and contentment. Whitney had never heard his voice sound stronger, booming out in contrast to his partner's sweet, soft tones.

No doubt the song would be a big hit, and every disc jockey who played it would remind the listeners about the song's history. *Remember the Brite Cola lady? The one who dumped her husband and kids? Well, here she is with her big hit.*

Before Whitney could quiet her thoughts, the song was over. Taking a bow, Carol gave the photographers an ironic smile, or at least, that was how it seemed to Whitney.

Then, with a jolt, she realized they'd been spotted. An expression of—was it guilt? or annoyance?—flashed across Carol's face.

"Jonas!" Whitney turned to him in alarm as the two singers abruptly headed offstage.

"Come on!" He jumped up and pulled her toward the exit. To a questioning hostess, he declared, "We've got to go backstage. I have an urgent message for Carol Truax. How do we get there?"

"I'll have to check," the woman said.

Whitney pointed to a door marked Employees Only. "There!"

"Wait a minute!" The hapless young woman tried to block their way. "I can't let you back without permission."

Jonas pulled Whitney around her. "I'll take full responsibility."

As they dashed through the door, they could hear the hostess calling, "But you can't . . ."

The door opened into a long corridor. Swearing softly at her hampering high heels, Whitney raced ahead of Jonas, barging through a door at the far end without knocking.

She found herself in a brightly illuminated dressing room littered with stage makeup and clothes. There was no sign of Karl or Carol.

"That way!" Jonas pulled her toward an exit, and they emerged into the parking lot. Several cars were pulling out onto the street, and it was impossible to tell whether their quarry might be in one of them.

"Why did she run like that?" With difficulty, Whitney suppressed the urge to pound on the nearest vehicle in frustration. "Why can't she just tell us what's going on?"

"At least she didn't make any statements to the press," Jonas pointed out. "If we stopped her from doing that, our trip here was worth it."

"She's trying to ruin me. Why? I never did her any harm." Whitney carried on a monologue as they trudged disheartened toward their car. "What did I do besides give her a dream vacation and a make-over? Launch her career and make her a star? You'd think she'd give me a commission, not destroy my company."

"I don't think Carol is operating rationally." Jonas seemed to have regained his composure as he started the car.

"Should we stick around in case they show up again tomorrow night?" Whitney asked.

They discussed it for a while, and decided against the idea. Carol and Karl wouldn't be foolish enough to appear at the same lounge twice in a row, if they were really trying to avoid capture.

"Let's go to the wedding and then head home tomorrow," Jonas said.

"Okay. I don't suppose we have much choice."

Neither said anything further until they arrived at their hotel room. Then Whitney registered the fact that there were two double beds in the room. Would he insist they sleep apart?

She needed Jonas's warmth tonight, even if they didn't make love. Apparently he felt the same way, because he didn't argue when she slipped into bed beside him and rested her head on his shoulder.

"This is driving me crazy," she murmured, studying the shadows on his face cast by the dim reading globe.

"You of all people should understand how she feels."

"Me?" Then Whitney realized he was referring to her own disappearance years ago. "Oh. You know, I'd almost forgotten how it felt. It was so—challenging. Kind of a game."

"Exactly." Unlike last night, Jonas was wearing pajamas. Whitney reached over to unbutton the top, but he caught her hand in his own. "I think we need some time to sort things out before we pursue this any further."

"We're not talking about a corporate merger here," she protested.

"All the same—"

Whitney sat up, debating the merits of smacking him with her pillow. *Darn Jonas and his caution!* "Then how come you're sharing a room with me?"

"Good question." His tone lightened. "Maybe I just enjoy verbal sparring. Or is that verbal abuse?"

"Jonas Ameling, if you *did* fall in love with me, you wouldn't admit it until you'd consulted your accountant and your lawyer."

"And if you fall in love with me, Whitney, you wouldn't admit it until you'd consulted your astrologer and your guru."

She began to laugh. "We are an odd couple, aren't we?"

"Odder and odder." He turned off the light. "Now let's get some sleep."

"Fat chance." But the next thing she knew, morning light was streaming through the window and she discovered she'd been nestled all night in the curve of Jonas's arm.

GAVIN AND MARIA'S WEDDING was held in one of the chapels for which Las Vegas is known, a cozy cottage designed to look as if it had been transported from a fairy-tale version of Olde England. Recorded music sweetened the air even more than the profusion of flowers, and, as Whitney and Jonas arrived, another couple was just driving away in a car with "Newlyweds" painted across the side.

Jonas frowned. "I don't suppose it really matters where you get married, but I think I'd prefer something a bit more traditional. And I'd rather not share my flowers with the couple before and the couple that comes after."

Adjusting the collar of her suit, Whitney said, "Remember when people were holding their weddings on the beach and reciting poetry they'd written themselves? I don't suppose their marriages are any better or any worse than if they'd tied the knot in church."

"All the same..." Jonas paused. "You weren't thinking—I mean, if we *should* decide to get married?..."

"I thought maybe we could both dress up as cans of Brite Cola and say our vows in the plant." Whitney took his arm as they strolled into the chapel.

"I wouldn't put it past you."

Inside, the minister was holding a prayer book and looking properly dignified. Maria, in a short off-white dress, was bending over a young boy, adjusting the bow tie on his miniature white tuxedo, which matched Gavin's.

Her brother, Whitney noted with an inward smile, looked as if he were afraid Maria might change her mind at any moment. He kept touching her, talking to her, fussing over her, even while all her attention was concentrated on her son.

Finally, Gavin gave up and knelt down by Bryan, chatting reassuringly to the boy. Maria smiled, and then she noticed the new arrivals.

"Whitney! Jonas! I'm so glad you're here. Would you mind being our witnesses?"

"We'd be honored," Jonas said.

Whitney stepped forward and gave her soon-to-be-sister-in-law a hug, careful not to crease the bridal dress. Then, after signing the legal documents witnessing the marriage, the two of them took their seats and waited for the ceremony to begin.

A couple of tall, striking women arrived a few minutes later. Friends and co-workers of Maria's, Whitney guessed. There was no sign of Lina.

Bryan led off the procession, holding a small cushion with the ring perched on top. Then Maria and Gavin walked up the aisle together.

The ceremony was short and traditional. Despite the prefabricated surroundings, the lack of a crowd of guests and the absence of bridesmaids and ushers, there was a sweet genuineness to the ceremony that brought tears to Whitney's eyes.

Years together stretched ahead of Gavin and Maria. They might come from different backgrounds, they might have weathered a variety of individual problems in the past, but now they were making a commitment to the future. To love, to cherish, to deal with whatever troubles came their way— and they were both old enough to understand that no life is all sunshine and cake.

Whitney had to force herself not to turn and look at Jonas. *Will we ever be able to take these vows? Can I give up some of my impetuousness, and can he learn to bend a little?* She wished she could read Jonas's mind. But then, he'd said earlier that he didn't know himself what he wanted.

And then Gavin was kissing Maria. They beamed at each other before almost skipping back down the aisle. Even solemn little Bryan was grinning.

Jonas and Whitney exchanged hugs and congratulations with the newlyweds, and Mr. and Mrs. Gavin Greystone and their son departed in a rented limousine.

A few hours later, Jonas and Whitney departed too, flying back to Orange County and the Truaxes.

Chapter Eight

"While you were playing whatever game you were playing in Las Vegas, we got another call from Carol." The intervening day hadn't added any charm to Ben Truax's personality.

"I told you, we saw her but she took off." Whitney didn't bother to disguise the irritation in her voice. "So she called. What did she say?"

"It was personal." Ben took a sip of Scotch and soda from the room service tray. The Truaxes, who apparently saw no reason to spare Brite Cola any expense, had ordered their entire dinner from room service and had been finishing up dessert when Whitney and Jonas arrived.

"I wish we could go home." Jimmy stared moodily at his father. "I'm tired of being cooped up here."

"You can if you want to." Whitney held her breath, hoping, but Ben was having none of it.

"We'll stay right here until your mother comes back. We haven't had a vacation in a long time, and it's the least Brite Cola can do for us."

"Well, it doesn't look like there's any more we can do tonight." Jonas stood up, his eyes betraying his annoyance with Ben's secrecy and selfishness. "And I don't see any point in chasing your wife around the country any further, since you won't even let us know what she's told you."

"What's the difference?" Gini swallowed the last of a huge fudge brownie topped with ice cream. "I'm not even sure I want her back."

"Gini!" Her brother glared at her.

"Well, honestly! Look at this mess! People are making jokes about her on the radio. Can you imagine what my friends will say? And here we are cooped up in this hotel room. I mean, we were going to go to the beach yesterday, and what happens? It rained! It never rains in Southern California!"

"I suppose you're going to blame Mom for that, too?" Jimmy shouted. "She probably ran away because of you in the first place. I'm tired of hauling your clothes out of the living room and answering your boyfriend's calls! Why don't you just grow up?"

"Cut it out, both of you," Ben growled. "We've got company."

"But, Dad!" Jimmy protested. "She's done nothing but whine since we got here. Why don't we just send her home? Then we could go to the Tar Pits and see the mastodons in peace."

"You're free to visit the Page Museum by yourself, Jimmy," Whitney said.

"We stick together as a family." Ben shot her a mind-your-own-business look. "We've seen enough of what happens when one member of the family goes gallivanting off on her own. Not that I begrudge Carol a little fun, mind you. I suppose her life has been kind of confining these past few years. We could all stand to make a few changes. But no more separate vacations!"

At least he seemed to assume that Carol was coming back eventually, a point that gave Whitney a spark of hope. "Let us know if she calls again. And—" There was no point in urging them to enjoy themselves. The Truaxes would do exactly as they pleased, she could see that.

"We'll see you later." Jonas pulled Whitney firmly out the door.

After checking in with Mattie, they collapsed at Whitney's apartment, eating canned chili while watching the evening news. At the very end, the newscast flashed a photo of Carol and Karl in performance.

"It seems the Brite Cola girl isn't going to go quietly home to Houston," the announcer said. "She and Karl Kauer gave a preview performance last night of a new song they've recorded in Nashville. The record producer says it will be at least a couple more months before the rest of us get to hear it, however."

He didn't add anything about the supposed romance going on between Carol and Karl. But there was an undisguised note of glee in his voice, all the same.

Whitney flicked off the set. "Anybody who hadn't heard about Carol and Karl certainly knows about them now."

But Jonas didn't look particularly upset. "I have an idea."

"Well, shoot."

"I think we should record a song of our own."

She stared at him dubiously. "You've got to be kidding!"

"It would have to be the right song, of course." Jonas tapped his fingers on the arm of her couch. "You wouldn't happen to have a guitar around, would you?"

"No," Whitney said regretfully, then remembered something. "But they do have a keyboard downstairs. Do you know how to play one?"

"I studied piano for years." Jonas nodded toward the door. "Why don't you see if they'll lend it to you?"

Whitney needed no further urging. She clattered downstairs and was relieved to find the girls at home. When she explained her mission, Sarajane darted into one of the bedrooms and came out with the portable keyboard, an inexpensive model with about a five-octave range. "See, you can make it sound like a piano or an organ or a violin or a flute, and there's a rhythm accompaniment, too."

"I think the piano will be fine. When do you need this back?" Whitney looped the cord around her arm and got a good grip on the keyboard.

"Oh, no hurry. I hardly ever use it."

"Thanks!" For once, Whitney reflected as she marched upstairs, she was glad she'd rented the unit to the ditsy trio.

Jonas was waiting at the top of the steps to help her with the instrument. "This ought to do it," he said as he settled the keyboard on the kitchen table and plugged it in.

"You're going to write the song yourself?" Whitney pulled up a chair.

"Who better? Although I could use a bit of help with the lyrics." Jonas was clearly enjoying himself. "Got a tape recorder? I wouldn't want to lose any of this."

"Oh, sure!" She bounced up and fetched a small, voice-activated recorder from the bedroom. "I got this to use on business but I never remember to take it to meetings with me."

"Is there tape in it? Do the batteries work?" Jonas cocked an eyebrow teasingly.

"Well, of course!" But she checked, just to make sure.

"Okay." Jonas played a series of chords, his eyes half closed. "Kind of an up-tempo number, maybe with a reggae beat."

"You're kidding, right?" But he didn't answer, leaving Whitney still unsure whether Jonas really intended to make a record or whether this was his idea of a way to blow off steam. In either case, she was glad for a chance to hear him sing again.

"Let's see." Jonas swung into a rhythm that reminded Whitney of Jamaican music. " 'The lady in the cola ad, the lady acting very bad, make a lot of people mad, naughty girl!' "

Whitney chuckled. "I think you're on the right track. Let's see...." She tumbled some rhymes around in her head as Jonas kept up the accompaniment. "She run off with a TV star... um..."

"But she not getting very far," Jonas improvised.

"Bar... tar... car..." Whitney mused. "She have a breakdown in her car, naughty girl!"

"Break-a-down, a break-a-down, the lady have a break-a-down," Jonas chorused, "In her car!"

For the first time in days, Whitney felt lighthearted. It was a pleasure to get a dig in at Carol, to vent all those pent-up emotions, even if nobody but them ever heard the song.

They experimented with a second verse, finally settling on

The lady dance, the lady sing,
The lady have a merry fling,
Kick up her heels and everything,
Naughty girl!

She say goodbye to all her friends,
A Christmas card is all she sends,
And this is where our story ends,
Naughty girl!

A break-a-down, a break-a-down,
The lady have a break-a-down,
In her car!

"Well, it won't win any awards, but it hits the spot," Whitney said.

"Too bad we can't actually record it." Regretfully, Jonas switched off the keyboard.

"Why not?" Caught up in the excitement of actually writing a song, Whitney couldn't bear to think of it dying an inglorious death. "I mean, as a joke, what they call a novelty song? I'm sure the disc jockeys would love it!"

Jonas reached over and clicked off the tape recorder. "Don't get carried away, Whitney. It isn't that good."

"It is, too!"

"And furthermore, by the time we could put out a record, the whole story will be yesterday's news. The last thing we'd want is to rake it all up again."

"I want revenge!" Whitney cried, not bothering to restrain the outpouring of frustration. "I want Carol to squirm at least a little bit for what she's done!"

"Did I ask for revenge after that stunt you pulled?"

"Quit bringing it up! That was years ago! Besides, you got your revenge."

"How so?" Jonas asked quietly.

Whitney paused for breath and a moment's reflection. "You made me keep my word."

"What word?"

"About running Brite Cola myself on a day-to-day basis." She'd never admitted this before, perhaps not even to herself. "It seemed like a good idea at the time, but I'm not sure I would have carried through with it. Only after you and Michael helped me buy up all that stock, I just couldn't let you down."

"You seemed eager enough at the time." It was impossible to read Jonas's reaction, even as well as she knew him.

"I was. Only…" Whitney paused to let her thoughts catch up with her tongue. "I hadn't figured on getting up early every morning—I know it must look as if I always oversleep, but that isn't true. And I hadn't realized how hard it would be, giving up those lazy days at the beach. And coping over and over again with routine details. I could have afforded to hire a competent manager long ago, but I couldn't allow myself to give in, not after all the faith you'd shown in me."

Jonas tilted his chair back at a dangerous angle and regarded her quizzically. "Does this mean you don't want to continue as head of Brite Cola?"

"Maybe for a while." Whitney was exploring new territory. "I'd like to stay involved, coming up with promotional ideas—yes, even after this fiasco—and making sure everything lives up to my father's ideals. But maybe I could take your job, as president, and hire someone to handle everyday operations. What do you think?"

"I think that sounds like a very mature decision," Jonas said, to her surprise. "You seem to understand where your strengths lie."

"And my weaknesses," Whitney said ruefully.

"We all have those."

"Not you."

"Can I quote you on that next time we have an argument?" he teased.

It was incredible, Whitney realized. She'd actually confessed to Jonas what she'd feared most to tell him, that she really wasn't cut out to be an executive day in and day out. And he hadn't thrown it in her face, or taken it as another example of her flakiness. "If you wanted to quote me, you should have left the tape recorder running."

"True." He regarded her with a bemused expression. "You never cease to amaze me, Whitney. But I hope this doesn't mean you want out of Brite Cola right away."

"Oh, no! Not until we're past the crisis and everything is under control." Whitney stretched, realizing suddenly what a long day they'd had and how tired she was. "And you're not giving up your job until then either, are you?"

"I guess not." He stifled a yawn. As Whitney was trying to figure out whether he intended to spend another night with her, the phone rang.

"Not again." Reluctantly, she reached for the receiver.

But it wasn't Bob Abernathy this time. It was Jimmy. "You weren't asleep or anything, were you?"

"No, of course not." In the background she could hear rustling noises and muted voices. "Where are you calling from?"

"The lobby." He paused for what felt like a long time, then added, "I don't know what to do about my sister."

"Strangle her?" Whitney suggested, mouthing Jimmy's name for Jonas's benefit.

"Think I could get away with it?" It was hard to tell if Jimmy was joking. "You know, I always thought Mom was a nag, trying to get me to pick up after myself and all, but boy, it really is a pain being around somebody who's so totally self-centered and sloppy. I don't know how Mom put up with us all these years."

"I suppose that's part of motherhood," Whitney observed. "Was there something you wanted me to do?"

There was a pause. Then he said, "I guess I just needed somebody to unload on. Dad figures that since he's willing to cut back on watching games if Mom comes back, that's all he needs to do. Oh, and he's willing to take her out to dinner once a week. But he won't put any pressure on Gini."

"Teenage girls can be pretty awful." Whitney didn't remember that she herself had ever been so terrible, but she was sure Jonas would disagree. "Maybe she needs time to see her way clear."

"But what if Mom decides not to come back? What if she really can't take it anymore?" Jimmy's anxiety vibrated into Whitney's heart. "I miss her. And I wouldn't be able to live with just Dad and Gini, not the way things are now."

"Got any ideas? I'd be glad to help bring Gini around, if you can think of something."

Jimmy mulled over the possibilities for a few minutes. Whitney put her hand over the mouthpiece and explained to Jonas what was going on.

"Progress at last," he whispered.

Jimmy came back on the line. "Well, it would be kind of expensive..."

"I'm willing to consider it."

"She's always talking about her boyfriend Huey, and how much more fun it would be if he were out here," Jimmy

. . . be tempted!

See inside for special
4 FREE BOOKS offer

 Harlequin American Romance®

Discover deliciously different romance with 4 Free Novels from

Harlequin American Romance ®

Sit back and enjoy four exciting romances—yours **FREE** from Harlequin Reader Service! But wait...there's *even more* to this great offer!

A Useful, Practical Digital Clock/Calendar—FREE

As a free gift simply to thank you for accepting four free books we'll send you a stylish digital quartz clock/calendar—a handsome addition to any decor! The changeable, month-at-a-glance calendar pops out, and may be replaced with a favorite photograph.

PLUS A FREE MYSTERY GIFT—a surprise bonus that will delight you!

All this just for trying our Reader Service!

MONEY-SAVING HOME DELIVERY

Once you receive 4 FREE books and gifts, you'll be able to preview more great romance reading in the convenience of your own home at less than retail prices. Every month we'll deliver 4 brand-new Harlequin American Romance novels right to your door months before they appear in stores. If you decide to keep them, they'll be yours for only $2.49 each! That's 26¢ less per book than the retail price—with no additional charges for home delivery. And you may cancel at any time, for any reason, and still keep your free books and gifts, just by dropping us a line!

SPECIAL EXTRAS—FREE

You'll also get our newsletter with each shipment, packed with news of your favorite authors and upcoming books—FREE! And as a valued reader, we'll be sending you additional free gifts from time to time—as a token of our appreciation.

BE TEMPTED! COMPLETE, DETACH AND MAIL YOUR POSTPAID ORDER CARD TODAY AND RECEIVE 4 FREE BOOKS, A DIGITAL CLOCK/CALENDAR AND MYSTERY GIFT—PLUS LOTS MORE!

A FREE
Digital Clock/Calendar
and Mystery Gift *await you, too!*

Harlequin American Romance®

Harlequin Reader Service ®
901 Fuhrmann Blvd., P.O. Box 1867, Buffalo, NY14240-9952

☐ **YES!** Please rush me my four Harlequin American Romance novels with my FREE Digital Clock/Calendar and Mystery Gift. As explained on the opposite page, I understand that I am under no obligation to purchase any books. The free books and gifts remain mine to keep.

154 CIH NBA8

NAME _____
(please print)

ADDRESS _____ APT. _____

CITY _____ STATE _____ ZIP CODE _____

Offer limited to one per household and not valid to current American Romance subscribers.
Prices subject to change.

Clip and mail this postpaid card today!

BUSINESS REPLY CARD

First Class   Permit No. 717   Buffalo, NY

Postage will be paid by addressee

Harlequin Reader Service
901 Fuhrmann Blvd.
P.O. BOX 1867
BUFFALO, NY 14240-9952

NO POSTAGE
NECESSARY
IF MAILED
IN THE
UNITED STATES

said. "And her girlfriend Nessa, who is a real airhead, and *her* boyfriend Rip—his real name is Roland, but he hates it. Suppose they were to fly out and Gini was in charge of showing them around? She's never been responsible for anything. I'll bet they'd drive her crazy."

"Give Mattie their phone numbers and we'll see if their parents will let them come out next weekend," Whitney promised. "It sounds like a terrific idea, Jimmy."

"The best part is, Gini'll think you're doing her a favor."

After they said goodbye, Whitney turned to Jonas. "We're flying her friends out here and letting her show them around. What do you think?"

"I think you're good at dealing with people," he admitted. "You know, I doubt if it would even have occurred to Jimmy to call me."

"You don't think this whole thing might backfire?" Now that her initial excitement was fading, Whitney began to consider the possible ramifications. "It's Brite Cola that's really going to be responsible for those teenagers. What a grown woman does is one thing, but kids are another matter."

Jonas pulled a pen out of his pocket and made a note on a spiral-bound pad. "As soon as the arrangements are firmed up, I know a private investigator in Santa Ana we can contact. Your father used him a couple of times to catch employees who were stealing crates of cola. We can have him keep an eye on the kids all weekend."

Reassured, Whitney let her thoughts return to the plan to bring Gini around. "We'll have to get two more rooms, one for the boys and one for Nessa. I don't want Gini and her sharing a room; that would make them allies. The point is for the other kids to dump all the responsibility on Gini and complain to her when anything goes wrong."

"Perfect."

And then there was nothing left to talk about. Except for the fact that Whitney felt uncommonly warm and close to Jonas. "You've been terrific tonight."

"Oh?" He leaned back in his chair. "What inspired that compliment?"

"Well, you didn't give me a hard time when I admitted I'm not cut out to be an executive, at least, not forever." Whitney reviewed the evening mentally. "And you backed me up on this plan about Gini."

"Something's got to be done." Jonas stifled another yawn. "I'm getting the impression Carol wanted to teach her family a lesson, and I think she's succeeding."

"You don't think she and Karl are—?"

"I'm doubting it more and more as time goes by." He stood up as if to leave. "I only hope the news media find out the truth—from Carol. They'd never believe it from us."

"Don't go," Whitney said.

"I didn't plan to." Jonas reached over and pulled her to her feet. "Earlier this evening I was making nefarious plans for your body, but I have to admit I'm kind of tired."

Now that he mentioned it, Whitney realized she was beginning to ache in muscles she hadn't even known she possessed. "Me, too."

"And since I checked out of my hotel before we went to Vegas, everything I have with me is in that suitcase right there. Makes things simple, doesn't it?" He reached over and rubbed Whitney's shoulders, which felt wonderful.

"You can stay here as long as you want." She leaned back, inhaling the masculine scent of his shirt.

"Unfortunately, I have to be heading up to Sonoma tomorrow for a few days. I do have a business to run there too, remember?"

Whitney sighed. "Rats."

"Come on, Lady Grey." It was the first time in years Jonas had used her old nickname. She'd loved it as a teenager; it had sounded so grown-up.

"Tuck me in?"

"I'll tuck us both in."

A funny thing happened on the way to bed. Whitney and Jonas found out they weren't as tired as they thought.

Their lovemaking was slow and tender, then fast and fiery. Within a few minutes after it ended, they fell asleep in each other's arms.

JONAS LEFT the next morning. Whitney, suppressing the urge to spend the next few hours on the beach, put in a call to Mattie. Although it was Saturday, she knew her secretary had planned to work for at least a few hours, catching up on the Truax's arrangements and other matters.

Whitney explained Jimmy's idea. "I hate to ask you to set all that up today, but the sooner we get in touch with these kids, the sooner we can get them out here."

"I don't mind." Mattie's voice over the phone was firm and unruffled. "Actually, I'm kind of enjoying the excitement."

"You can assure their parents we'll have an investigator following the kids the whole time, but warn them not to tell. The kids would only resent it, and they might try to lose him."

"Good idea." Whitney could picture Mattie taking notes. She would never stop admiring her secretary's gift for organization. "They'll just be here for two days, next weekend? Their parents will probably be glad to get rid of them." Mattie had two teenagers of her own.

"And when this is over," Whitney said, "you can take your choice of overtime for all the extra work or an all-expenses-paid vacation to Hawaii. With or without any members of your family."

"With," Mattie said decisively. "Carol Truax I'm not." Then she added thoughtfully, "On the other hand, my husband isn't exactly Karl Kauer, either."

Then at last Whitney had a chance to duck out and work on her tan. The early April sunshine was thin compared to what it would be later, but the day was warming up rapidly. The beach was practically empty, a rare luxury.

Yet as she lay there, soaking up the sunshine and inhaling the fresh ocean breeze, Whitney's thoughts roved restlessly over the past week, over Gavin and Maria, Carol and Karl, Las Vegas and the phone call from Lina....

Darn it, would she ever be able to enjoy a life of indolence again?

When she finally gave up and went back into the apartment, her phone was ringing.

It was Mattie. "All systems are go. The parents are delighted; Nessa's mother told me she'd been hearing nothing all week but how lucky Gini is, and why couldn't they send Nessa to California this summer. The boys' parents said they were thrilled about the investigator, not to protect their sons but to keep them out of trouble."

"Wonderful. It's enough to make you wonder whether you want children," Whitney said.

"Oh, mine aren't so bad. Most of the time. And they were real cute when they were little," Mattie said. "Besides, how else can you get grandchildren?"

"That's something I hadn't given much thought to." Whitney returned to the plan. "So they're arriving Friday?"

"In the evening. And they'll leave Sunday afternoon. I've already told Gini and she's planning for them to spend all day Saturday at Disneyland. There's a dance band there in the evening, so there should be plenty to do."

"And there's no way they can sneak any alcohol," Whitney added. The fact that Disneyland refused to serve drinks even at its best restaurants had sometimes annoyed her, but now she was glad. "And you've booked two rooms? Oh, sorry. I know you're always way ahead of me."

"It's all set."

As she hung up, Whitney noticed the tape recorder still sitting on the table. She rewound the tape and played it back, enjoying over again the intimacy of creating a song with Jonas.

She wished she could be sure that, after this whole mess was over, she and Jonas wouldn't drift back to their old brother-sister relationship. But for right now, it was enough that he would be flying back in the middle of the week. Even if their romance was a short one, Whitney intended to enjoy every minute of it.

Chapter Nine

Jonas loved the wine business. He loved the oak smell of the vats where the wines aged, the dark coolness of the cellars, the green sturdiness of the vines in springtime, even the distinctive blue and white oval labels that marked the Ameling Vineyards products.

And he loved his home, a rambling farmhouse that looked as if it had been constructed piecemeal over the years, which it had. The screened wraparound porch might have come from a Norman Rockwell painting, and inside the decor had been executed with a Mexican sensibility— clean spare lines, gleaming wooden floors overlaid with colorful woven mats, large pots filled with dried flowers and herbs, windows that swung open without screens to darken the view.

Most of the furniture had been handed down through three generations of Amelings, of whom Jonas was the only surviving member. Without Whitney, he would have felt very much alone in the world these past few years, he had to admit as he prepared to fly back to Orange County on Wednesday.

Casey and Flanigan, his two russet Irish setters, barked in annoyance as Jonas shut them into the house and carted his suitcase down the steps. He knew the dogs would calm down as soon as Lupe, his housekeeper, set out their food.

His four-wheel-drive vehicle bounced down a rutted road to the airstrip his father had built. Leaving the vehicle for his foreman to collect, Jonas settled into the Piper Cub, running quickly through his checklist to make sure the plane was flight-ready. Within minutes, he was on his way south, not even needing to consult a map for the trip he'd made countless times.

Whitney. Damn, but she was full of surprises. He hadn't expected her to admit that running a company full-time wasn't her favorite thing to do. She had a stubborn streak as long as the California coastline, and a longstanding unwillingness to admit to any weakness, at least in Jonas's presence.

It was true what she'd said, that she was growing up. Of course, he would never want to see Whitney change entirely. Her spontaneity and enthusiasm were delightful, as was her essentially optimistic view of life. He'd been afraid, after Whitney's mother died when she was a teenager, that she would never recover from the grief. But she had, after long spells of weeping on Jonas's shoulder. He was glad he'd been able to help.

They certainly shared a long history. The question was, could they share a long future?

Jonas had had his share of lovers over the years, but never anyone like Whitney. She brought out a daring side of him, a youthful fervor where the nerve endings tingled close to the surface. He felt young when he was with her.

And they had managed to get through some trying times these past few weeks without murdering each other. It was hard to imagine any other woman who could be so consistently fun and surprising.

And yet—

Jonas knew himself well enough to understand that he needed order and stability in his life. He enjoyed formal dinners and fine wines, and the respect of others was important to him. He wasn't going to take part in any wild stunts such as the ones Whitney had become famous for—dressing up as a gypsy and playing the tambourine in front of Newport Beach City Hall when the council considered banning fortune-telling, for instance, or entertaining inner-city children on her yacht with a fireworks display for which she hadn't bothered to obtain a permit, and nearly getting arrested as a result.

But, he had to admit, that had been years ago. Before she became chief executive officer of Brite Cola.

Now, well, she still wasn't anyone's stereotype of a yuppie, and she maintained an off-the-wall approach to almost everything, but she no longer struck him as a rebel with too many causes. In a little over a year, Whitney would be thirty. It was hard to believe, and yet . . .

Had she changed enough? Could they really make a life together? Jonas wished he could be sure.

His attention returned to his flying as he entered Southern California airspace. The skies had become increasingly crowded in recent years, and he had to make sure to avoid the landing and takeoff patterns for LAX and the Long Beach airport, as well as the military airspace at Los Alamitos.

Finally, his plane safely tied down at John Wayne Airport, Jonas picked up a rental car and was on his way to Balboa Island.

He'd had a phone call from Whitney on Monday, to fill him in on the plans for Gini's friends. They would be arriving on Friday, two days from now.

Jonas didn't bother getting a room at the hotel. Usually he liked the predictability of hotels, of knowing he could go back to his room and be alone, that there was plenty of closet space so his suits wouldn't get wrinkled and that the plumbing would work and a maid would change the sheets every day. But the prospect of being with Whitney more than outweighed the disadvantages of her helter-skelter housekeeping.

Why, he wondered for the umpteenth time as he parked and started toward Whitney's apartment, didn't the heiress to the Brite Cola fortune simply hire a cleaning lady?

The sound of an angry female voice cut into his reverie as he neared the top of the steps.

"You were there! You could have stopped them!" The stentorian tones and the affected finishing-school accent unquestionably belonged to Lina.

"Why didn't you fly out yourself?" came Whitney's calm rejoinder. "Gavin notified you in plenty of time."

"That isn't the point!" Lina's diatribe stopped abruptly as Jonas rapped on the door.

Whitney opened it cautiously, then gave Jonas a broad smile. "Boy, am I glad to see you!"

He returned her greeting warmly and said a polite hello to Lina, as if he hadn't heard anything on the steps. It was always possible the argument would be postponed, perhaps until tempers had cooled.

No such luck. No sooner had Lina finished answering a courtesy question about her flight to the West Coast than she added, "Can you believe what's going on? This tramp has a son—an *illegitimate* son—and neither my son nor my stepdaughter bothered to notify me!"

Jonas wasn't sure that Whitney qualified as Lina's stepdaughter, but he saw no merit in raising fine points of etiquette under the circumstances. "Perhaps they thought you'd be pleased to be a grandmother."

The tall, aristocratic woman stared at him in mute shock. Obviously, the idea of being a grandmother, particularly a stepgrandmother, didn't appeal to her in the least. "Hardly!" she managed to say at last.

"Coffee, anyone?" Without waiting for a reply, Whitney darted into the kitchen. Since it was partially in view from the living room, however, she remained part of the conversation. "You might be interested to know, Jonas, that

Lina has just paid Gavin and Maria a little visit—on their honeymoon.''

"You interrupted their honeymoon?" Jonas couldn't quite believe that even Lina would be so insensitive.

"Well, they took that boy along!" the first Mrs. Greystone returned huffily. "I'd say it was a pretty public sort of honeymoon."

"She never plans to speak to them again," Whitney called to Jonas. Sounds of water dripping through a coffee filter mingled with the hum of the microwave oven. The air smelled like a bakery, and Jonas guessed that a coffee cake from the freezer was being pressed into service.

"I've said all I have to say." Lina stalked over to the window and stared out. "Look at those little tramps on the beach. I think it's disgusting what girls wear these days."

"I'm sure Gavin would agree with you," Whitney observed from the kitchen.

Lina ignored the sarcasm. "I wash my hands of him. I'll admit, Gavin has his faults. He does drink too much, and I've never liked the way he ran around with women. But this is out of the frying pan into the fire!"

Jonas wished he had an excuse for joining Whitney in the kitchen. He didn't know what to say to Lina, and was afraid that if he did speak, he would insult her. He'd never liked the woman, even in the days when she and George Greystone were still married and they'd been friends of his parents. And he certainly disagreed with her assessment of Maria.

The silence threatened to stretch out awkwardly, until Whitney bustled in with a tray. Not coffee cake but bran muffins, Jonas noted. No doubt Whitney had chosen them during one of her occasional health food kicks, but at least they smelled good.

Lina poured herself a cup of black coffee without bothering to say thanks. She always behaved as if she had grown up surrounded by servants, and occasionally dropped references to her Boston upbringing. Actually, Jonas recalled, she came from a poor Irish family, had grown up in south Boston and had been christened Eileen.

"I'm going to cut Gavin out of my will," Lina announced as she spread butter on one of the muffins. "I've already told Anston that all my money is going to charity."

Whitney and Jonas exchanged looks. They both knew that Lina had no sympathy whatsoever for poor people, despite her recent pose as a benefactress. On the other hand, Lina probably never expected to die, either.

The best tack, Jonas decided, was to change the subject. "Speaking of Anston, how was the charity ball?"

A smile lit Lina's face. "A smashing success! We were written up in all the papers, and positively *everyone* was there!"

"And you raised a lot of money, I hope?" Whitney dug into her second muffin.

"Oh, well, of course." Lina waved a hand dismissively. Then she waved the hand again. It was her left hand. On its third pass through the air, Jonas realized there was a ring on it.

"You're engaged," he said. "Congratulations. Or is it 'best wishes' that one says to the lady?"

"Either one will do." Lina gazed smugly at the ostentatiously large diamond, which was surrounded by an adoring horde of little diamonds. "Anston popped the question on Sunday. So you see, I was absolutely right not to tear off to Las Vegas at such a crucial time."

"Of course." Whitney covered her mouth with one hand, no doubt to hide her amusement. Lina's transparent selfishness was a subject Whitney had burlesqued—out of Lina's hearing—for years.

"I'm sure Gavin thought I should have been there," Lina continued, "to cheer him on as he shackled himself to that fortune hunter!"

"So you swore never to speak to them again." Jonas didn't like allowing such remarks about Maria to pass unchallenged, but neither did he want to get into a pointless squabble with Lina. If she would just go home...

"*And* disinherit him," Lina reminded him. "That ought to do it!"

"Do what?" Whitney poured more coffee into each of their cups, although none of them had drunk much.

"Bring him to his senses. Make him see that it's not too late to get the whole business annulled."

For once, neither Whitney nor Jonas could think of anything to say.

Nor did they need to. Because outside on the sidewalk, the sound of voices was growing louder. And the voices were familiar.

"I really don't think she'd come here." That was Gavin, sounding harried. "Not to Whitney's, of all places."

"She wouldn't just have hopped on the first plane back to New York." Maria's voice was much calmer. "Goodness, what are all those men in business suits doing on the beach?"

"Is that a TV camera?" Bryan's voice was shrill with excitement. "Look, Mom! Somebody must have drowned."

"I don't see any emergency vehicles," Gavin corrected the boy. "It's probably some kind of feature story."

Lina set down her cup in a hurry. "Is there a back way out?"

"I'm afraid not." Whitney strolled over to open the door. "Up here, guys! Your mother's been waiting for you."

The look that Lina gave Whitney's back could have frozen lava, Jonas judged.

Maria led the procession up the stairs. "What a charming place you have." She stopped inside the doorway, facing Lina with the calm of a skilled diplomat. "Mrs. Greystone, we didn't have a chance to finish our conversation at the hotel."

"As far as I'm concerned, it's finished." Lina's hand shook slightly as she lifted her coffee cup to her lips once more.

Gavin paused beside his wife, holding Bryan's hand. The boy took in the scene with frank curiosity, as if it were some new soap opera on television.

"I'd better heat up some more muffins." Whitney went back into the kitchen.

"I'll help you." Jonas was half afraid he might get shot in the course of the hostilities.

As soon as they were out of view of the others, he leaned over to give her a kiss. "I missed you," he whispered.

"Me, too." Whitney wound her arms around his neck. "I was hoping we could be alone."

Jonas shrugged. "They can't stay long."

"Mrs. Greystone," they heard Maria say. "Gavin didn't want to come here. But I don't want to see him estranged from his only family."

"She's not my only family any more," her husband corrected.

"Damn right," said Lina. "And don't try to pull the wool over my eyes. I know what brought you here—it was when I said I'd cut him out of my will. I meant it and I still mean it!"

"We don't want your filthy money!" Gavin snarled. "I've got my own, Mother. And furthermore, Maria and I are starting a restaurant together in Corona del Mar. We've already scouted out locations. We're going to work together and build something worth having."

"My son, wearing a chef's hat and waiting on people?" Lina moaned. "I can't bear it."

"If I'd learned the value of honest work a long time ago, I wouldn't have wasted so many years of my life." This didn't sound like the Gavin that Jonas knew. This sounded like a man who was beginning to grow up.

"Honest work?" Lina nearly shrieked the words, then stopped herself. "Well, Gavin, you can do whatever you please. Anston and I will be very busy and we would appreciate not hearing from you."

"Not even when the baby's born?" Maria asked.

There was a long silence. Outside, Jonas could hear a strange sort of murmur on the beach—masculine voices, mixed with giggles. Apparently the girls downstairs had met some new men.

"Congratulations!" Whitney barreled out of the kitchen, nearly dropping the basket of newly heated muffins. "Maria, that's wonderful! I'm going to be an aunt twice over! When's the baby due?"

"September," Maria said.

"Now I understand." Lina sneered at her son. "She trapped you. Well, that can be taken care of."

"Don't be ridiculous." He stood his ground. "We'd planned on having children right away. This just happened a little earlier than we expected."

"That's your decision." Lina clinked her cup down onto the coffee table. "I want nothing to do with any of this."

As she stood up and headed for the door, Jonas decided it was time to intervene. He was, he judged, the only person in the room for whom Lina held any real respect, minimal as it might be.

"Lina." She stopped and turned, her body rigid with tension. "I'm sure we all know this has come as a shock to you. But you do realize that this child will be your own flesh and blood. You don't want to miss seeing your grandchild grow up?"

"I—" Lina hesitated "—I might allow him—or her—to visit me in New York."

Gavin shook his head. "We won't be separated from our children. And they're both to be treated as equals. Neither one gets privileges above the other."

"Well, I suppose..." The rest of Lina's reluctant concession was lost in a pounding at the door.

Gavin, who was standing closest, jerked it open impatiently. "Yes?"

"Excuse me, I'm looking for Whitney Greystone," came a deep, mellifluous voice.

Jonas was astounded at the hot rush of jealousy that scorched through him. If this man thought himself a competitor for Whitney, he had another think coming.

Grimly, Jonas stalked through the room and stood in the doorway. As he opened his mouth to speak, he realized that the tall, slickly handsome man standing there looked familiar. Like someone he'd seen on television. Like a newscaster.

The impression was bolstered by the fact that, standing behind him, a young woman in jeans and a flannel shirt was holding a Minicam.

"I'm Jonas Ameling," he said. "Can I help you?"

The man looked momentarily disconcerted. Franklin Estrada, that was his name, Jonas recalled. "We, uh, in the news media have learned that Carol Truax's family is staying at a hotel here in Newport Beach. We wondered if we might talk to Whitney about that."

"Her name is Miss Greystone and I'm president of Brite Cola, so you can talk to me." Although he knew it was unwise to antagonize the press, Jonas resented the man's assumption of familiarity with Whitney.

A thumping at the bottom of the staircase drew his attention. A rangy young woman carrying a notepad and a camera was pelting up, looking as if she might elbow Franklin Estrada right over the railing.

"Yes, what can you tell us about the Truaxes?" she demanded. "Is it true that Carol is asking for a divorce? Did Ben Truax really threaten to kill himself?"

Jonas held up his hands to stop the flow of words. "As far as I know, none of that is true."

More people were surging toward the staircase. Where had all these reporters come from? Someone must have stirred them up—maybe even Carol herself. *It must be a slow day for news,* Jonas reflected with growing annoyance.

Moreover, some of the reporters were stopping to query people on the beach, including the dizzy girls from downstairs and that cartoonist who lived next door. Heaven knew what questions they were asking. Did they expect to uncover wild orgies? Where Whitney was concerned, people were likely to believe anything.

He turned back into the room. "It's a madhouse out there. You'd think they were covering a visit from the Pope."

The camera woman was shooting over Estrada's shoulder as he said, "Who are these people with you? These wouldn't be more of Carol's family, would they?"

"I'm Bryan." The little boy wrinkled his nose as he stared up at the newscaster. "I'm six."

Franklin knelt. "How do you feel about your mommy's behavior?"

"I'm real glad," Bryan said.

"You're glad she ran away?"

The little boy looked confused. "She's right there."

It was Estrada's turn to look confused.

"Excuse me, but you're intruding on a private family gathering." Jonas reached to close the door. Immediately, he saw an air of determination settle on the newscaster's chiseled features.

"Oh? I think the public has a right to know about this," he said.

Before Jonas could frame a reply, Whitney appeared at his shoulder. "Frank! Frank Estrada! Hey, it's nice to see you again!"

The man's features softened instantly. "There you are! Listen . . ."

"Yes, I know what you heard about the Truaxes." Whitney sparkled like a girl madly in love, which would have made Jonas furious except that he knew perfectly well she would never feel anything even approaching affection for an egotist like Estrada. "Frank—and Mina!" She was addressing the woman reporter, who was busily snapping a photo of her. "Let me introduce you to my brother Gavin. We're celebrating his wedding! This is his bride, Maria..." She ran through the introductions in one breath.

"Pleased to meet you." Even as he shook hands with Gavin, Franklin had clearly lost interest in the occupants of the apartment. "Now about the Truaxes..."

"Oh, yes. Let's just step outside, shall we? The light's so dim in here, I know it will mess up your pictures." The landing was small, so in order for Whitney to come out, the others had to retreat to the beach. A masterful stroke, Jonas had to admit as he followed his bouncing blond friend down after them.

She stopped a couple of steps from the bottom, which gave her a commanding position over the reporters clustering around. "Hey, Roger! How's the wife? Mary, you're back at work! I've got to see that baby one of these days! Sam—you're not flying a desk anymore?" They all cooed back adoringly, and it occurred to Jonas that the press probably got tired of turning the spotlight on other people all the time and enjoyed getting a bit of attention themselves.

It was a fact Whitney appeared to have grasped instinctively.

When silence finally reigned, she said, "I'm sure you've all heard that Carol and Karl Kauer cut a record in Nashville. As a matter of fact, Jonas and I were there." She filled them in on the title and the Las Vegas appearance as if it had all been planned and organized by Brite Cola Inc.

Questions flew at Whitney. She held up her hands. "I know this looks funny, but it was Carol's idea of a publicity stunt. I have to admit, I was pretty worried at first, but she's been in regular contact with her husband and everything's all right.''

''Why are the Truaxes out here, then?'' someone called.

''We at Brite Cola—'' Whitney spoke loudly in the direction of the TV camera with its built-in microphone ''—felt they deserved a vacation of their own. They've been such good sports about this whole thing.''

''Aren't the kids missing school?'' one of the women asked.

After a brief hesitation, Whitney improvised, ''Their father is thrilled at the chance for them to visit our museums here in the L.A. area. He considers it a rare educational experience and frankly, I agree!''

There were a few more questions, which Whitney handled neatly, and then the reporters began wandering away. Jonas choked down his impatience as she hung around until she'd satisfied the last request for a photo and the last probing innuendo about the Truaxes' marriage.

''Brilliant,'' he admitted as they went back upstairs. ''Those people drive me crazy. I don't know how you stand it.''

''Easy!'' Whitney gave him a cocky grin. ''We just got thousands of dollars' worth of free publicity for Brite Cola, and managed to throw them off the track at least for the time being. Not that the rumors won't take on a life of their own, but think how much worse it would look if we'd refused to talk to them!''

''I know, I know.'' And he did know, but somehow Jonas's common sense was always transformed into truculence whenever he was confronted with pompous snoops and intrusive cameras.

Inside the apartment, they found Lina calmly drinking coffee with her son and daughter-in-law. ''They're going to name the baby Linette if it's a girl,'' she informed Jonas. ''Isn't that sweet?''

Maria was smiling calmly, and Bryan was wolfing down bran muffins. Gavin looked moderately pacified.

"Keep in touch," Whitney said as the rest of the Greystone clan headed for the door. "Maria, let me know if there's anything I can do to help."

"Don't worry. We will!" she sang out.

Jonas was relieved to see them go. "What a zoo," he said when the door had closed behind them and he was alone with Whitney at last.

"I kind of enjoyed the excitement." She was still glowing with an adrenaline high.

"I hope you never grow up," Jonas heard himself say. "If I ever married someone like me, we'd probably rust."

"Your hair already did," she teased, brushing it gently with her hand. "Wanna make some whoopee?"

"Conservatively speaking, that sounds like a hell of an idea," he said.

So they did.

Afterward Whitney filled him in on the details of what she was calling Gini's Jaunt. "They're all arriving on Friday evening. I wish I could be a fly on the wall, but at least we'll have that detective watching them."

"I'll look forward to reading his report." Jonas grinned. "Assuming he survives."

"If I were you, I'd be more worried about Gini." But Whitney didn't look worried at all. In fact, she looked downright ecstatic. And, lying naked in bed, entirely irresistible.

"Let's do some more research into the differences between men and women," Jonas suggested. "I don't think I've quite got the hang of it yet."

Her answering chuckle was all the encouragement he needed.

Chapter Ten

Gini couldn't remember ever feeling so excited before. She wished she'd been able to go to the airport, but those people at Brite Cola had arranged to meet her friends and bring them to the hotel. So here she was, sitting in the lobby, swigging root beer out of a can and trying to picture the expressions on their faces when they got here.

They were going to be so impressed! Gini glanced down at her brand-new prewrinkled shrink skirt and fingered the soft bleached-out material of the ragged top. It was just perfect, and she'd bought it at Neiman Marcus, too! Nessa had said more than once that she'd simply die to have something from Neiman Marcus. Actually, she'd said she would sleep with the devil, but everybody knew Nessa was still a virgin and just liked to talk a big story.

And Huey—wait till he saw Gini's new hairstyle, with pink and orange stripes down the side. She'd found all sorts of fabulous hair products at South Coast Plaza, not to mention some glittery makeup that made her eyes look twice as big. She couldn't wait to hear the compliments.

With a leap that sent root beer fizzing down the side of her skirt, she sprang to her feet as a limo stopped in front of the hotel. They were here!

"Hey! Guys!" Gini sprinted through the doorway. "Hey, you made it!"

"Yeah. How ya doing?" Nessa bounded out of the car as soon as the driver opened her door. "Whadja spill on your skirt?"

"Nothing!" Gini gave her best friend a hug. "Huey! How do ya like California?"

He shrugged. "It's dark. Who can tell?"

Then Rip got out of the car, waving his cigarette so the smoke stung Gini's eyes. "Would you believe the airlines wouldn't let me sit in the smoking section? I mean, man, I'm finally rid of my parents for a whole weekend and I have to sit in a dumb nonsmoking section!"

The driver of the limo handed their bags to the porter. "Come on." Gini led her friends into the lobby.

"Wow, looka this place!" Rip practically shouted.

"Shh!" Why was he being so obnoxious? People were staring at them.

"Never mind him." Nessa giggled. "We're all just excited."

"Yeah. Me, too!" Gini felt better.

They followed the porter up to their rooms, which unfortunately were one floor down from the Truaxes' suite. "You're gonna stay with me, aren't ya?" Nessa asked as the boys ambled down to their own room.

"Dad won't let me." Gini flopped onto the bed. It was great, being able to put your shoes up on the spread and everything without some grown-up nagging at you. "He's got this thing about us sticking together as a family, because of Mom."

"Yeah, exactly what is your mom up to, anyway? We keep hearing all these wild stories."

"She's just acting like a spoiled brat. No big deal."

"Well, everybody's talking about it." Nessa began pulling clothes out of the suitcase. Gini had never seen that skirt before, or those sweaters. . . .

"Where'd ya get those?"

"Oh, my mom took me shopping at Neiman Marcus so I'd have something to wear on the trip." Nessa tossed everything into a drawer. "You mean I get my own bathroom? Hey, great!"

The girls pawed through the bathroom together, whooping over the complimentary tubes of shampoo and hand cream and tearing the paper off all the little bars of soap.

Someone thudded furiously on the door. It was, of course, Rip and Huey.

"Where's the action?" Huey said.

"Well, we hadn't really planned anything tonight." Gini had figured everybody would be worn out after going to school most of the day and then flying out here. "We could order up something from room service and watch TV."

"And make out." Nessa giggled.

"Hey, can I sleep here?" Rip bounced on the bed. "It's about time we got it on, Nessa."

She ducked behind a curtain of hair. "Well, I don't know, Rip, honey."

"If I know those people from Brite Cola, they've got the room bugged," Gini complained. "They're probably watching us like hawks."

"Man, I didn't come to California to sit in some hotel room and watch TV." Huey started for the door. "Let's go find the action."

Everybody trooped after him, screaming and howling on the elevator. It made Gini feel good, although it bothered her a little, too. She was glad her friends were having a good time, but she half wished somebody from Brite Cola would show up. They weren't really expecting her to keep everybody under control, were they?

Downstairs, they could hear dance music blaring from one of the restaurants. Huey led the way, only to be stopped at the door when he couldn't produce an ID.

"ID, man?" He snorted in disgust. "I thought this was California! Well, let's go get a hamburger."

"We'll have to get a car," Gini said. "There's no place you can walk to."

"So hurry up!" Huey said.

Just as she was about to give him a piece of her mind, Rip added, "Yeah. We don't want to stand around here all night."

Two sleek young women walking by stared at Rip as if he were some extra slimy kind of slug. It made Gini mad, but kind of embarrassed, too.

She went to a house phone and called upstairs. "Dad, can we borrow the car?"

"Only if Jimmy and I come with it," he said.

"Dad!"

"You argue with me, and the answer will be a flat no."

"Oh, all right." She slammed down the phone and went to tell the others.

They muttered and complained, and after her dad and Jimmy came down, everybody scrunched into the back seat of the car, Nessa on Rip's lap. The others kept poking each other, and her, with their elbows.

"Yeah, man, this is really what I wanted," Huey announced as they stopped at a signal light. "To come to California and be driven around by somebody's dad."

Jimmy turned in his seat and gave Huey a look of pure disgust, but at least he didn't say anything.

It took them half an hour to find a hamburger joint, and then Rip complained because he couldn't get a beer, and Huey dumped his French fries into the trash because he said they weren't crisp enough.

The least they could do was be good sports about it! Gini thought.

As they drove back to the hotel, she comforted herself with the thought that tomorrow they were going to Disneyland, and everybody was going to have a terrific time.

"I'M SORRY, SIR, but you can't come in here without shoes," a shiny-faced young man at the turnstile told Rip.

"Hey, man, I thought this was California!" Huey interjected.

"You can buy a pair of thongs over at that souvenir counter." The man pointed.

"What a pain," muttered Rip as they all slogged over to buy the sandals. At least they didn't cost much. Gini had a wad of spending money that her father had given her this morning, courtesy of Brite Cola, but she had a feeling it might not last long.

"Just think, guys," she reminded them as they paraded down Main Street between the small shops. "A whole day with nobody watching us."

"I don't believe it—Mickey Mouse?" Huey flared his nostrils at the sight of someone in a giant mouse costume posing for photographs with a little girl. "Man, this is medieval."

"Kindergarten stuff," Rip said.

"Wait'll you see the rides." Gini thought the costumed people were fun, but she didn't want to argue. "Pirates of the Caribbean is the best one, and the Haunted House is really cute."

"Cute?" said Huey. "Did you say cute? Oh, God, this whole place is one big Saturday morning matinee. Let's cut out and go to Hollywood."

"We're going on the Universal Studios tour tomorrow," Gini promised.

"I meant like Hollywood Boulevard, you know, the bar scene," Huey said. "Oh, yeah, I forgot. In California, you gotta have an ID." He pronounced the letters with exaggerated sarcasm.

"When are we going to the beach?" Nessa demanded.

"Tomorrow afternoon, if there's time. I mean, the weather's kind of overcast, so I didn't think you'd be too interested."

"You coulda asked us." Rip was slogging along, making a big deal out of having to wear the thongs.

"Yeah," Nessa said. "You coulda asked us, ya know."

Gini glared at them. "Well, excuse me! I was trying to figure out what would be fun. I mean, you can lie around a swimming pool at home, right? When's the last time you went to Disneyland in Houston?"

"When's the last time I wanted to go to Disneyland in Houston?" Huey sneered.

"Hey, guys." Rip jerked his head back toward his shoulder, as if he'd gotten a cramp, but finally Gini figured out he was trying to call their attention to someone behind them. "Don't look now, but I think that guy in the hat is following us."

"What guy in the hat?" Nessa turned around and stared.

"Don't look at him!" Rip grabbed her arm. "Maybe he's some kind of pervert."

"Naw. If a pervert wanted to come to Disneyland, he'd dress up in one of those mouse outfits. Matter of fact, I'll bet they're all a bunch of perverts." Huey stopped in the middle of the ramp to Sleeping Beauty's Castle. "What is this, anyway? Fairy tales? Gimme a break, Gini!"

She looked down at the map she'd picked up near the entrance. "We're going the wrong way. Pirates of the Caribbean is in that direction."

"I'm thirsty," Rip said. "They got a bar around here?"

He asked a young woman who was sweeping up microscopic bits of litter. She told them Disneyland didn't serve alcoholic drinks."

"Aw, no!" Rip exclaimed.

"Come on." Nessa grabbed his arm. "Gini's right. We're here to have a good time and go on some of the rides, and tonight they've got a rock band and everything."

"You expect me to dance in flip-flops?"

They were walking toward New Orleans Square, the site of the Pirates ride. "That weird guy is still following us," Huey said.

Gini got a tight grip on her purse. "He wouldn't dare do anything at Disneyland."

"Nobody does anything at Disneyland," Rip grunted.

It was a big relief when they got to their destination. *Now,* Gini reflected with a sigh, they could start to have fun.

INVESTIGATOR'S REPORT.

Location: Disneyland. 2-3 p.m.

Subjects leave Haunted House, wait in line at Matterhorn ride. Female N kicks male R in ankle. Argument ensues. Male H pours soft drink over female G. She stalks away in direction of It's a Small, Small World. After a brief discussion, others follow.

3-4 p.m.

After a short wait in line, subjects ride through Small World. Male R sings along with music loudly and off-key. Female G pounds him on back. Verbal altercation ensues.

4-5 p.m. Subjects consume hot dogs, tacos, pretzels and ice cream. Female N clutches stomach, races to ladies' room.

5-6 p.m. Subjects take sky ride. Male R tries to lean out of gondola. Female N screams repeatedly. On conclusion of ride, they are spoken to by Disneyland personnel.

6-7 p.m. Female subjects part from males. Using best judgment, follow females. They apparently become aware that someone is behind them, begin to run. Female N stumbles, loses heel on shoe, begins to cry. Observation curtailed at this point due to subjects' being aware of investigator.

IT WAS THE WORST DAY of Gini's life, even worse than that day in the seventh grade when she let out a loud belch while singing a solo in church.

She'd never realized how selfish and childish Huey and Rip and Nessa could be. You turned yourself inside out to make sure they had a good time, and all they did was complain about it.

And Sunday wasn't much better. Huey complained that the special effects at Universal Studios were fake and Nessa grumbled because she didn't see any movie stars and then there wasn't time to go to the beach, and anyway it was starting to sprinkle.

Gini had finally figured out that the man in the hat must be working for Brite Cola, which made her feel better, but then he didn't show up on Sunday. Where was Whitney, or even that grim-faced man called Jonas?

For once in her life, she would have liked to have a grown-up around, somebody who could tell Huey to shut up when he whined about not being able to buy a beer. Even Nessa, who was Gini's best friend, kept taking the boys' side and making Gini out to be the bad guy, as if everything that went wrong was her fault.

It seemed like they'd never get back to the hotel, and then that the limo would never get there to take them to the airport. She nearly had a heart attack when Nessa complained about being sick to her stomach and said she might have to stay for another night.

Not if I have to personally stuff you into that airplane myself, you won't! Gini thought as she packed Nessa's clothes for her.

And then, finally, they were gone, without so much as a thank-you. Gini had the feeling that if they'd been here another day, they would've expected her to do their laundry, too.

Unreal!

She dragged herself back up to the suite, wondering why she ached all over, as if she'd had a double dose of gym class.

Funny how it made Gini think of her mother, how Carol had collapsed in her chair one day after taking Gini shopping and moaned about feeling drained. At the time, Gini had figured that was just part of getting old.

Now she was beginning to wonder.

"Have a good time?" Jimmy asked when she trudged in the door.

"Get me a Coke, wouldya?"

"Get your own Coke. I'm not your mother."

Gini let it pass. She didn't have enough energy for an argument.

Dad came out of his bedroom. Apparently the ball game was over. "You kids want to go out and get something to eat? Maybe some pizza?"

"Yeah." As she went into the bathroom to brush her hair, it occurred to Gini all of a sudden how good it felt to know there was someone else in charge.

Chapter Eleven

The drizzle cleared up Sunday afternoon, and although it was still too cool and damp for sunbathing, Whitney took a chair and a couple of cans of soda onto the beach. She left the door to her apartment open so she could hear the telephone if it rang, but she hoped it wouldn't.

Jonas had gone to Fashion Island to pick up a few things. Whitney loved being with him, but it was nice to be alone with her thoughts once in a while, too.

Things were changing between them. Not just because they were lovers, but because they both seemed to be mellowing. Maybe it wouldn't last, maybe Jonas would rigidify again and Whitney would begin to feel stifled, but for now, it was heaven.

There'd been no further word from Carol, but at least the teenagers from Houston had behaved more or less as Whitney had hoped. According to her reports from Jimmy and the private investigator, the weekend had been a disaster. What remained to be seen was whether Gini had learned anything from it.

Carol would get a chuckle out of it when she learned what had happened. That was, if she ever stayed in one place long enough for Whitney to tell her.

Whitney looked up as her neighbor, Larry, brought out his beach chair and began sketching one of the seagulls poking about for sand crabs. She carried over a spare can of Brite Cola and offered it to him.

"Thanks." Larry squinted at the bird, then made some rapid strokes on his pad. Peering over his shoulder, Whitney saw that the cartoon bird bore an unmistakable resemblance to an outspoken senator who had been in the news recently.

"I don't know how you do it." She picked up a newspaper that lay by his side. "I missed your strip this morning. Must have been in a pre-coffee fog."

"You didn't miss much. It's not my best work." Intent on his gull, Larry didn't even look up. That was the funny thing: even though he lived a casual kind of life, there was a tautness about him that Whitney couldn't quite figure out. One of the other neighbors had told her that before he began cartooning a few years ago, Larry had been a heavy-drinking playboy in a self-destructive spiral. Obviously he'd gotten his act together since then, yet he was still an oddly solitary figure.

"How come you're so hard on yourself? I always think your stuff is terrific." She sneaked another peek at the sketch, delighted to see the gull taking on richer detail. It was wearing a tuxedo now and officiously laying an egg.

"I know my own strengths and weaknesses, that's all." Larry flipped his sketchbook shut. "I'm at my best when I've got a real juicy target, some pompous public figure who deserves to be brought down a few notches. Usually there's no shortage of them, but lately nobody's interested me much. Maybe I'm getting stale, sitting around here. Maybe I ought to get out and find some excitement."

"You want some of mine?" Whitney sighed. "I've had more than enough since Carol disappeared."

"Oh, she'll turn up." Larry popped open his can of cola. "Where's Jonas?"

"Buying shirts."

"Stuffing them himself these days?"

She kicked a little sand in Larry's direction. "He's not so bad."

"Ah, a reconciliation. Or is the first time called a conciliation?" Larry regarded her thoughtfully. "Don't blow it, Whitney. The two of you are damn lucky to have each other."

He sounded envious, which struck Whitney as strange, considering the way Larry practically had to chase women away with a stick. But then, she knew what it was like to have a lot of suitors, all of them the wrong ones.

Since he was engrossed in his sketch again, Whitney opened the newspaper and found Larry's strip. One of his main characters, a tuxedo-sporting hippo, was dumping a load of dollar bills into his washing machine and taking a few digs at a financier recently indicted for money-laundering. "This is cute."

"Isn't that your phone?" Larry said.

"Oh, rats." Whitney jumped to her feet and raced up the steps, tracking sand across the carpet. "Hello?"

"It's Sarah." Her friend didn't waste any time on idle chitchat. "I just heard on the radio that Carol is going to be making an appearance at a baby and child products show at the Anaheim Convention Center."

"When?"

"In about an hour."

Whitney checked her watch. It would take at least half an hour to reach the center, and she had to change into something more presentable than cutoffs and a sweatshirt. "Any details, like which booth?"

"Sorry."

"Oh, well, I ought to be able to find her by the swarms of envious homemakers. Thanks, Sarah."

After collecting her belongings from the beach, Whitney pulled on a pair of slacks and a hand-knit sweater made of thick, soft blue wool. It wasn't exactly fancy, but where Carol was concerned, she'd learned to dress for running.

Just to be on the safe side, Whitney laced on her jogging shoes.

As she was finishing, masculine footsteps came up the steps. "Jonas?"

"Fortunately, yes." Appearing in the doorway, he looked so relaxed and handsome in his blue plaid shirt and designer jeans that Whitney had a sudden urge to forget all about Carol and drag him into bed.

She suppressed the thought. "Sarah just called. Our runaway is supposed to turn up at the Anaheim Convention Center in forty-five minutes."

"Let's go." Dropping his purchases onto the bed, he caught Whitney's arm. "I'm getting tired of this game."

"You and me both."

They didn't need to say much on the drive to Anaheim. Whitney fiddled with the radio, hoping to hear some further details, but all they could get on this Sunday afternoon was music and commercials.

"What do you suppose she's up to now?" Whitney asked as they turned off the freeway at Katella. Signs pointed them toward Disneyland, which was across the street from the convention center.

"I don't know, but it had better be good."

There was a long line of cars entering the convention center parking lot, and all the spaces near the building were taken. In the end, they parked at the far side of the lot and hiked an interminable distance.

"Let's split up." Jonas went right to the battle plan. "That'll double our chances of finding her. Did Sarah say whether Karl was supposed to be here?"

"No, she didn't."

"Hmm. I wonder if there's trouble in paradise," he murmured, cutting between a motor home and a Porsche. "Look at all these women!"

There seemed to be hundreds of them, many pushing strollers, some accompanied by bored-looking husbands, all heading for the convention center. Whitney wasn't even sure what exactly a baby and child products show had to offer. How many cribs and blankets did one baby need, anyway?

They bought tickets and asked directions at the door, and were told Carol would be somewhere in the main display area.

Pushing through the crowded lobby, Whitney and Jonas paused as they entered the huge hall. Dozens and dozens of brightly colored booths merry with balloons and streamers were almost lost among the thousands of people. The air vibrated with music, the jingling of uncounted toys and the wails of babies.

"I may go deaf." Whitney had to shout to make herself heard.

"There seem to be a lot of people gathering over there." Jonas pointed to one side of the room. "You circle around that way and I'll meet you there."

"Right."

Easier said than done, she reflected a short time later, trying unsuccessfully to edge past a flotilla of slow-moving strollers. Besides, the little folks were so cute—tiny girls dressed up in crocheted dresses and bonnets, chunky boys wearing Superman sweatshirts, and one set of triplets trundling along between their parents, strung together hand to hand like cutout dolls.

Watching a couple of women examine a domed display of dried baby food, Whitney had a disconcerting thought. *These are the people I've been trying to reach with my Brite Cola promotion!*

In her mind, the grocery shoppers of America had so far been a faceless mass of figures in housedresses. In real life, they consisted of an infinite variety—teenage girls with spiky haircuts, sophisticated matrons, professional-looking women efficiently steering their tots along, round-faced grandmothers with knowing eyes.

How on earth could anyone hope to persuade them to do anything with a single promotional campaign? They were so different that Whitney felt as if she hadn't even begun to grasp what might appeal to them.

A male voice over the loudspeaker said, "Ladies and gentlemen, in a few minutes Carol Truax will be signing autographs at the Bottoms-Up Diaper booth."

To Whitney's amazement, a chorus of cheers rose into the air.

As an experiment, she turned to a heavyset woman next to her. "Who's Carol Truax?"

The woman smiled as if imparting a treasured bit of lore. "You know, that housewife who won the Brite Cola contest."

Another woman in front of them turned. "The one who ran off with Karl Kauer. Boy, does that sound tempting!"

The mother of the triplets looked over. "Let me tell you, I've had days when I'd have run off with King Kong."

"But don't you think what she did was wrong?" Whitney asked.

"Honey, my oldest just turned thirteen, and let me tell you, if I could get away from her for the next couple of years, I'd jump at the chance," said the heavyset woman.

"Besides, some advertising guy probably dreamed the whole thing up," added the lady in front.

"Whoa!" The mother of triplets halted suddenly, setting off a whiplash effect that nearly toppled her husband. "Aren't you Whitney Greystone?"

There was no use denying it. "Well, yes."

"Can I have your autograph?" The heavyset woman reached into an oversized purse and pulled out a pad and pen. "You're the first celebrity I've ever met."

"Well, sure...."

By the time she was through writing her name, Whitney found herself surrounded by autograph-seekers. It reminded her of the scene at the pizza parlor, but this time the people weren't mistaking her for a pop singer.

In fact, they seemed to know an amazing amount about her. "When you took over that company, a lot of people said you'd fall right on your fanny," one lady informed her. "But I knew they were wrong. Women can do anything they set their minds to!"

"I took the Pepsi challenge and I picked Brite Cola," another told her.

There was a volley of unsolicited comments.

"I like that lemon cola you're putting out, but the name Lemon Brite sounds like some kind of cleanser," one woman said.

"I can't ever find your stuff at my supermarket. They bury it behind the Dr. Pepper," complained another.

"Those cents-off coupons you put out expire too soon," lamented a third.

"Can you have another contest like this one? I'd just die for a chance to run off with Karl Kauer," asked yet another.

Apparently the public wasn't as disgusted with Carol's behavior as Whitney had thought.

The problem was, with all these people gathering around her, she didn't have a chance of getting to Carol. She only hoped Jonas was having better luck.

"Do you have children?" one young woman asked.

"No. I'm not married," Whitney admitted.

"Oh, that's right." With a sigh, the woman brushed back a strand of hair. "Well, they're great but—have fun while you can."

"Mommy!" A toddler tugged on her hand and pointed to a balloon. "Gimme!"

"Honey, those aren't for sale, they're decorations." The woman's response was met with an ear-splitting shriek. She gave Whitney a helpless look. "He's a balloon freak."

It was at least fifteen minutes before Whitney signed her name for the last time and resumed her trek toward the Bottoms-Up Diaper booth. So she caught only a glimpse of what might have been Carol's head, disappearing in the other direction.

Doggedly Whitney continued her pursuit, but it was hopeless. Not only had she lost sight of Carol, but her hair was askew, she'd chewed off all her lipstick and there was no sign of Jonas anywhere.

"Well, great," Whitney muttered, rearranging the purse strap that was digging into her shoulder.

"Whitney! This way!" Startled, she turned to see Jonas straining toward one of the exits, not even waiting to make sure she'd heard him.

The whole thing was beginning to feel like a Keystone Kops caper. Or maybe some absurdist play in which everyone turns into a rhinoceros.

There wasn't much choice but to press on in Jonas's wake, but Whitney was seeing less and less sense to this chase. After all, hadn't the mothers themselves let her know they liked and admired Carol? Wasn't it obvious that, far from backfiring, the promotional campaign had succeeded beyond anyone's expectations?

Of course, they would still have to look at the sales figures; you couldn't get around that. But goodwill was important, too, and obviously Carol had stirred up a lot.

At the exit, Whitney spotted Jonas loping across the parking lot. She couldn't see Carol, but apparently he could.

Thank goodness for jogging shoes.

Whitney took off at a run, clutching her purse to keep it from flying off. "If I'd wanted to take up exercise, I'd have joined a health spa," she muttered as she dodged behind a slow-moving Cadillac.

She sped around a motor home and halted, only a couple of feet behind Jonas. He was glaring at a van as it pulled away—or rather, at Carol and Karl in the front seat.

The van turned down the next aisle and slowed as it came alongside them.

"I'm sorry!" Carol was leaning out her window. "We're late already! It isn't what it looks like, honest." The van was heading toward the street. "Watch *Celebrity Hotline* tonight. You'll see."

"If I had a gun, I'd shoot out their tires," Jonas snarled. Whitney had never seen him so angry.

She had to admit she was pretty disgusted, too. It was hard to feel charitable toward Carol when your feet hurt and the snap on your purse had just fallen open, spilling half your belongings onto the pavement.

"Great. Now she's going on television." Whitney knelt and scooped up her junk.

"*Celebrity Hotline.* I never watch that garbage." Obviously, Jonas didn't have a kind word for anything right now. But he did kneel down and retrieve a lipstick that had rolled under a car.

Whitney wasn't crazy about celebrity interview shows either, but she had been on enough of them to appreciate their value.

"Maybe things aren't as bad as they seem." As they hiked back toward their car, Whitney's thoughts returned to her earlier experiences. "I got inundated by envious housewives who think Carol is the greatest thing since toaster ovens."

"So that's where you were." Jonas strode along rapidly, making no allowance for the fact that her legs weren't quite as long as his. And that her feet were aching in spite of the cushioned shoes.

"Well, why didn't you catch her?"

"What did you expect me to do, wrestle her to the ground in front of all those people?" Jonas's temper certainly wasn't improving any. "You could have waltzed right up there, but in my case, the security guards would probably have hauled me off to jail."

"I couldn't get through. All these women wanted my autograph." That sounded lame even to Whitney's ears. "I couldn't exactly trample on them, could I? Besides, they had a lot of interesting things to say about Brite Cola."

"I'll just bet they did."

"No, really." Surely when he heard, he'd feel better. "They think the whole thing is one big promotional stunt. And they wish it were them instead of Carol. They're not sneering at her or at us, Jonas. I think it worked. In fact, this may turn out to be the most successful promotion in the history of the beverage industry!"

Jonas swung around, his face tight with fury. "Don't go congratulating yourself too soon, Whitney. What people say and what they do are two different things."

"Yes, but we're talking about goodwill...."

"This isn't a game, Whitney." His voice was raw around the edges. "And we're not amateurs. At least, I'm not. So what if a few women paid you a few compliments? Has it occurred to you that people who are fed up with Carol's shenanigans wouldn't have come here to get her autograph?"

"Well, no, I guess not." Whitney wished she'd thought of that herself. "Maybe it wasn't a representative sampling, but..."

"That's the problem with your whole approach to running Brite Cola," Jonas ploughed on furiously. "Nothing's done scientifically, nothing's thought out. It's all off-the-wall fun and playtime, with Whitney acting on hunches and impulses."

"I thought you liked the way I was handling things!" She was beginning to get angry.

"I'll grant you've worked hard, and some of your efforts have paid off." Jonas looked as if it hurt him to concede even that much. "But maybe it's a good thing you don't plan on sticking it out as CEO. You're right, it's time we hired a competent professional."

"Do you know what you sound like?" They'd reached the car, and Jonas leaned over to unlock the door. "A stuffy, self-righteous stick-in-the-mud who resents the fact that I've carried off this promotion. What's the matter? Can't you stand the fact that I might be good at something? You can't keep me under your thumb forever, Jonas."

"Is that really how you feel about me?" He observed her coldly over the open car door.

"Well, just think about it! You've always been like the big brother and I've been the giddy kid sister. Okay, my style's a lot looser than yours, but I've grown up, Jonas. That's what I've been trying to tell you. You've got to start treating me as an equal." Whitney paused for breath.

"That's what I thought I was doing." He sounded angry again as he swung into the car.

"Well, you haven't! You were lecturing me as if I were your student or something." Whitney plopped herself into the passenger seat.

"That's because you still act that way. Damn it, Whitney, we're running a multimillion-dollar business here. You can't treat it like a game of Monopoly."

About to snap back at him, she paused to think it over. As soon as she did, a rush of pain replaced her anger.

I can't go through life having my behavior and my ideas dismissed as childish.

Whitney leaned her forehead against the glass, fighting back tears. This was what she'd been afraid of all along, that she would fall in love with Jonas and then discover that it simply wouldn't work.

"Whitney?" He reached over and touched her cheek lightly. "Please don't cry."

"I'm not." She swallowed hard against the lump in her throat. *Darn it,* why did she have to do something adolescent like getting all weepy?

"Maybe we need some time apart." Jonas guided the car into the freeway. "I'm going to fly back to Sonoma this evening."

"You'll miss *Celebrity Hotline*."

"I'll call Lupe and have her tape it." He let his breath out slowly. "I'm sorry I lost my temper. Not that some of what I said wasn't true, but maybe not all of it."

"Oh, Jonas." Whitney still couldn't bear to turn and face him. "We've known all along it would come to this. We're just too different to get along for more than a short time. We always end up fighting."

"Let's not jump to conclusions." His tone was carefully controlled. "Neither one of us is functioning at our best. There's been a lot of stress and frustration these past few weeks."

She started to say that it hadn't been all stress and frustration, at least not for her, but she managed to keep silent. He was right. They needed some time apart, time to think.

Time to get over each other? That didn't seem possible. She'd loved Jonas for most of her life. He simply wasn't replaceable.

"I'm going to send the Truaxes home." The decision came to Whitney already made. "I've had enough babysitting and cajoling Ben and his wayward kids. They've got to work this out on their own. If Carol wants to screw up her marriage, that's her business."

"We've done as much as anyone could," Jonas said.

In an odd way, Whitney realized, she was going to miss those scrappy kids and their bullheaded approach to growing up. And watching Jimmy take on a sense of responsibility and an appreciation for what his mother had gone through *had* been rewarding. But it was hard to tell whether that new maturity would last much beyond the return to Houston.

Jonas left Whitney at her apartment, packing his clothes with hurried efficiency and departing with a rather impersonal kiss on the cheek.

"I'll call you," he said.

"Don't forget about watching the show tonight."

"I'll call Lupe from the airport."

Then he was gone.

Whitney slumped onto a chair, gazing half-heartedly out her window at the sunset.

She knew she ought to be glad for these past few weeks, to relish the time she and Jonas had been able to spend as lovers. Maybe when the pain receded she would find that it satisfied her need for him, that now she could get on with her life and learn to love someone else.

Maybe pigs could fly.

Feeling as if her feet weighed five hundred pounds each, Whitney dragged herself over to the refrigerator and pulled out a frozen dinner. There was no point in starving herself to death.

After all, she would probably need her strength to bear up under whatever Carol was going to say on TV tonight.

Chapter Twelve

At about a quarter to eight, the girls from downstairs came trooping up to Whitney's door.

"We're really sorry to disturb you," said the one that Whitney thought was Mindy.

"We've got kind of a problem," added Candy. She was blonder than the others; Whitney was almost certain she remembered that correctly.

"It's all my fault." Sarajane slouched with her hands in her jeans pockets.

They looked so dejected, it was hard to keep a straight face. On the other hand, Whitney wasn't in much of a laughing mood right now. "Well?"

"It's the carpet," Sarajane said. "See, I promised my boyfriend I'd take care of his dog for the weekend, and he assured me it was housebroken."

"Well, it was," Candy corrected. "I told you we shouldn't have left it alone all afternoon."

Whitney stared at them grimly. "How bad is the damage?"

"It's this big spot right by the front door," said Sarajane.

Whitney didn't know a lot about carpeting, but she'd heard somewhere that dogs were pretty hard on it. "I suppose you've already tried to clean it?"

"We didn't want to make the damage any worse," Mindy offered.

Glancing at her watch, Whitney saw that it was almost time for the program. "There's something I've got to see on TV. Carol Truax is going to be on."

"Can we join you? We get such lousy reception downstairs." The girls sidled in the door, their faces alight. They'd been thrilled by the whole Brite Cola promotion, although Whitney hadn't talked to them about it much since Carol's disappearance.

Not sure she wanted any company if the news was bad, Whitney had to think for a moment before deciding that she needed all the moral support she could get. "Well, all right."

Mindy joined her on the couch while the other two girls sat on the floor. The program was just starting. The first guest was a young actor who'd been in trouble recently for punching out a photographer.

"Wow, is he cute!" Sarajane giggled.

"Not as cute as Larry." Mindy sighed. "He doesn't seem to know I'm alive."

"He knows *I'm* alive," Cindy groaned. "He just doesn't care."

A commercial came on.

"About the carpet." Whitney had their instant attention. "You will look in the Yellow Pages and arrange to have it cleaned. And you will pay for it yourselves. Understand?"

There was a chorus of yeses.

"And you will do this tomorrow before the stain has any more time to set."

"We promise," said Sarajane.

Why stop now? "And since I rented it to you so cheap," Whitney said, "you will also take the curtains to the dry cleaners before you move out. And scrub the kitchen top to bottom. There will be an inspection. Got it?"

"Got it," Candy said.

"And no more dogs."

When the program returned, the host said, "We have a special guest with us tonight. You've been hearing a lot these past few weeks about Carol Truax, who vaulted to fame after winning a contest sponsored by Brite Cola—" Whitney thanked him silently for the free plug "—and who has just cut a record with Karl Kauer."

The camera angle widened, and Carol came into view, seated beside him.

She looked a little tired, Whitney thought, scrutinizing the screen image carefully. Well, that was only fair. After all, Whitney was exhausted.

On the other hand, Carol looked sophisticated and trim in a glittery blue gown that had been part of her prize wardrobe. Her new hairstyle had been carefully groomed and her makeup was expertly applied.

"Carol, welcome," the host said.

"Thank you, Bob." The response was carefully modulated, as if Carol had been appearing on TV talk shows all her life.

The three girls watched intently. Whitney resisted the urge to throw something at the screen.

"We're glad to have a chance to talk to you about some of the rumors that have been going around," the host was saying. "I suppose you've heard some of them."

"Actually, I take full responsibility for starting them." Carol smiled ruefully. "I want to say right now that this wasn't a ploy by the Brite Cola people. Whitney and Jonas and Mattie have been absolutely wonderful to me, and I'm sorry for any distress I've caused them."

"Any distress?" Whitney grumbled, then caught herself. She didn't want to miss any of this.

"First, tell us about your record," said the host. The girls hooted and Whitney joined in.

"Hurry it *up*!" she grumbled.

After Carol had announced the name of the song, the record label and the release date, she took a deep breath. So did Whitney.

"I have something to announce," Carol said at last. "Something important."

IT WAS ALMOST EIGHT-THIRTY by the time Jonas reached home, and he was glad he'd called ahead to have Lupe tape the show. He glanced into the den, and was rewarded by the sight of glowing lights on the VCR, indicating it was still recording.

His phone machine was also aglow, although he'd called in this afternoon to collect messages. Had Whitney called? Jonas almost didn't play it back, not wanting to hear the bad news about the TV program before he witnessed it himself.

On the other hand, maybe something urgent had happened.

The house was very still around him. Lupe had gone home by now to the cottage in the vineyard grounds that she shared with her husband and nearly grown son.

After spending so much time at Whitney's apartment, where there were always ambient noises from the harbor and the neighbors, Jonas was struck by how remote his farmhouse felt. So quiet. So empty. So far from Whitney.

Pushing aside a growing sense of loneliness, he played back the tape.

"Jonas? Hello, this is Cynthia." The throaty voice brought back a rush of memories that seemed to come from another lifetime. "Give me a call when you get a chance." Efficient as ever, she left both her work and her home phone numbers.

Impulsively he dialed her home number, although it wouldn't have surprised him had Cynthia been at work, even on a Sunday. She answered on the third ring.

"Thanks for calling." Jonas sat on the edge of his bed and began pulling off his shoes. "I'm afraid things have been rather hectic." He waited, not sure why she'd called, and feeling vaguely guilty, even though it was Cynthia herself who'd suggested he resolve things with Whitney.

"I've been rather busy myself." She sounded slightly strained. "Jonas, the reason I called was—well, there's something I think you have a right to know."

Jonas shrugged off his jacket. "Shoot."

"I've met someone else," she said. "He's a lawyer, too, so we both work long hours, and we both realize it would be impractical to consider having children under these circumstances. So you see we have a lot in common."

Trust Cynthia to analyze a man from a purely objective viewpoint. Although, to be fair, Jonas conceded no woman as diplomatic as Cynthia would regale a former boyfriend with extravagant praise of another man. Maybe she really was in love with him. Maybe she too felt the waves of exhilaration and the gentle radiant glow he sometimes experienced with Whitney. "Congratulations."

"You're not angry, are you?" He could picture her sitting in the perfectly decorated cream and brass living room of her Victorian-style house near Golden Gate Park. "I mean, I assume you've been seeing your friend down in Orange County."

"Yes, I have, although…" Jonas realized he didn't want to discuss his concerns with Cynthia, or with anyone except perhaps Whitney herself. "Yes, I have. And I'm pleased for you, Cynthia. He sounds like a very fine man."

"Sometimes I wish my life weren't quite so regulated," she admitted, and Jonas remembered why he'd liked Cynthia, for those brief glimpses of the lively girl she must have been once. "But I think this is the wisest choice."

"Good luck," was all Jonas could think to say. "I hope everything works out for you."

"And for you," Cynthia added before saying goodbye.

Jonas hung up the phone with the sense of turning a page in his life, in a book that could never be reread. And with a sneaking sense of relief that he had no further obligations to Cynthia.

After changing into his gray velour robe, he went back into the den and rewound the videotape.

As he waited, he glanced at a photograph on the mantel of Whitney with her father and himself. It had been taken at her high school graduation. The tassel hung rakishly across her forehead and she was grinning as if there were nothing in the world she couldn't do.

How much younger she had looked then, her face rounder and her eyes less troubled. Jonas was struck suddenly by the fact that, while he still pictured Whitney as a kid, she really had changed, outside and in.

And damn it, she *had* done a good job with Brite Cola. Why had he been so hard on her today? Was it just frustration over Carol, or was it because he was afraid of his own feelings?

Slowly, Jonas gazed around the den, at the furnishings his parents and grandparents had selected, at the abstract painting he himself had bought in San Francisco. For a long time this place had been his refuge and his hideout, an orderly safe base from which to live an orderly safe life.

Sometimes I wish my life weren't quite so regulated.

What Cynthia had said might apply to him, too. Surely there were a lot of women in the world who would happily fit into his existence and live by his rules, staying in the background while he went about his work and accompanying him on trips, raising a couple of quiet respectful children and serving carefully prepared meals on a perfectly laid table.

And then there was Whitney—who was part of his soul and his youth and his heart, even if she did drive him crazy sometimes.

With a frown at his own turmoil, Jonas turned on the TV and pressed the Play button on the VCR, using the fast-forward key to bypass the first segment of the interview show. Then he watched impatiently as Carol chatted about her record. "I have something to announce. Something important." At Carol's words, Jonas felt his fists tighten. *This had better be good.*

"You mentioned the rumors about Karl and me." Carol addressed the show's host. "We got them started on purpose, but the truth is, there's nothing to it."

The host smiled. "Now, do you really expect people to believe that?"

"Yes, because..." Carol cleared her throat. "Karl has authorized me to announce his engagement to Susan Sager. She was his high school sweetheart in Nashville and they recently got reacquainted. In fact, that was part of the reason we went to Nashville. And I wish them every happiness."

"So do we," the host added quickly.

"Karl agreed to pretend to run off with me because he wanted to help." The camera moved in for a close-up of Carol. "You see, I had a problem that a lot of women share."

Jonas reached for a bowl of cashews that Lupe kept filled on the coffee table, and took a handful.

"I've devoted most of my life to my family, and I don't regret a minute of it," Carol went on. "But it's the old story. Everybody takes Mom for granted. By the time I realized it and tried to do something about it, they were set in their ways. And I realized I couldn't go on like that any longer."

"So you ran away to teach them a lesson?" the host said.

"In a way." Carol smiled ruefully. "My husband and I have had some of the most meaningful discussions of our marriage these past few weeks—by telephone. And my son Jimmy has been terrific, taking on a lot of responsibility."

Jonas scooped up another handful of nuts.

"The funny part is that the only holdout was my daughter Gini, and she's the one I mostly did this for." Carol looked a trifle less nervous now. "You see, she and girls like her never realize that they're going to grow up to be a lot like their mothers. Not that I don't want her to have a career; she deserves to make her own choices."

The camera shifted to the studio audience. They were leaning forward, many of the women nodding in agreement.

"But one of these days she's probably going to take on the most important job on earth, which is motherhood," Carol said. "And she too is likely to find herself undervalued. And if the center of the family isn't respected, isn't held in high esteem, then the whole family becomes a collection of strangers who just happen to share the same dwelling."

"What does your daughter think about all this?" the host asked.

"I don't know. I wanted to wait a little longer, until I was sure she'd come around, but I miss my family." Carol smiled gently. "I miss them a lot. You know, I've learned a few things myself while I've been gone. Like that my husband has pressures on him at work that I wasn't aware of. And that, irritating as kids can be, there's sure a big empty space when they're not around."

The studio audience erupted in claps and cheers. For once, Jonas felt sure it was spontaneous, rather than the result of some assistant holding up a sign saying Applause.

"Well, we wish you the best of luck," the host said. "And when we come back, we'll be talking with…" Jonas switched off the VCR and the TV.

He thought briefly about calling Whitney but decided to wait until morning. He was tired from the flight and besides, what the hell was he going to say?

Jonas collected his mail from his desk and went to read in bed. But his eyes wouldn't stay open, and finally he gave up and turned off the light.

Just before he fell asleep, it occurred to him that it would have been interesting if he and Whitney had thought to bug the Truaxes' hotel room. He'd have given anything to know what they were saying right now.

"WELL?" JIMMY GLARED over at Gini. They were both sitting on the carpet, which was littered with room service dishes that had once held cake and ice cream.

"Don't push her." It wasn't like Dad to go easy, but Gini was grateful. What Mom had said was kind of embarrassing, real sentimental stuff, but it made her feel guilty, too.

"So when's she coming back?" Gini asked, since everybody seemed to be waiting for her to say something.

"Tonight." Dad had known about this all along, she could tell. "We're going home tomorrow. I'm sure you'll be glad to be back with your friends."

Oh, no. Gini hadn't thought about that. How could she ever put up with Huey again after the way he'd behaved? Nessa hadn't been so bad, but if she kept seeing Rip after the creepy way he'd acted, Gini wasn't sure she could stand to be around either of them.

"What about the housework?" she muttered. "I guess Mom is going to insist I start vacuuming and everything."

"It wouldn't kill you." Jimmy stopped at a look from their father.

"We're hiring a cleaning lady. Your mother's going back to school to take some music classes," Dad said. "But that means you kids will be responsible for preparing some of the meals."

"I'm pretty good at barbecuing," Jimmy said.

"Oh, all right." Gini didn't want to give in too easily, but in fact she was feeling relieved. For one thing, Jimmy had turned into a real nag, and at least Mom would keep him off Gini's neck. "What was all that stuff about me having a career? I've never wanted a career."

"I feel sorry for the guy who marries you." Jimmy began stacking the plates onto the room service tray. "What if he gets laid off or sick? You'll hang around whining that he was supposed to support you.

Actually, being around Huey for the past two days had made Gini understand a little better why some women got divorced. Being stuck with a guy who acted like a baby could be pretty awful. "Well, I don't mean I want to get married right away. I might want to go away to college for a while." It was a new thought but a pleasant one. Studying wouldn't be so bad if your friends didn't all make fun of you when you took it seriously. "I mean, I'm only fifteen. What's the hurry?"

Jimmy turned to their father. "When's Mom getting here?"

He looked at his watch. "It's about an hour's drive from the studio."

"Is Karl Kauer coming with her?" Gini wasn't much of a country music fan, but she wouldn't mind getting his autograph. After all, the kids at home would be impressed.

"No." Dad didn't look too happy.

Gini tried to put herself in his place, which was a new experience. *Yeah,* she could see how, if Huey had run off with some actress, she wouldn't feel too good about it even if it all turned out to be a joke. She might forgive him, but the actress could go stick her head in a barrel of peanut butter.

"Maybe we ought to straighten up," she said.

"Good idea," Dad said. For once, Jimmy kept his mouth shut.

SARAH CALLED a few minutes after the Terrible Trio had gone back downstairs. "Whitney, did you see? . . ."

"Yes. What a relief."

Her friend laughed. "I knew you'd pull it off somehow. It couldn't have worked out better if you'd planned it. The publicity is priceless! And hey, I was nearly in tears, and I'm not even sentimental. This'll put an end to those dumb jokes about serving Brite Cola at your next affair.''

"I guess it really did work out for the best." Whitney knew she ought to sound more excited, but she just couldn't whip up much enthusiasm.

"Uh-oh." *Trust Sarah not to miss a trick.* "Something wrong with you and Jonas?"

Whitney told her about their fight. "So he's gone home. Sarah, I thought after we spent all this time together that our differences would kind of melt away, but they haven't. And it really hurts."

"I can imagine. I think he really does love you, Whitney, but he's stubborn."

Thank goodness, Sarah wasn't the type to rush in with blithe assurances.

"I guess I'd better get off the phone, in case he's trying to call me." Whitney thought briefly about phoning Jonas herself, but decided not to risk another quarrel. Besides, he might not have watched his tape yet.

Sarah clicked off, and Whitney wandered around the apartment getting ready for bed and jumping at any noise, even though none of them turned out to be the telephone.

She knew she ought to feel great about what this would mean for Brite Cola. But as she finally gave up on hearing from Jonas, she had to admit it was a hollow victory.

Now he could safely give up his position as president, and largely remove himself from her life.

Whitney lay awake for a long time that night, wondering how she was going to get along without Jonas. And not coming up with any answers.

Chapter Thirteen

The sound of the radio woke Whitney. She groped around to turn it off and then realized she didn't have a radio at her bedside.

In fact, the only radio in the apartment was the one hooked to her stereo system, and it couldn't possibly be on.

Someone was singing on the beach. Several someones, actually. A ragged chorus accompanied by a guitar was working its way through a song that sounded faintly familiar.

Getting up and pulling on a bathrobe, Whitney dragged herself over to the window. Obviously the Terrible Trio was up to something, and at—she checked the Mickey Mouse clock—eight in the morning, she was in no mood to be charitable.

The song, she realized as she struggled with the recalcitrant loop that opened the curtains, was "The Teddy Bears' Picnic."

Finally she jerked the curtains aside and she could see. Yes, there were Candy, Mindy and Sarajane, along with a knot of early-morning bicyclists and joggers, but they were merely standing around watching the show.

The song was being sung by Carol and Ben Truax, Jimmy and Gini, who were staring up at Whitney with bright grins on their faces.

She opened the window. A fresh salt-tinged breeze blew in. "I see the prodigal has returned."

"We brought you some breakfast," Carol called up, and pointed at a sack. "Doughnuts and coffee. Come on down!"

"Okay." Pulling on a sweatshirt, Whitney realized it would have been kind of embarrassing had Jonas been here, too. On the other hand, it was the kind of embarrassment she could learn to live with.

A few minutes later she was down on the beach, spreading out an old blanket that she kept handy, and trying to decide what to say to Carol.

Fortunately, Jimmy and Gini were whooping and chuckling enough to fill in the silences. It was nice to see the two of them getting along, for a change.

As soon as the doughnuts had been offered around and the coffee suitably adulterated with sugar and powdered creamer, Carol said, "I want to apologize. Whitney, you and Jonas were innocent bystanders, but I was afraid if I said anything to you, well, my plan just wouldn't work."

The childish side of Whitney wanted to scold her, to complain about what a pain in the neck it had been, but she had to be fair. "I pulled something like that once myself. I guess it was only fair for me to learn how it feels to be on the receiving end."

It was Ben's turn to apologize. "I suppose I could have been a lot more gracious; after all, what's between my wife and me isn't your fault. The kids and I put you folks to a lot of trouble, and we spent a lot of your money. I want you to know I plan to reimburse you for the money Gini spent on clothes and personal items like that."

Whitney waved her hand. "Thanks, but the publicity we've gotten from Carol's escapade is worth a thousand times what we spent."

Gini licked chocolate icing off her fingers. "Yeah, but you really went out of your way. I mean, flying my friends out here and all."

Her mother looked startled. "What was that?"

"Huey, Duey and Dopey," explained Jimmy, using what appeared to be his accustomed nicknames for his sister's friends. "Brite Cola flew them out for a weekend of fun and games."

"They nearly drove me crazy." Gini debated between a maple-covered cake doughnut and a frosted one, and finally took both.

"That was the point," Whitney admitted.

Her mouth full of doughnut, Gini couldn't answer at first. Finally she asked, "You mean you *planned* it that way?"

"Grown-ups aren't entirely stupid," Whitney told her.

"Oh, ick. You mean we're that predictable?" Gini twisted a lock of hair around her finger and managed to get it full of icing. "Maybe I ought to read up on this psychology stuff."

Carol shot Whitney a grateful look. "I have to say, you're a genius in your own way."

"I wish I were a genius in some other way." Whitney sipped her coffee, watching a boy skim by on a skateboard. The crowd that had gathered earlier had finally dispersed.

"Where's Jonas?" Jimmy asked.

"In Sonoma." Whitney tried to sound nonchalant. "That's where he lives."

"Most of the time." They all looked up at the sound of a deep, familiar voice that sent tingles down Whitney's spine.

"Jonas!" She barely restrained herself from jumping up and running to him. "I thought you were going home."

"I was. I came back." He looked refreshed and glowing in the morning light, wearing a navy cashmere sweater and a casual pair of slacks. Jonas folded his long legs easily onto the blanket and reached for a peanut-coated doughnut. "My favorite."

Whitney ached to hug him, to reach out and touch his soft sweater and feel the hard chest underneath. Instead, she clasped her hands around her knees. "I guess you saw Carol on TV."

He nodded. "I didn't want to miss out on the reunion. Besides, I have a business proposition to make."

"Shoot," Carol said. She and Ben were holding hands, Whitney realized.

"I figure after all your shenanigans, the public's going to identify you with Brite Cola anyway," Jonas said. "So I'd like you to star in a series of commercials. We can shoot them in Houston, if you like, and of course you'll be well paid."

Carol looked at Ben. "Would you mind?"

"I've kind of had my eye on a motor home," he said. "I guess the money wouldn't hurt."

"Sounds good to me." Carol turned back with a smile. "Okay. Do you need me to sign something?"

"Not at the moment." Jonas picked up Whitney's coffee without asking and took a drink.

She felt half annoyed and half admiring. Just as he'd commandeered her coffee, he'd also lined up Carol for the commercials without consulting Whitney. It was a high-handed thing to do—and yet, of course she would have approved. It was a terrific idea.

"I hate to interrupt this, but we've got a plane to catch." Ben Truax reached over and shook Jonas's hand. "Thanks for everything. I hate to admit it but—I've learned a lot."

"Yeah." Gini stood up, brushing her hands against her jeans. "Jimmy and I got a lot out of it, too."

"Hey, you're the one who caused all the trouble."

"Oh, yeah?" Gini pointed to the sack her brother was filling with napkins and empty Styrofoam cups. "When did you ever bother to clean up before?"

"I just don't want Mom to change her mind and leave again." He sounded wistful, and Carol gave him a hug, following it with one for her squirming daughter.

"The next person to leave home is going to be you, when you go away to college," she told Jimmy.

"We'll be in touch about the commercials," Jonas promised. Amid a flurry of farewells and promises to see each other again, the Truaxes departed.

"A happy ending at last." Whitney watched them go. "I always did like happy endings."

"Me, too." Jonas rested his arm around her waist.

"What does that mean?" She was instantly cautious. By now, she'd come to realize that Jonas's mellow moods were far from permanent.

He withdrew his arm. "We've got a few things to talk about."

Whitney bent to grasp the corners of the blanket and shook out the crumbs, grateful for the chance to hide her face. She wasn't sure what she expected from Jonas now, or what she was willing to offer. But he was right. They needed to talk. "Okay."

She folded the blanket and led the way up the steps.

As soon as they were alone inside the apartment, he said, "I missed you last night."

"Me, too." She tucked the blanket away in the linen closet, making a mental note to have it dry-cleaned one of these days.

"You're not just going to leave that there, with the crumbs on it?" Jonas said. "You'll get bugs."

"Is that what you wanted to talk to me about?" Whitney turned to face him.

"Well, no."

"Then I think we'd better stick to the subject." She was surprised at how businesslike she sounded.

"Right." Jonas turned one of the kitchen chairs around and sat in it, stiffly upright. "We make a very good couple, Whitney."

"Tell me something I don't know."

"Okay. Half the time I want to spend the rest of my life with you, and the other half I never want to see you again."

"You, too?" She flopped onto the carpet. "Jonas, this is impossible. We're no further along than we were weeks ago, in spite of—all that's happened."

"One thing has changed," Jonas said ruefully. "I don't think I could ever be happy making love to another woman."

"That's some consolation, anyway." Whitney propped her feet on a cushion and leaned back against the edge of the couch. "I've always felt that way about you."

"So I noticed." His expression softened. "Whitney, damn it, you're part of me."

"An irritating part?"

"Sometimes."

This wasn't getting them anywhere. "Okay, so we're talking," she said. "Now what are we going to do?"

"I think we need to spend more time together." Jonas spoke slowly and thoughtfully. "In spite of the fact that we've known each other for years, we've only been lovers a short time. And we've been under a lot of pressure."

Whitney let her breath out slowly. So he didn't intend to hide out in Sonoma, after all. "That sounds good to me."

"And I think I was premature, about giving up my position at Brite Cola," he went on. "Not that you haven't been doing a good job, but I want to see how the sales figures pan out after this business with Carol. Doing a little better isn't enough; we've got to go head-to-head with the majors."

He was right. "I guess I hadn't wanted to face up to that," Whitney admitted. She knew as well as he did that the supermarket business was a highly competitive one; every inch of shelf space was fought for intensely. With Coke and

Pepsi bringing out new products all the time, Brite Cola sales had to be high enough to make it worthwhile for the markets to continue giving it some of that precious space.

"That's why I thought of doing the commercials with Carol, to capitalize on what you've started." At least Jonas was giving her a fair share of the credit, Whitney had to admit. "So far we've been lucky. But we've got to streamline our operation and make sure we're ready for the big time."

Whitney sighed. Now that Carol was back, she'd been indulging in daydreams of relaxing and of hiring an experienced executive to run the company.

But she knew that would be the wrong thing to do just now. There wasn't room in the market anymore for the equivalent of Mom and Pop businesses. Food companies were mostly conglomerates with plenty of bucks behind them and lots of clout, too. Along with millions of dollars spent on television advertising.

"Let's go for it," she said. "You'll stay here, with me?"

Jonas nodded. "If we don't kill each other, maybe we'll work things out."

"I hope so." Whitney bit her lip. "Well. I guess we'd better get to work, huh?"

"I guess so."

She knew, as she went to change into something more businesslike, that she was glad for this chance to let her relationship with Jonas develop and mature.

But at the same time she found herself looking back wistfully on that crazy chase after Carol, when she'd been free to be impulsive and spontaneous. There wouldn't be much time for that in the weeks to come.

Whitney already seemed to hear the clang of a prison door closing behind her. Her suit coat felt like a straitjacket, and the makeup she was carefully applying suddenly looked like a mask.

She closed her eyes and took a deep breath. *You're not going to lose yourself, Whitney. This is what growing up means. Self-discipline and all that. You can do it. For your sake, for Brite Cola and for Jonas.*

She had to do it. Because if she failed, she would lose him. And that would hurt too much even to think about.

Chapter Fourteen

"Brite Cola brought me and my family closer. I can't promise it will do the same for you—but I can promise you'll enjoy the same great taste we do."

The video cut from the smiling faces of Carol, Jimmy and Gini—her hair now restored to its natural light brown—to a closeup of a can of Brite Cola, dressed up in sunglasses and a bikini, lolling on the beach.

The commercial was over. Whitney rewound the tape with a sense of relief.

Finally. Finally.

She looked around her office. Things had changed over the past few months. A VCR and TV screen had been installed. There was a new filing cabinet, already crammed full of papers, and the updated phone system had enough flashing lights and buzzers to accommodate a rocket launch.

Mattie stuck her head in the door. "I'm off now. Don't work too late."

"What time is it?" Whitney checked her watch, a new digital model that Jonas had bought her as a sign of appreciation for working through the Fourth of July, a month ago. It was after six, although still light out. Usually she enjoyed the lengthened days of summer, but this year she hadn't had time to notice. "Yes, I guess I'll knock off soon. Did Jonas say when he'd be back from L.A.?"

"The meeting was at three." Mattie shrugged. "Who knows?" Then the secretary regarded Whitney closely. "Are you feeling all right?"

"Just a little tired." Whitney frowned. "Why?"

"You seem kind of subdued. With the commercials finally ready to air and all, I thought you'd let up a bit."

Whitney unthinkingly ran her fingers through her hair, then stopped short as her hand encountered a bun secured by half a dozen pins. "I suppose I will. One of these days."

"Go home and take a nice hot bath," Mattie advised.

"Sounds like a good idea."

Whitney sat staring into space for a while after Mattie left. It was true that she hadn't been herself for a while. She certainly felt like a toned-down version of the old Whitney.

But it was worth it. Things were going smoothly between Jonas and herself, although their lovemaking didn't have quite the same zip. But she supposed that was to be expected, as lovers got used to each other.

Whitney stood up slowly, stretched, and locked up the office before leaving.

It was strange, she reflected as she took the elevator down to her car, but she was almost glad Jonas had had to go into L.A. and would be flying up to Sonoma tomorrow for a few days. Not that she didn't still love him and enjoy his company, but sometimes it was a strain being around him. It was as if she were being tested; as if she were on trial.

That's not fair. Jonas has a right to make sure we can be happy together before we make any commitments.

But what about me, another little voice asked. *Am I happy?*

It didn't make Whitney feel any better that today was her twenty-ninth birthday. Jonas had greeted her with flowers this morning and taken her out to breakfast, where he'd presented her with a stunning pair of diamond and pearl earrings.

She checked them out in the rearview mirror. They looked dazzlingly sophisticated. Elegant. Not at all the sort of thing the old Whitney would have worn. She'd kept touching them all day, half afraid one of the valuable gems would fall off.

The rush hour traffic was heavy, and Whitney had to concentrate on her driving for the rest of the trip home. As always, she experienced a rush of relief when she turned onto the narrow bridge leading to Balboa Island and drove between the quaint shops. The beach community had a relaxed, informal air that helped her recover at least a little from her hectic day.

She tried to look forward to the pleasures of soaking in the tub, but, as she parked her car, Whitney found that she didn't want to go back to the apartment right now. It was so silent since the Terrible Trio had moved out six weeks before. Who would have believed she would actually miss them?

The downstairs unit looked so empty now. And it struck her as wasteful, even if she *had* bought it for the benefit of VIPs and special promotions.

What she needed was a walk. Whitney started off, walking away from her apartment.

Thank goodness, the heels on her pumps weren't very high. Still, it was awkward, strolling along in her linen suit while half-naked teenagers rattled by on roller skates. A small mop-shaped dog sniffed at her ankles curiously, until the owner pulled it away. *Am I that out of place?*

Twilight was dimming the harbor, and lights began to flicker on. Two children ran by, shrieking and waving leftover holiday sparklers. They were the only fireworks Whitney had seen this year, except for a brief glimpse, driving home late on the Fourth, of a red and yellow rocket exploding over the ocean.

Whitney blinked her eyes, and found that they felt dry and sore. What a long, long haul it had been.

But things were going to get better, she reminded herself, summoning up a ghost of a pep talk. Carol's first commercial would begin airing this weekend, and beefed-up supplies of Brite Cola had been shipped out in anticipation of an increase in sales. Jonas's meeting today was with an executive search firm that would be looking for an experienced CEO to take over the running of Brite Cola.

And, Jonas had hinted with a grin, maybe it was time he and Whitney took a long trip. He hadn't said so, but she got the feeling he intended it to be their honeymoon.

So why wasn't she overwhelmed with joy instead of kicking at a stray candy wrapper and battling a sense of impending doom?

Up ahead, a group of people had gathered in the sand, and Whitney heard whoops and giggles. She pulled off her shoes, and heedless of the damage to her stockings, picked her way across the beach.

Gazing over a surfer's shoulder, she saw two clowns with bright red noses and carrot-stick hair tumbling in the sand, pretending to fight over possession of a plastic lobster. They whacked each other with plastic shovels, dumped toy buckets of sand through each other's hair and carried out a fencing match with a pair of toy rakes.

The female clown spotted Whitney, let out a piercing shriek and clomped forward on oversize shoes to haul her into the fray. The beachgoers cheered, apparently enjoying the contrast between Whitney's yuppie image and the zany costumes.

Whitney's first response was an urge to snatch her hand away. She'd worked so hard to keep her appearance neat and professional. What would Jonas think if she wound up rumpled and messy?

But Jonas probably wouldn't be home for at least an hour. He'd said something about having dinner in L.A. to avoid the rush hour traffic.

Seeing uncertainty flicker in the clown's eyes, Whitney couldn't resist. She caught the woman's arm and swung around, hoisting the clown onto her back and twirling her in a circle before dumping her on top of her partner.

At least Whitney's stab at martial arts training a few years back hadn't been entirely wasted.

The crowd cheered as Whitney triumphantly hoisted the fake lobster, then pretended to use it as a weapon to keep the two clowns at bay. Finally they swept a low bow, conceding defeat.

The audience clapped and tossed coins into a black stovepipe hat that sat upside down on the beach. Whitney reached into her purse and pulled out a five-dollar bill, which she added to the pot.

"Wow! Thanks." The female clown found her voice, now that the act was over. "You really took me by surprise."

Whitney reached down and brushed off her suit. "I sort of took myself by surprise," she admitted.

"You look familiar," the male clown said. Up close, she could see that the pair were quite young, perhaps in their early twenties, with intelligent eyes and mobile, quick-to-smile mouths. They seemed a lively pair.

"Are you two related?" Whitney asked, glad for an excuse to change the subject.

The boy nodded. "I'm Tom and this is my sister Mimi."

"Screaming Mimi." She shrieked for emphasis. "And you are?"

"Whitney Greystone." No point in trying to hide her identity, which, she could see from their expressions, was about to be guessed, anyway.

"Oh, the Brite Cola lady," said Mimi. "You look different. More dressed-up. I saw you on TV one time and you were wearing some kind of Mideastern thing, or maybe it was from India."

"I used to have a lot of dresses like that," Whitney admitted, strolling alongside the mimes as they headed toward a van. "What are you guys doing here?"

"We've been traveling around the country since we got out of college." Tom unlocked the van and slid open the side panel. "We're twins, you might have guessed. We both graduated from NYU in June."

"Want some cocoa?" Mimi scrambled inside and helped Whitney up.

"Sure." It beat going home to a silent apartment.

The van had been cleverly fixed up to resemble the inside of a gypsy wagon, or at least the way Hollywood would have depicted one. Paisley curtains hung at the windows, a matching cloth was draped across the small round table, and perched on a small table there was even a crystal ball.

As they heated water and mixed up instant hot chocolate, the twins worked in unison, seemingly unfazed by the cramped space. Although the day had been warm, the temperature was already dropping here at the beach, so the cocoa tasted wonderful.

"So where are you going next?" Whitney asked.

"Actually, we're staying," Tom said.

"We got a job," his sister added.

"With a mime troupe."

"Here in Orange County."

"That visits nursing homes and hospitals, that kind of thing," Tom finished.

"I thought those were all volunteers," Whitney said.

The twins explained that they'd been accepted into a new troupe operated by a resident theater company, which had won a grant. Their income wouldn't be much, so they'd be living in the van for a while.

It didn't have a bathroom, Whitney noticed, but Mimi explained that they had no trouble finding rest rooms in stores and public buildings.

Still, Whitney couldn't help thinking about the vacant apartment downstairs from her. Maybe just for a few months...

No. Jonas had been so proud of her for finally behaving like an executive, instead of a goofball. Right now, she felt too worn out to face battling him, having to prove all over again that just because she had a soft heart didn't mean she had a soft head.

"Will you be parked around here for a while?" she inquired. Jonas would be leaving for Sonoma tomorrow, Whitney reflected, so at last she might be able to take these two home to dinner over the weekend. She was relieved when they nodded. "Then I'll probably be seeing you."

Reluctantly she said goodbye and walked home. After all, she *was* hungry, eager to get out of her suit, and expecting Jonas to arrive any minute.

It was almost dark now, and the apartment certainly didn't look inviting as Whitney clumped up the steps and fished in her purse for the keys. She nearly had to turn her purse inside out to find them, then the lock stuck and she had to kick the door and curse a few times before it opened.

The place was dark and silent. Whitney just stood there for a minute, almost too weary to step over the threshold.

Suddenly the lights flashed on. She blinked, confused. The whole place was draped with colored streamers and bright balloons proclaiming Happy Birthday, Whitney!

She picked out Jonas's face, smiling from ear to ear, and Mattie, of course. Along with Sarah and little Kip, Gavin, Bryan and a very pregnant Maria, and—Carol Truax.

"Surprise!" they shouted.

Whitney blinked. Then she spotted the cartons of pizza on the table. "Wow. Dinner!" she said.

Everybody laughed.

"That's my Whitney—right to the point," Jonas said.

"You took the long way home," added Sarah, already cutting a slice of pizza into little tidbits for Kip. "We were ready to start without you."

"Oh, sorry." Whitney kicked off her shoes and found an apron in the kitchen to cover her suit. "If I'd known, I'd have hurried. But then it wouldn't have been a surprise."

"Michael's sorry he couldn't be here, but he had to go to San Francisco on business," Sarah said. "He sends his love."

Bryan pointed to a pile of gaily wrapped packages. "Aren't you going to open your presents?"

Whitney downed a slice of pizza in three gulps. "Maybe you could help me."

"Okay!"

Soon she was seated on the floor, surrounded by pieces of paper, making the appropriate enthusiastic comments about the books, records and sweaters her friends had brought her.

The gift from Jonas was a very small box. "But you already gave me these," Whitney said as she touched her earrings. Then it occurred to her it might be a ring. If it was, she didn't want to open it in front of all these people, even if they were her best friends. "I'll save it till later."

Jonas didn't object. In fact, he was amazingly mellow tonight, after the tense way he'd gone about business all summer. Maybe he too was glad the ad campaign was just about wrapped up. At any rate, he was busy playing host, refilling glasses with Brite Cola and Ameling wines.

"What are you doing here?" Whitney asked Carol as they stuffed the wrapping paper into a grocery sack. "Not that I'm not glad to see you."

Her friend laughed. "I wouldn't blame you. The more I think about it, the more awful I feel."

"But things are going okay? With Ben and the kids?"

Carol nodded. "I was afraid the effect might wear off, but they seem to have made a real transition. What you did with Gini was amazing. Sometimes she catches herself in the middle of whining and just stops with her mouth open, and looks embarrassed. Like she's remembering the way her friends behaved."

"Are they still her friends?" Whitney watched as Maria began lighting the candles on the chocolate-frosted birthday cake. Gavin hovered protectively nearby. The baby was due sometime next month, Whitney remembered, watching her sister-in-law's slightly clumsy movements with a touch of envy.

"Nessa still comes over once in a while," Carol said. "But she's dating someone else, a senior in high school who wants to be a doctor. Not just a doctor: an open-heart surgeon. Kids are a lot more focused about their careers now than when I was in school."

Whitney studied the candles, trying to figure out how to blow them all out in one breath. "You still didn't explain why you're in town."

"Oh!" Carol chuckled. "Well, you know, 'Texas Girl' is being released this week, and Karl's getting married, so I came out for kind of a double celebration. Ben decided he'd better stay and keep an eye on the kids. I'm glad he trusts me out of his sight."

"What're you going to wish for, Aunt Whitney?" Bryan asked.

Kip toddled over to the table and tried to stick his finger in the icing. Sarah, snatching him away, said, "If she tells you, it won't come true."

"Oh. I forgot," Bryan said.

What did she want to wish for, Whitney wondered. A few months ago, there wouldn't have been any question. But now...

I want to be able to be myself, and still have Jonas love me. The realization squeezed so tightly at her heart that she felt as if she might cry. Quickly Whitney closed her eyes as if making the wish, then blew out the candles to distract everyone.

"Wow! She got 'em all!" Bryan said.

Whitney busied herself cutting the cake, and somehow the next hour sped by, filled with chitchat and good-natured joking. Maria seemed to enjoy being part of the family group, and Whitney was glad.

Finally all the guests were gone, with lots of hugs and promises to call soon, and Jonas was cleaning up the apartment while Whitney changed into jeans and a sweatshirt and brushed out her hair.

"Aren't you forgetting something?" he asked as she came out.

Puzzled, Whitney glanced around, and then spotted his gift still sitting on the table. "Oh!" she exclaimed guiltily, crossing the room and opening it.

Inside was a small box, but not the kind jewelers use. Curious, she opened it, to find not a ring but an old-fashioned oversize key. "What's this? The key to your heart?"

"More or less." Jonas ducked his head, as if suddenly touched by shyness. "Actually, it's the key to the farmhouse in Sonoma."

"The key?" Whitney repeated, feeling rather stupid. She couldn't quite figure out what it meant. After all, anytime she went to Sonoma, she would be with Jonas, and Lupe would be there, so why should she need a key?

"Well, it's been fun staying at the beach this summer, but there isn't exactly a lot of room here," Jonas pointed out. "Not to mention when we have children. I presume you still want them?"

"Of course." Whitney stopped. He meant that he expected them to move to Sonoma. "I—" She couldn't sort this out yet. Weakly she said, "Thanks, Jonas."

He gave her a hug. "Are you ready to set a date yet?"

I'm not ready for any of this yet. "Why don't we talk about it when you get back from Sonoma?"

"Okay." He looked a little disappointed, but obligingly went into the other room and switched on the TV. Their favorite sitcom was on Thursday nights, and a few minutes later Whitney joined him.

Her thoughts buzzed for most of the night. Whitney would wake up from a dream and realize that somehow she'd been thinking about Jonas and marriage and Sonoma. The funny thing was that the dreams all had something to do with being trapped, isolated, stuck.

Why, she wondered as they kissed goodbye in the morning, was she feeling so apprehensive?

It was actually a relief to get to the office and forget her concerns for a while in her work, but by afternoon Whitney's musings had begun to take on solid shape.

Yes, she loved the vineyards, and Jonas. *Yes,* it would be a relief not to have to show up at the office every day. In fact, with Lupe around, Whitney wouldn't even have to worry about occasionally running the vacuum cleaner.

But she didn't belong in a farmhouse, at least not permanently. Whitney loved people, the unexpected, excitement, having lots of friends. She liked being around a beach, with its offbeat atmosphere. She would die of boredom, living at Jonas's farmhouse all year.

It was partly her fault, Whitney admitted silently as she drove home. These past few months, she'd intentionally given Jonas the impression that she had settled down. And in a way it was true; bit by bit, Whitney could feel herself maturing. But she hadn't changed *that* much.

She took a deep breath of salt air as she neared her street. Now that the pressure was easing up at work, it was time to reassert herself. To remind Jonas that Whitney was still Whitney.

If he couldn't accept that, they weren't going to make it as a couple.

Whitney parked and turned off the ignition, then laid her head back against the seat. She missed him so much already, missed his grin and his warmth. And she'd already fantasized, in odd moments, about the children they would have, so much that the little guys almost seemed real.

For some reason, thinking of the children reminded her of Tom and Mimi. Whitney sat upright. If she was going to show Jonas that she was still herself, what better way than by helping the two mimes?

Without even stopping by her apartment, she charged down the sidewalk, checking out all the dead ends for a sign of the van. Unfortunately, it wasn't still parked where it had been yesterday, and after half an hour her shoes were pinching and her purse felt as if it weighed fifty pounds.

Just as she was about to give up the search, Whitney heard the sound of applause. Turning toward the water, she saw a crowd breaking up on the beach and, in the center, two figures in brightly colored costumes.

"Tom! Mimi!" Whitney waved, and the clowns started toward her, picking up their coin-filled top hat on the way. When they got closer, she said, "How would you guys like a place to stay for a month or two, until you can afford an apartment?"

The twins exchanged looks. "You're offering to let us move in with you?" Mimi asked. "We're kind of rambunctious."

"We might be in the way," Tom added.

"Downstairs from me," Whitney said, and explained about the apartment.

A few minutes later, the whooping pair had escorted her back to their van, and they drove to her apartment. "Fantastic!" Mimi proclaimed when Whitney opened the door to the downstairs unit. "This is great!"

Tom inspected the kitchen. "Some of the handles on the cabinets are loose. I'll be glad to fix the place up here and there, if you like."

"And we'll pay you as soon as we can," Mimi added.

"Just don't break anything." Whitney handed them the key. "My boyfriend thinks I'm flaky enough as it is."

At their insistence, Whitney joined the pair for dinner, which consisted of canned beans with cut-up hot dogs. Actually, it didn't taste too bad.

Later, going upstairs, she listened with delight to the banging and chortling as the pair moved in their few belongings. Mimi uttered an occasional shriek, just for the heck of it, and Tom paused from time to time to tootle on a small recorder.

Whatever Jonas might say, Whitney knew she'd done the right thing.

She woke up the next morning feeling more high-spirited and enthusiastic than she had in weeks. After all, the hardest part of the work was nearly done, and she would have the whole weekend to relax and finally start on a tan.

As she was debating whether to wear a suit to work again or indulge herself by dressing in slacks and a knit top, Whitney was dismayed to hear the phone ring. Now who could that be?

It was Mattie, sounding uncharacteristically distraught. "Whitney, I just got to the office and it's a mess. The building manager says there was some kind of electrical fire last night—don't worry, the place didn't burn down, but between the sprinklers and the firemen, it's just chaos. One of the file cabinets got knocked over, and everything's soaked. I don't know how we're going to get it straightened out." To Whitney's amazement, her secretary's voice choked with frustration, as if she might burst into tears at any moment.

"Don't worry," she heard herself say in a calm, authoritative voice. "I'll be right there. We'll get that place in order if it takes all weekend."

"Should we call Jonas?"

"We can handle this ourselves," Whitney said. "He's got his own work to do."

Mattie sounded reassured. "Thanks. I just—it's just such a *mess*, Whitney!"

"Get the coffee ready and don't lift a finger till I get there," Whitney said, and rang off.

She picked out a pair of jeans, a work shirt and a bandanna for her hair. It looked as though this was going to be a tough weekend, after all.

Chapter Fifteen

On Saturday, Jonas had to drive into San Francisco to meet with his export agent, so he called ahead to Michael McCord's hotel room and arranged for them to have dinner together.

Michael was one of those people Jonas had always meant to get to know better, but somehow never had. They hadn't met under the most favorable of circumstances; at Michael and Whitney's engagement party, some three and a half years ago, Jonas had felt stiff and uncomfortable, doing his best to hide his jealousy and not at all mollified by the fact that Michael turned out to be a solid, respectable fellow.

He'd developed a grudging admiration for Michael during their search for Whitney, despite, or perhaps because of, the fact that it had become obvious Michael was growing seriously attached to Sarah. It had been a relief when the engagement was amicably broken off, and something of a surprise when Whitney served as a bridesmaid at Sarah and Michael's wedding.

And McCord had certainly come through like a gentleman, helping buy up the remaining shares of Brite Cola and then entrusting the business to Whitney and Jonas. Of course, as it turned out, he'd made a tidy profit on it. But then, as a successful magazine publisher, Michael hardly needed the money.

Well, they'd undoubtedly be seeing a lot more of each other, with Sarah being Whitney's best friend. So it was about time the two men got to know each other on a more than superficial level, Jonas told himself.

But, as he navigated his way to Chinatown that evening, he had to admit that wasn't his only reason for arranging this meeting.

He'd been getting the strangest feeling about his relationship with Whitney. As if there was something not quite right, a piece out of place. And yet she'd been everything he could ask for these past few months; mature, self-disciplined and responsible, as well as warm and loving.

Maybe Michael could set his mind at ease. After all, Michael must have gotten to know Whitney fairly well during their engagement—even though, as Jonas now knew, the two hadn't been lovers—and perhaps had learned even more through Sarah.

It was ironic, Jonas had to admit, that he should turn to a virtual stranger for reassurance about a woman he'd known most of his life. Until recently, Jonas would probably have dismissed the possibility, but these last few months had shaken up some of his previously impenetrable self-assurance.

Where Whitney was concerned, it was true that Jonas had assumed the role of know-it-all big brother. But she'd shown him quite clearly that there were times when her instincts were superior to his cautious analyses. So he was willing to face the likelihood that there were areas in which someone else could enlighten him, even when it came to his own lover.

Michael had suggested they meet at a Chinese restaurant, which suited Jonas well enough, although his usual taste ran to French cuisine. A bit of variety now and then wasn't a bad thing.

However, Chinatown's location at the heart of the city made driving tricky. After half an hour's search through the steep, narrow streets, he managed to find a parking lot with a vacancy, albeit at an exorbitant price, and hiked along the crowded sidewalk. Flashy signs and a garishly ornamented arch announced that he'd reached Chinatown.

Following the directions Michael had provided, Jonas found his way to a rococo restaurant with enough red velvet in the lobby to decorate half a dozen bordellos. The maître d' showed him immediately to a corner table, where Michael was already ensconced.

Even if they hadn't been acquainted, it would have been obvious that Michael was someone Jonas could feel comfortable with. The publisher wore a conservative business suit and had neatly trimmed dark brown hair, with a hint of humor softening his blue-gray eyes.

The men shook hands and took their seats, exchanging the customary pleasantries. Jonas flashed back to a breakfast meeting three years ago, when he and Michael had met to thrash out the details of the Brite Cola takeover. Then, he'd felt a sharp rivalry with the man who had still been Whitney's fiancé; now he felt somewhat unsure how to begin, so he asked about Michael's business trip.

"We're acquiring a new business magazine here in the city." Michael, although a year older than Jonas, looked young and rakishly cheerful as he sipped at his drink. "It's about the Pacific Rim, trade and exports, mostly."

"The coming thing." Jonas nodded. "We're shipping Ameling wines to Japan now." They talked for a while about the growing importance of California as a center of U.S. international trade, a subject that carried them through ordering but began to peter out as the almond chicken and *k'ung pao* shrimp arrived.

Jonas tried to figure out how to bring up the subject of Whitney. He knew that women friends gossiped easily about their acquaintances, but that wasn't the way men usually talked to each other. Or at least, not in his experience, and certainly not tonight. The conversation seemed to be stuck on financial topics, and he was damned if he could figure out an unobtrusive way to steer it away.

It was finally Michael who cut to a more personal topic. "You and Whitney getting married?"

Jonas took a deep breath, caught off guard in spite of the fact that he'd arranged their meeting to talk about this very thing. "It looks that way."

"About time." The publisher helped himself to a second serving of fried rice. "You two have been crazy about each other for years. Sarah and I had a bet going on how long it would take."

"You seem to have had more confidence than we did." Jonas didn't like the idea that other people, even good friends, had been speculating about their romance, but he supposed it was only natural. He could see that getting close to a woman meant figuring prominently in her friends' lives as well, a prospect that he wasn't entirely comfortable with.

"Well, Sarah noticed it right away," Michael said. "As soon as she met you, in fact."

"How did you and Sarah happen to meet, anyway?" Jonas was glad of a chance to dance around the subject for a while. "She seemed to pop up out of nowhere after Whitney disappeared."

Michael looked slightly embarrassed. "Actually, I met her when she broke into my house."

"Broke into your house?" Jonas wasn't sure he'd heard correctly. "Why on earth would she do that?"

"She pictured herself as some kind of amateur detective." Michael signaled the waiter to bring another round of drinks. "I'd gone to the library looking for information on missing persons, to help locate Whitney. Sarah, you'll recall, was a librarian. She got suspicous of me for some reason and decided to follow me home."

"I can't picture it." Sarah had always seemed like such a down-to-earth person. And certainly librarians didn't make a habit of spying on their patrons.

"She was a lot wilder then," Michael conceded. "Actually, I realized she was following me and I set a trap for her, leaving a window open and pretending to drive away, and she went right in. Caught her in the bedroom, as a matter of fact. I meant to scare her, but she didn't scare easily. She knew all about Whitney from the newspapers and was a big fan of hers, and when she figured out Whitney was missing, she insisted on helping find her."

"So she's settled down a lot since then." Jonas hoped that was a good omen. "She certainly seems happy enough."

"There was a process of adjustment," Michael conceded. "She had to learn to be less impulsive, and I had to learn when to follow and when to lead."

"Tell me more," said Jonas dryly, wondering what he would hear next.

"Well, for example, I've been thinking about winding down my role in the business over the next few years. Sarah's always wanted to do some writing; she's a big fan of romance novels and wants to try her hand at one. We don't want to put Kip in day care, so that means I'll have to free up more time. Which may not be a bad thing."

Jonas tried to picture himself taking care of a baby, and couldn't do it. On the other hand, he would enjoy taking an older child tromping about the vineyards, showing how the grapes were trellised and explaining the winemaking process. Maybe he'd discover some new sides to himself if he had a child.

He could see that marriage wasn't going to be as predictable as he'd always supposed. His parents had been traditionalists, his mother reserved and home-centered, his father hardworking and stern. Neither one of them had been forced to display a lot of flexibility. But neither one of them had fallen in love with anyone like Whitney, either.

The topic of conversation shifted to whether the Dodgers had a chance at winning the World Series this year, and it wasn't until he was on his way back to Sonoma that Jonas had a chance to reflect further about his chat with Michael.

He wasn't sure he'd learned anything new about Whitney, but the discussion had been worthwhile, nevertheless.

Michael, it seemed, had learned to adapt himself to Sarah during their courtship. Jonas, on the other hand, hadn't really had to change at all. He wondered if that might be a problem, but didn't quite see how.

True, Whitney hadn't seemed exactly thrilled by his suggestion that they move to Sonoma. But she could hardly expect them to make a permanent home in that cramped apartment, could she?

And certainly, Jonas told himself as the miles slipped by, he'd shown a lot of tolerance for her zany side. He'd even learned to respect the value of intuition in business, particularly when it came to promotions.

Yet all the next day he couldn't squelch a feeling of unease. He and Whitney hadn't been separated for more than a few hours since April. Left to her own devices, was she likely to backslide? And if she did, what would that mean to their future?

Jonas wanted to trust her. He forced himself not to telephone on Sunday, because he knew that if he did he'd find himself checking up on what she'd been doing and whom she'd been seeing. And Whitney would have every right to resent that.

Still, by Monday he was impatient to get back to Orange County, although he wasn't due back until Tuesday. And his employees here at the winery had demonstrated they were more than capable of running operations with only occasional input from Jonas.

Why not fly back early and surprise her?

Jonas liked the idea. In fact, he'd discovered on her birthday that it was fun catching Whitney off guard. She'd certainly seemed to enjoy the party, and he'd enjoyed planning it.

Whistling to himself, he went into the house to pack.

BY THE TIME noon rolled around on Monday, Whitney was wiped out.

The weekend had turned out to be hour after hour of hard physical labor. Determined to get things in shape before Jonas returned, Whitney had outworked even the dedicated Mattie, whom she'd sent home on Sunday afternoon to spend some time with her family.

Mattie's description of the offices had been, if anything, an understatement. It had taken several hours on the phone just to find an electronics repairman who worked weekends, to check out the computers and VCR equipment.

Copies of all the vital computer data were kept in a fireproof and waterproof safe. But the files and other paperwork hadn't been so lucky. Page after page had to be laid out to dry—Whitney and Mattie had pressed their hair dryers into service—and then methodically refiled. The whole office had to be scrubbed, the curtains taken down for cleaning, the desks polished. Although the offices were cleaned once a week, the crew usually did a fairly perfunctory job, and Whitney wanted to make sure everything was done right.

As a result, her arms, legs and back ached, and she could hardly concentrate all morning.

I think this is what they call burnout.

Finally, about noon, she gave up. "Mattie, let's both take the afternoon off. The receptionist can let me know if there are any urgent calls."

Her secretary looked dubious. "There's still a lot to do...."

"It can wait till tomorrow."

Mattie nodded. "You're right. We're exhausted."

On the way home, Whitney stopped to pick up a pizza. Discovering she had a two-for-one coupon in her purse, she bought two.

When she got home, she was pleased to find Tom and Mimi rehearsing some tumbling on the beach with a couple of other mimes from their new troupe. Larry was sitting in front of his house, sketching the flying bodies.

"Anybody hungry?" Whitney called as she came down the walk.

Heads turned. The pizza cartons evidently spoke for themselves, because there was a chorus of yeses.

"I'll get paper plates and napkins," Larry offered, folding up his sketch pad.

"I just made a big salad," Mimi called. "And we've got a lifetime supply of plastic forks."

Whitney turned the pizza over to Tom and gestured to one of the other actors. "Come help me carry down some Brite Cola."

A few minutes later she had changed into a swimsuit and spread a blanket on the beach, and half a dozen of them were picnicking.

Just as they were finishing, some more friends of Tom and Mimi's arrived with several half gallons of ice cream. Whitney ran upstairs and turned her stereo on full blast so they could dance.

She felt a momentary twinge of guilt as she rejoined the others. It was, after all, a workday, and Jonas would never approve—but Jonas was in Sonoma and, besides, didn't she deserve a break after laboring all weekend?

Not to mention that the sun was warm, the harbor was dotted with brightly colored sails, the music was infectious and her feet itched to kick up sand.

With a whoop, Whitney gave herself over to a frenzied dance.

A FEELING OF APPREHENSION dogged Jonas on the entire flight to Orange County. The clear weather gave him plenty of leisure to think about what lay ahead, but he couldn't for the life of him figure out why he was so tense.

Maybe he *was* too much of a worrier, as Whitney had sometimes charged. Or maybe he'd picked up that same feeling she'd mentioned the night before Carol disappeared, that things were going just too smoothly.

He'd known Whitney a long time, since she was a little girl. It was still hard to believe the change that had come over her these past few months, even though she had of course been maturing ever since she'd taken over Brite Cola.

Those crazy impulses must still be there. But she loves me too much to let them take over again.

It was a touching thought. Jonas smiled to himself. He was going to do everything in his power to make sure Whitney never regretted her decision.

Because he was spending so much time in Orange County, he'd bought a car to keep there, and it was waiting for him at the airport. Tossing his suitcase into the back seat, Jonas decided to drop it off at the apartment before heading to the office.

Maybe he'd give Whitney a call from there, so his turning up unexpectedly wouldn't look as if he were snooping. She had a right to expect his trust; she'd certainly earned it.

The radio was playing Carol and Karl's song, "Texas Girl." Jonas whistled along, his spirits soaring.

After they moved to Sonoma, he would make sure that Whitney didn't die of boredom. They'd go into San Francisco for dinner and shopping a couple of times a month, and maybe take some trips, too. He'd heard Australia was an interesting place to visit, and not too foreign; at least, everyone spoke English.

And, now that he thought about it, he recalled that Sarah was writing a weekly book review column for a newspaper. Maybe Whitney could do something like that, so she wouldn't be completely cut off from the professional world. Sarah's desire to be a novelist struck him as reasonable, although he wasn't sure he wanted to encourage Whitney in the direction of romances. Maybe something along the line of light comedies . . .

Loud music rocked the car as Jonas turned into the dead end near Whitney's apartment. Now who the hell was blaring rock 'n'roll on the beach on a weekday afternoon? He knew it was irrational to be so annoyed—after all, it *was* summer—but he couldn't help thinking even students ought to be doing something useful with their time.

Then he stepped onto the sidewalk and halted in shock.

The beach in front of Whitney's apartment was jammed full of people dancing. There were sunbathers in bikinis, skateboarders boogying on the sidewalk, and even a number of people in clown costumes.

The rock music, he realized now, was blasting through an open window in Whitney's apartment. And there she was, long blond hair flying over her bare shoulders, wriggling away in the middle of everything.

A dark, bitter disappointment welled up in him. For a few moments, Jonas couldn't even move. Then the feeling began to transform into anger.

It was as if Whitney had deliberately been acting out a lie, playing the part of an executive while he was around, but hopping right back into her usual irresponsibility the minute he left town. Maybe on Sunday he could have understood her cutting loose like this, but there was simply no excuse for leaving the office on a weekday. Assuming, that was, that she'd gone there at all today.

To make matters worse, Jonas had to harness his fury. Nothing would be more distasteful to him than a scene in front of all these people.

The music stopped for a moment, and a breathless Whitney turned in his direction. He could tell from the way her eyes widened and her mouth dropped open that she'd spotted him.

At least she has the grace to look guilty.

"Jonas!" Whitney started toward him. *Damn,* but she looked stunning in the swimsuit, her legs long and shapely, her waist nipped in, her shoulders straight and her chin high. "This isn't the way it seems."

He tightened his jaw to stem the angry words and gestured toward the clowns. "And who, may I ask, are these—persons?"

Whitney looked him straight in the eye. "A couple of them are staying in the unit downstairs. For the summer."

He couldn't restrain the sarcasm. "As long as you're backsliding, might as well go all the way, right?"

"Jonas—"

One of the clowns did a series of flips, landing in front of them. "Hi! I'm Mimi!" She stuck out a gloved hand. "Why don't you take off those clothes and join us?"

Jonas ignored her. "I'm going upstairs," he told Whitney. "I'd like to speak to you alone." Without waiting for an answer, he stalked up to the apartment, where he clicked off the stereo. Below, he could hear the people grumbling at the sudden silence.

The door slammed, and he turned to face Whitney.

He'd never seen her so angry. "You had no right to do that!" She didn't look the least bit self-conscious, standing there wearing a minuscule swimsuit while he was fully dressed. But then, things like that never bothered Whitney.

"Did it ever occur to you that other people live in this neighborhood, and that they might not enjoy the same music you do?" he snapped back.

"I wasn't talking about that!" She paced angrily across the room and slammed the window shut. "I'm talking about the way you snubbed Mimi. That was inexcusable!"

She did have a point, but Jonas was in no mood to admit it. "What I find inexcusable is that, the minute my back is turned, you feel free to act like an adolescent. Of all the irresponsible..."

"Irresponsible?" She swung around and glared at him. "You certainly get your exercise jumping to conclusions, don't you, Jonas?"

"What else am I supposed to think?" He didn't like fighting, and suddenly wished that he hadn't been quite so high-handed. "Look at it from my point of view. This is the first time I've been away from you in months, the first time I've even gone back to check out my own business in Sonoma, and—"

"Speaking of Sonoma!" Whitney wasn't about to let him finish. "I love your house there and everything, but I can't live there. Not all the time, Jonas."

She couldn't mean it. "You wanted to be with me as much as I want to be with you," he reminded her. "Isn't that what we've been working toward all summer?"

"Right now, I don't know!" She inhaled deeply. "Jonas, I love you, but damn it, I'm tired of feeling like a prisoner! I need more freedom."

"Freedom?" He couldn't believe it had come to this, not after all their plans, all the time they'd spent together, but here it was, the same old devil-may-care Whitney wanting to have her own way. "Or license? You say you don't want to be a prisoner—well, I don't want to be a jailer, either. I don't like feeling that you can't wait for me to go out of town so you can cut loose and act like a spoiled brat."

To his surprise, tears of fury—or was that something else?—glistened in her eyes. "You always assume the worst about me. I don't think I can live with that, Jonas. You've got to learn to trust me."

"That's what I thought I was doing."

They stared at each other for a long, silent moment. Then the phone rang.

A rueful expression came over Whitney's face as she crossed to answer it. "Maybe it's Bob Abernathy." Her mouth quirked wistfully. "Maybe he could send us on another wild-goose chase.... Hello?"

She listened for a moment, then said tautly, "We'll be right there," and hung up.

"What's wrong?"

"That was Gavin." Whitney raced into the bedroom, and he could hear her scrape the closet door open. "They're at St. Joseph Hospital. Maria's labor pains started and they can't get them stopped."

"But the baby's not due for another month." Suddenly Jonas understood why Whitney sounded so shaky. "I'll drive."

She changed into slacks and a blouse in record time. "Let's go."

Locking the door behind them, he hurried down the steps behind her. It was odd, he reflected, how natural it seemed that Gavin would take the time, even at a moment like this, to call Whitney.

Whatever her faults, she was the most caring person he knew. And Jonas realized as something squeezed painfully at his heart, that he couldn't bear to go through life without her.

Chapter Sixteen

Maria had never been so terrified in her life.

Everything had gone normally in her pregnancy until this morning. Having had an easy delivery with Bryan, she'd been expecting the same thing to happen again.

Then, while fixing breakfast, she'd felt the muscles contract in her abdomen. *False labor,* she'd told herself firmly, pouring out pancake batter.

After all, the sun was shining, and through the window of the cottage they were renting in Corona del Mar she could see roses and petunias brightening the neighbor's flower bed. The world was healthy and lush, and nothing could go seriously wrong, could it?

But the contractions hadn't stopped. In fact, they'd intensified until they were coming only a few minutes apart. That was when Gavin had called the doctor and, after quickly arranging for Bryan to stay with their neighbor, had rushed her to the hospital.

There was an air of unreality to the whole thing: the lobby dotted with people, the intake clerk, the wheelchair in which they rushed Maria off while Gavin answered questions about insurance.

Disjointed thoughts fleeted through her mind: that it was too bad she hadn't already preregistered, which would have saved time; that she was glad St. Joseph was adjacent to

Children's Hospital, just in case the baby needed extra help; and that this couldn't be happening to her.

I can't bear to lose this baby. It would break Gavin's heart.

A small, cold voice within warned that Gavin might turn away from her, might blame her somehow. Until now, the men in Maria's life had all shirked responsibility, and it was hard to believe that even someone as loving as Gavin would stick by her in such awful circumstances.

Take the money and run, one of her co-workers at the casino had said. *His kind will never really accept you, you know.*

Maria was vaguely aware of riding up in an elevator and being wheeled through corridors until the orderly pushed her past doors marked Labor and Delivery.

It was too soon. They had to stop the baby coming.

Nurses helped her onto a hard, narrow bed and began attaching monitors to her stomach. Moments later, Maria heard the reassuring amplified sound of her baby's heartbeat.

"The doctor is on his way," one of the nurses told her, jabbing a needle into Maria's arm to start an intravenous solution. "You're how far along? Thirty-five weeks? I'm sure you'll be fine."

Where was Gavin?

The contractions were coming faster, and more and more painfully. Had it really hurt this much last time? Maria didn't think that was possible. Surely no sane woman would have chosen to go through this again, if it had.

One of the nurses gave her some ice chips, but her mouth still felt parched.

"Did you eat anything this morning?" the woman asked.

A contraction eased, and Maria shook her head weakly. *Thank goodness,* she hadn't had time to eat breakfast.

A masculine voice in the corridor sent her heart skittering, but it turned out to be the doctor. Dr. Bloome. His name had always reminded her of flowers. She hoped that was a good omen.

"How're we doing?" he asked Maria as he strode in and checked the graph paper emerging from the monitor machine. "Looks like the baby's coming early, huh?"

"My... husband?" Maria managed to gasp.

"He's getting cleaned up," the doctor said, but she wasn't sure whether to believe him. Would they tell her if her husband had decided to skip out?

He wouldn't do that. I couldn't bear it if he did.

The doctor did a quick examination. "I'm afraid you're too far along for us to stop the labor," he said. "But don't worry. Everything looks good. I'll be back in just a minute."

People came and went. A woman was admitted into the next bed, separated by a curtain. Then one of the nurses returned to check the graph.

"Doctor!" The woman leaned out into the corridor. "I think you should see this."

Maria felt as if she were drifting between fire and ice. Was something else wrong? Surely this had to end soon. Surely she'd wake up and find she'd dreamed the whole thing.

The doctor popped in and looked at the graph. "Maria." His eyes were stern, worried. "We're picking up a little irregularity in the heartbeat. I don't think it's anything to get excited about, not yet."

For the next few minutes, nurses shifted her position, the doctor examined her again, and still Gavin didn't come.

"I think we're having a little problem with the umbilical cord." Why did the doctor keep referring to everything as "little?" Was he afraid she'd panic if she knew the truth? "I'm going to perform an emergency caesarean section." He squeezed her hand. "We do this all the time. In just a few minutes, we'll have the baby safely out of there. Okay?"

"Okay." What else could she say? *Please let my baby be all right.*

Within seconds, Maria was wheeled into a gleaming operating room and an anesthesiologist was asking her questions about what she'd eaten and whether she'd had any anesthetics before. He did something to the IV bottle and the world began to spin away from her. The last thing she thought was, *Why isn't Gavin here?*

It seemed like only moments later that she began drifting upward through a well of darkness. Up, up into the light. She was lying on a gurney behind a curtain. *Oh, my gosh, I must be dead.*

Then she heard the murmur of a woman's voice and realized it might be a nurse. Tentatively Maria shifted her hand until it was touching her abdomen. She could feel bandages, and her stomach still protruded. But the baby was gone.

She had never felt so alone in all her life. Not even when her father had run out on Maria and her mother while she was in junior high school; not even when her mother had died, when Maria was barely eighteen. Not even when Bryan's father had refused to acknowledge paternity and had promptly disappeared.

Closing her eyes, she tried to visualize herself going back to Las Vegas and working as a show girl again. She could still smell the stale perfume, sweat and cosmetics in the dressing room, could feel how the feathers on her costume itched. It had seemed glamorous at first, but she'd quickly learned the job was hard, hard work for barely adequate pay. You had to watch your diet constantly, fend off the advances of men who considered you fair game, and hope you found some better way to make a living before your wrinkles began to show through the makeup.

She didn't see how she could do it. They might not even want to hire her back.

Where, oh where, was Gavin?

Someone was pulling apart the curtains that surrounded her. "Mrs. Greystone?" the nurse said. "Your husband is here."

Maria clenched her hands into fists. What was he going to say? Had the baby died? Was he going to disown her?

When Gavin came in, she almost didn't recognize him. He was wearing a white gown over his clothes, and a white cap covered his hair.

"How do you feel?" he asked.

"Numb," she said, and waited.

"You sure scared the hell out of me." Gavin pulled up a chair and took her hand. "By the time I got up to maternity, you were already out cold."

"The—baby?"

"She's just fine. That's where I was now, at the nursery." His eyes were alight. "Maria, she's beautiful. Little Linette. She's six and a half pounds, something like that. They're going to keep her here a few days for observation, but then, you'll be in the hospital for a few days yourself."

Maria closed her eyes. She had a daughter, a healthy little girl. But what if the child had died, or been born handicapped? Would Gavin be so loving and attentive then? Would she have to live the rest of her married life with the fear that he might run out on her when she needed him most?

But he was talking again. "You know, the funny thing is, I wasn't thinking about the baby at first. When I saw you lying there unconscious, I thought you were dying. You really scared the hell out of me, Maria. I guess it sounds terrible, but I almost hated the baby for doing this to you."

He couldn't really be saying this. Men didn't talk that way. At least, not in Maria's experience. "But if—if we'd lost her..."

"It certainly wouldn't have been your fault." Gavin was toying with her fingers, nibbling at the tips. "We'd have tried again, that's all. And anyway, we've got Bryan."

But he's not even your child. Almost at once, the response came back to her: *Yes, he is. Because you love him. We're a family.*

Maria felt thick hot tears slide down her cheeks.

"Honey? Are you hurting somewhere? Do you want me to call the nurse?"

She managed to smile and blink up at him. "I love you, Gavin."

"Hey, that's no reason to turn on the waterworks."

Suddenly she felt wonderful. "When can I see the baby?"

"Maybe this afternoon, the doctor said." Gavin sat there beaming at her. "Oh, I called Whitney. She and Jonas should be here any minute."

"Let's not tell her how bad it was, okay?" Maria said. "It might scare her off having children; well, probably not, but Linette and Bryan deserve to have lots of little cousins. That's what families are for, isn't it?"

"Among other things." Gavin bent down to kiss her forehead. Relaxing, Maria let herself drift off to sleep. Now she knew that Gavin would be here when she woke up, and whenever she needed him, for the rest of their lives.

Chapter Seventeen

"She's beautiful." Whitney gazed through the glass of the intermediate care nursery. "Look at those little hands! Are all newborn babies that tiny, Jonas?"

"Well, she's smaller than most." He stared at Linette, a frowning red bundle swathed in a blanket and held up by a nurse. "Six pounds something, Gavin said."

"They're cute small," Whitney announced, then felt rather stupid. After all, wasn't that the reason people cooed and fussed over babies? "I mean—well—I used to think babies were icky."

"Icky?" Jonas's mouth twisted in amusement.

"I was never much interested in babies when I was a teenager," Whitney admitted, watching intently as the nurse laid Linette in a plastic-covered bassinet—no, isolette, that was what they were called, she remembered from somewhere. "All I could think of was dirty diapers and drooling toddlers. But she's so precious."

"There haven't exactly been a lot of babies born in our families, have there?" Jonas observed. "That's the problem with being an only child."

"I was half an only child," Whitney reminded him, taking a wistful look at the other dozing babies in the nursery. Each one was distinctive, some with shocks of dark hair, one with adorable Oriental eyes, another with a teddy bear perched atop her isolette. Would she ever be lucky enough to have a baby of her own? Well, there was no sense dwelling on it now. "Let's go find Gavin again."

They'd arrived at the hospital half an hour before, nerves tight as rubber bands. Whitney shivered to think that something awful might have happened to the baby. She'd been looking forward so much to having another nephew or a niece. And besides, Maria and Gavin deserved a break.

It had been a great relief to find Gavin glowing with pride. Maria was being moved from Recovery into a semiprivate room and couldn't be disturbed just now, he told them, but he'd directed them to the nursery.

Now they wandered back down the corridor and ran into Gavin near the nurses' station. "She's stunning," Whitney said. "You should be thrilled. And so should Lina."

"I couldn't reach her, actually," Gavin said. "She and her fiancé are traveling in France. I left a message on her machine."

"Was she planning to be here for the birth?"

"I hope not." Gavin grinned. "I can't imagine my mother playing nursemaid to Maria and Linette, can you?"

As she shook her head, it occurred to Whitney that, whenever she had children, there wouldn't be any mother or even mother-in-law there to help her. That was, assuming she went ahead and married Jonas, which was beginning to look less and less likely.

At the thought, her spirits took a dive. In the anxiety and excitement over the baby, she'd almost forgotten about the quarrel they'd been in the middle of.

But now it came back to her in a cloud of anger. That had been Jonas at his worse: judgmental, haughty, unwilling to listen. She couldn't spend her life within rigid guidelines, always afraid that the least misstep would bring down his angry disapproval.

"Congratulations." Jonas reached out to shake Gavin's hand. "We're both thrilled for you."

"Can we come back tomorrow?" Whitney asked. "Will they let me hold the baby?"

"I'm not sure. Probably not for a few days," Gavin admitted. "But I'm sure Maria would love to see you."

"I'll be here."

She and Jonas stopped in the gift shop on the way out and ordered a bouquet of flowers to be sent up to Maria's room, along with a fluffy white teddy bear.

"It's so sweet." Whitney held the bear in her arms, and Jonas wasn't sure whether she was talking about the stuffed animal, the baby or about Gavin and Maria.

And then, to his astonishment, tears began coursing down Whitney's cheeks.

"Are you all right?" He reached out to touch her, but she moved quickly away.

"Of course." She handed the bear to the clerk and paid in cash. "Just nerves, that's all." She ducked her head as she gave the clerk Maria's room number.

But they weren't more than a few steps out of the lobby when Whitney's shoulders began to shake. Jonas hadn't seen her cry this way for more than ten years, since her mother died.

"Whitney?" He stopped on the walkway, catching hold of her arm. "What's going on?"

"I can't—it isn't—" She fished in her purse for a tissue and blew her nose. "Oh, Jonas. This is awful."

"Tell me about it." He led her gently toward the privacy of the parking garage.

"That's the awful part!" Whitney sputtered. "You're the person I always talk to when something's wrong. But this time what's wrong is you!" She fumbled with the tissue again.

"I'm sorry about today." He was glad that she'd brought the subject up. "I really went off half-cocked. I'm sure there was a good reason for you to throw a party like that."

"There was!" She led the way up the narrow steps to the second level, where they'd left the car. "I worked all weekend. There was some kind of electrical fire and the water left a big mess and Mattie and I worked like slaves. I'm so tired, Jonas! I just couldn't do it anymore. So I came home and Tom and Mimi were there, and I had this pizza, and well, it just sort of happened."

He decided it wasn't a good time to point out that Tom and Mimi wouldn't have been there if she hadn't let them move in, that he didn't quite see where the pizza came in, and that things had a tendency to happen to Whitney that wouldn't happen to anyone else.

What did all that really matter, anyway?

"I'm sorry I jumped to the wrong conclusion." He opened the car door. "That was unfair of me, Whitney. I know you've matured a lot, and I think we can work things out."

"I hope so." She sank into the seat. "I hope so, Jonas."

So did he. And maybe, he reflected more cheerfully, when she was calmer she'd be willing to reconsider about moving to Sonoma. Maybe her defiance had been the result of a weekend of overwork, followed by his own unfair accusations.

After all, one had to expect a little backsliding, he decided. If she could forgive him, then he could certainly forgive her.

All the same, he couldn't quite convince himself that the issue was really resolved once and for all.

BY THE END OF SEPTEMBER it had become clear that the new ad campaign was having a significant effect on Brite Cola's popularity.

Sales had nearly doubled, and while still far short of the giants like Pepsi and Coke, Brite Cola was clearly improving its share of the market. The company was even branching out into ice cream novelties laced with a syrup developed from the classic Brite Cola formula.

Best of all, from Jonas's point of view, they'd hired an outstanding executive to take over the day-to-day running of the company, a woman named Mona Artukian who had held several high-level positions at major food companies but wanted the challenge of being chief executive officer.

Which meant there was no longer any reason that he and Whitney couldn't get married. Yet somehow both of them kept postponing a decision.

He wasn't sure what was going on in her head, but he knew what he was concerned about: he didn't want to lose her. And there was always the possibility, if he forced the issue, that he might.

But he didn't want to wait forever. *Damn it,* what did Whitney want, anyway? She'd told him that she'd been in love with him for years, that she'd never found another man to measure up. And *he* certainly hadn't changed.

Moreover, except for that one incident over a month ago, she'd more than lived up to his expectations. If anything, Whitney was growing more beautiful as she got older, and was beginning to take on the air of dignity that he valued so much in a woman.

He'd even reluctantly admitted that Tom and Mimi were delightful, and that it would have been a waste to leave the apartment empty. In fact, brother and sister were now paying rent, and had done some much-needed repairs to the plumbing.

It was time to bring matters to a head, Jonas decided one Saturday night as he dressed laboriously in his tuxedo, wriggling the cuff links into place and tieing the bow tie. He was tired of having his clothes crammed into Whitney's closet, tired of sloshing around at night on her water bed; and he was good and ready to get on into the next stage of their lives.

"Where did I put my shoes?" Whitney stepped out of the bathroom. "The silver ones—have you seen them?"

"You look fabulous." No other woman could take his breath away the way Whitney did, Jonas reflected, his eyes studying hungrily the way she looked in her evening gown.

It was an off-the-shoulder, sea-green and silver designer ensemble stunningly set off by Whitney's height and coloring. And she'd had her hair done today, piling it up with some kind of tiara that made her look like a queen.

But her lips were pursed irritably as she scuffled around the floor. "Where the hell are they?"

"Don't you think this apartment is getting a bit cramped?" he asked.

She continued her search in silence, then stooped to peer under her bed. "Oh, *there* they are." A minute later she was ready, her feet tucked into the evening sandals and a crisp silver wrap draped about her shoulders. "Okay."

"Our employees are going to be bowled over," Jonas said as he held the door. It had been his idea to hold a formal dinner and give awards to their best workers, but Whitney had added her own inimitable touch to the occasion. "I'm sure they'll be impressed that you've gone to so much trouble to dress up for them."

Whitney clomped down the steps ahead of him, managing to make it sound as if she were wearing boots instead of high heels. "Oh, pooh. They know what I'm really like. It's Mona I'm worried about. She's such a knockout, I don't want to look like a slouch by comparison."

Was that a hint of jealousy? Jonas smiled to himself. Maybe it was a good sign.

They took his new Mercedes. He'd hoped to ease the topic around to marriage on their way to the hotel, but almost at once Whitney dialed her brother's number on the car phone and got into a long conversation with Maria about colic and pediatricians. By the time she finished, they were pulling up in front, and the doorman was waiting to hand Whitney out.

Later, Jonas told himself.

The dinner went well. At Whitney's request, speeches were kept to a minimum, and she'd ordered a hearty meal of steak and potatoes that was downed with genuine enthusiasm. Moreover, the workers seemed especially pleased by the fact that their award plaques came with hefty bonus checks.

Mona did indeed look striking in a tailored blue dress, but Jonas was reminded all over again that Whitney had nothing to fear from their new chief executive. There was a single-minded devotion to work about Mona that reminded him of Cynthia.

Maybe a year ago he would have considered that appealing, but now that he knew he could have Whitney *and* the kind of well-ordered life he wanted, no other woman could interest him.

The toasts were drunk with Brite Cola, but Ameling wines were served afterward. Whitney didn't seem to be eating or drinking as much as usual, Jonas noted, but then she *had* mentioned last week that she was concerned about gaining weight.

He considered it merely another sign that her body, along with her mind, was growing up.

At the end of the brief ceremony, Whitney and Jonas symbolically handed over the keys of the office to Mona.

"We're not promising to keep our noses out entirely," Jonas told the executive afterward.

"I wouldn't want you to." Her smile was friendly but impersonal. "After all, you're the ones who rescued Brite Cola from disarray—you're something of a phenomenon in business circles, you know. And of course you're majority stockholders."

"But I expect we'll have a few things to keep us busy," Jonas added. He looked at Whitney, but she was focused entirely on Mona.

"I'm glad somebody likes to handle these things," Whitney said at last. "Running that company was exciting, but it nearly drove me crazy."

"I expect most people would find the day-to-day details boring," Mona answered. "But of course, I find it a challenge."

It was a relief to Jonas when the evening was over and he could escort Whitney out to the car again. *Time to get to the point.*

However, as soon as he got the car started again, she began to chatter. "Did I tell you about Mimi and Tom's new job? They're making a TV commercial for some kind of nasal decongestant."

"Sounds thrilling." Jonas paused at a signal light. "Whitney, I think it's about time . . ."

"Mimi said they want to pay me back for the rent they couldn't afford last month." She didn't seem to have heard him.

"Let's get married," Jonas said.

There was a brief silence, and then Whitney repeated slowly, "Married. What does that mean to you, Jonas?"

It was a legitimate point, he supposed. After all, he'd always heard that couples should discuss every aspect of their relationship before they got married.

"Well, it means living together, of course," Jonas said. "I know you aren't crazy about the idea of moving to Sonoma, but I hope you'll reconsider. It's perfect for children."

"Go on." He couldn't get a clue to Whitney's emotions from her impassive expression, which was unusual.

"Well..." Jonas was relaxing a bit now, getting into the swing of it. "And I assume we both want children, right?"

"Mmm-hmm." It sounded like agreement, but of a very noncommittal variety.

"And of course marriage means planning for the future." Jonas thought he sounded a bit stuffy, but she *had* asked him. "Financial planning, which shouldn't be difficult considering we're both in great shape, and other kinds of planning."

"Such as?"

He wasn't sure he liked being pressed this way, but no doubt Whitney was taking the matter seriously and wanted to be sure she understood it all. "The children, for example. What kind of education we want for them. What kind of environment we want to create, in terms of our life-style and our friendships."

"We're going to plan all that out?" Whitney asked.

"I think we should set goals." Jonas was rather pleased with his improvising. "Where we want to be in five years, that sort of thing. Then we can evaluate our decisions in that light. Not go off half-cocked."

She didn't answer.

"Whitney?"

"I'm thinking."

The silence continued all the way to Balboa Island. There weren't any parking spaces near Whitney's apartment, and Jonas had to park two streets away. But it would be pleasant on a night like this to walk along the beach.

Whitney hopped out of the car before he could come around to help, and took off her shoes.

"You're going to wreck your stockings," he pointed out as he locked the car.

"Okay." Whitney reached down and, to his astonishment, stripped off her panty hose. Although she didn't actually reveal anything embarrassing, the gesture itself was inappropriate to a public place, and Jonas checked around them, relieved to find they were alone.

"Why do you do things like that?" he demanded, beginning to get fed up with her lack of response. "Are you trying to prove something?"

"Maybe." Whitney stood there in the moonlight, holding her shoes in one hand, her chin tilted up defiantly. In the dim light, her hair glowed as silver as her dress. She looked like a creature newly arrived from fairyland. Like a princess that he wanted desperately to carry off and keep for himself.

But from the angry look in her eye, he knew with a surge of pain that Whitney had no intention of marrying him. Like a magical spirit, she refused to be caged.

Jonas tried to think back over what he'd said. It had all been perfectly sensible, he told himself. There was no reason for Whitney to be regarding him as if he were some kind of monster.

"Don't give me that look," he said. "I don't deserve it."

"Don't you?" Whitney whirled and began to march away. It was one of her more infuriating habits, to assume that he would follow. And of course he did.

"Tell me what I've done to make you so angry." Jonas gritted his teeth as he felt sand begin to slip into the patent leather shoes that went with his tuxedo.

"I thought—" She turned, a dark figure against the moon-touched harbor. "I thought I'd proved something to you, not that I'd have to go on proving it for the rest of my life."

"You misunderstood me. Look, do we have to have this conversation on the beach, where everyone for miles can hear us?"

"Yes," Whitney said. "Right here. Right now."

"You haven't answered my question."

"What you did to make me angry?" Whitney shook her glowing hair. "I proved I could fit into your world, didn't I? Well, it's your turn to bend a little. When people get married, they live the rest of their lives together, or at least, that's the idea. That means they have to be able to be themselves."

"Have I asked you to be anything else?" Uneasily, Jonas suspected that maybe he had, so he added hastily, "I was trying to bring out the best in you, the mature, levelheaded Whitney who's so capable and so—so strong. What's wrong with trying to help the woman you love be the best person she can?"

"Because you aren't willing for me to do the same for you!" she flared. "I thought you'd ease up, Jonas, living here at the beach with me, but you haven't. You haven't even tried to! You grudgingly accept my friends like Mimi and Tom, because you figure they won't be around for long. You indulge me as if I were some kind of child. That isn't the same as accepting! That isn't the same as meeting me halfway!"

"Whoa." Stunned by her tirade, Jonas wondered if he'd missed something along the way. Had Whitney been giving him signals these past few months that he hadn't picked up? He'd never suspected that she intended him to change. The idea was startling and a bit unnerving. "What exactly is it you want from me?"

"What I'm never going to get." Her voice was thick with misery. "A man in touch with his own spontaneity, his own lovable childlike qualities. A man who isn't afraid to let things get a little out of control once in a while. A man who knows how to play as well as work. A friend and lover, not a taskmaster!"

Part of him wanted to debate the issue, to prove her wrong with logic and perhaps even a bit of sarcasm. And if he did that, he knew instinctively, he would lose her forever.

"I love you, Whitney."

"Don't talk about love!" He still couldn't see her clearly, but he knew she was crying. "To you, love is nothing but a straitjacket to throw on someone else!"

"Damn it...." The truth struck Jonas with a jolt. *Yes,* he was proud of Whitney's increasing maturity, and *yes,* he adored the sophisticated woman who'd stood beside him tonight, but *damn it,* he *didn't* want Whitney to turn into Cynthia. She was the only part of his world that was thoroughly, stunningly, and sometimes shockingly alive.

He'd never been as good with words as she was, and they failed him now. How could he tell her what he was feeling without sounding patronizing?

"Where do we start?" he asked, and gesturing at his formal attire. "I take it you don't like my clothing."

Whitney's shoulders sagged. "Once in a while it's okay, but Jonas, you never take it *off*."

He knew she didn't mean it literally, but he chose to take her words that way. "Maybe not until now, but things are going to change around here. Starting with what I'm wearing." He reached down and tugged off the bow tie, then flung it toward the harbor.

"Jonas—"

"Let's see—we're going barefoot tonight, right? Good. These are pinching and besides, they're full of sand." He bent down and pulled off the patent leather shoes, which he tossed up into the air. "What else?"

"Jonas, this is silly." She hopped on one foot, squirming like a youngster. "You don't have to do this."

"Yes, I do. Damn it, Whitney, you know I'm not as good as you are at expressing myself. If I have to strip myself naked to get you to marry me, I'll do it."

A tentative giggle was quickly stifled. "That's ridiculous. Besides, I already told you, I'm not going to marry you."

"So you say now." He shrugged off his jacket. "Hold this, will you?"

She clutched it awkwardly. "Come on, let's go inside."

"Fine." He struggled to get the suspenders loose, then flung them away and broke into a trot in the direction of her apartment. "Have you changed your mind yet?"

"About marrying you? This had nothing to do with—"

Getting the cuff links off proved the biggest challenge of the evening, but Jonas was up to it. His cummerbund followed, and then he began fumbling with the buttons of his shirt.

"You've got to be kidding!" Whitney was panting behind him, trying to collect the garments as he dropped them. "Jonas—"

"I'm just trying to prove a point." He pulled off the shirt. "Okay, so I'm a little stodgy. I like things neat and organized. But I love you, woman, and I intend to keep you, no matter what I have to do."

"This doesn't settle anything!" She swooped down to catch the shirt.

"No, but it sure is a lot cooler. Don't you think it was hot in there tonight?" He stripped off his socks and pitched them toward her. "You know, I get a little tired of being in a straitjacket myself. Maybe you could take me shopping at an army surplus store tomorrow. Or how about the thrift shops? I hear they're great."

"Jonas, you're not—" She gasped as he bent to unzip his pants. "You can't!"

"I might get arrested," he agreed calmly, wondering what demon had taken possession of him as he proceeded to lower the slacks, leaving him clad only in his tight-fitting black shorts. "That's up to you."

They'd reached her apartment, and Whitney tugged at his arm. "Come inside."

Jonas, his ankles still entangled in his slacks, hopped twice in an attempt to keep his balance and then tumbled on top of her.

With an "Ooph!" Whitney sank into the sand, designer gown and all.

"Are you all right?"

"What if somebody sees us?" Whitney hissed. "Jonas, you lunkhead!"

"They'll just think we're drunk," he pointed out in his best commonsense manner.

"That's the whole point!"

"Maybe we could get picked up by the harbor patrol," he suggested. "The Coast Guard doesn't come into the harbor, does it? I always thought it would be exciting to get arrested by the Coast Guard." Maybe he *had* drunk one glass too much of the wine tonight, he reflected. On the other hand, maybe that was a good thing, if it kept him from losing the woman he loved.

"Jonas, we're not a couple of kids!" Whitney was struggling to get to her feet, but she kept stumbling over his arms and legs. "What would people say?"

"That you put me up to it," he responded promptly. "And they'd be right."

"I never did anything *this* lame-brained!" She pushed up with her hands and finally got into a crouching position, from which she proceeded to reclaim her shoes and his various tuxedo parts. "Pull your pants up!"

"Will you marry me?" he asked.

"This is blackmail!"

"I'll take what I can get. Do you want to see the man you love hauled off to the hoosegow, his reputation in tatters?"

"You idiot!" Whitney began to laugh. "Do I have to go live on your farm? Can't we buy a house where I can still send out for pizza?"

"I suppose that point is negotiable," he conceded.

"And do I have to agree to set down five-year plans?" she pressed. "I'd feel like some Russian peasant."

"I don't suppose we need to get that precise about it." Jonas remained sitting where he was, although the night air was beginning to chill his bare skin.

"And that business about our life-style and friendships," Whitney pushed on. "Are you going to restrict who I can associate with?"

"I positively refuse to entertain convicted felons in my home," Jonas teased, then added quickly, "with the exception of former peace protesters, environmental activists and—did I leave anybody out? Oh, animal rights activists."

"And fortune-tellers," Whitney added.

"Right. With the exception of mystics, soothsayers and psychics," he agreed.

"Well, okay," she said.

"Then you'd better give me back my tuxedo." He stooped up and brushed sand from his legs. "I'm going to need it for the wedding."

She opened her mouth as if to protest, then closed it again. "Oh, well, I suppose it won't hurt to have a conventional wedding."

He pulled up and secured his pants before leading the way up the steps. "You had in mind perhaps something during lunch hour at the pizzeria? We could take orders as we trot down the aisle."

Whitney gave him a shove as they reached the landing. "Did I ever tell you sarcasm was one of your worst faults?"

His arms stopped her as she turned the key in the lock. "I'm not going to let you out of this, Whitney. You're going to marry me if I have to parachute out of a plane to say my vows. Got that?''

''I got that, Jonas,'' she whispered as his mouth closed over hers.

THEY LAY IN BED, aglow with the aftermath of lovemaking. Jonas reached over and picked up the guitar he'd brought down from Sonoma.

''What are you doing?'' Whitney murmured

''Writing a song.'' He strummed chords thoughtfully, then began to sing.

Lady Grey, won't you stay
Don't you ever go away.

Something came back to him that Michael had said about his marriage to Sarah, about having to learn when to lead and when to follow.

Hold my hand, show the way,
Never leave me, Lady Grey.

He sighed and set down the guitar. ''Not very original, I'm afraid. I guess I just wasn't cut out to be a songwriter.''

''No, but you can't be good at *everything*,'' Whitney teased. A languorous feeling of satisfaction was washing through her veins.

''I'm glad to know I meet with your approval in other areas.'' He bent over her tenderly. ''You won't change your mind, will you? About marrying me.''

''Never.'' Whitney smiled to herself. Did she dare confess what she was thinking? But if she didn't, then she wasn't being completely honest. And whatever she demanded of Jonas, she had to be willing to do herself. ''Actually, out there on the beach, I was surprised to find how concerned I was about what people might say.''

"Turning conservative on me?''

"Not entirely.'' She reached up to touch his cheek. "But I guess I'm not as much of a rebel as I used to be.''

"Don't lose it entirely,'' he warned. "I might get bored.''

"Not likely.'' Whitney lay back, her mind drifting. "I want to have a baby—well, maybe not right away, but soon. Maybe even a big family. Linette and Kip are so cute.''

"I hear babies are a lot of work,'' Jonas cautioned.

"I won't mind,'' Whitney said dreamily. "They'll be so darling, it'll be worth it. Is that okay?''

"However many kids you want,'' Jonaes promised. "And wherever you want to raise them. As long as it has indoor plumbing.''

At that moment, Whitney didn't think she could ever ask for anything more.

Epilogue

"She's just *got* to be home!" Whitney muttered to herself, letting the phone ring for the seventh time before slamming it into the cradle. "Oh, Maria, where are you when I need you?"

"Mommy! Mommy!"

Hank and Hannah were pulling at her pant legs, both of them snuffling through runny noses.

"Are you two ready to take your medicine?" Wearily Whitney bent down and reached for the bottle of cold medicine. Immediately the twins darted away through the kitchen and into the den, where Hank climbed onto the sofa and grabbed at the window shade, which promptly snapped upward. Hannah snatched up two pieces of a puzzle and raced away with them, no doubt to lose them forever.

"I can't stand this!" Whitney sank into a chair, rubbing her temples. She'd hardly slept last night for the twins' fussing, and Hank had spat up all over the crib the last time she tried to give him his medicine.

Not only that, but the house was a mess. It had seemed like a good idea, buying a two-story house right on the beach in Corona del Mar. Whitney hadn't counted on the fact that the twins would track sand all over everything, usually five minutes after she'd finished vacuuming.

Why had she thought it so delightful when the doctor told her she was going to have twins? Why had she cooed over them eighteen months ago, the first time she saw them lying side by side in the nursery?

In all honesty she had to admit she still thought they were adorable, at least when they weren't sick. And just recently they'd begun spontaneously running up and hugging her, usually around the kneecap, and chattering away in a delightful mixture of words and gibberish. But then there were days like today.

If only someone had warned her that it wasn't just a question of a few problems now and again, the way the books made out. If only someone had prepared her for the fact that no sooner had the kids gotten big enough to sleep through the night than they began teething. And for the fact that early walkers had a knack for climbing up on chairs and finding those vases and other fragile items she'd thought were safe.

Maria and three-year-old Linette had been Whitney's comfort, reminding her that kids did after all grow up, and that there were really a lot of joyful moments—those first words, the emergence of personality quirks, the sleepy "Night-nights" and kisses at bedtime.

But Maria wasn't home today. And the twins had colds and refused to take their medicine. And Jonas was off at Brite Cola, communing with other adults while Whitney sat here going out of her mind.

Snap out of it. It isn't so bad.

Holding onto the thought that colds didn't last forever, Whitney managed to corral the twins, pen them in their respective cribs and squirt medicine down their throats. Handing them each a bottle of milk, she slouched away toward the bedroom.

Time for a nap.

The house was, amazingly, quiet, and Whitney felt her body begin to relax. Sleep crept over her slowly. *Ah, blessed release...*

The doorbell rang.

She tried to ignore it, but someone pressed the buzzer again, and she was afraid the kids would wake up. *Darn it,* couldn't people read the No Solicitors sign?

Grumbling aloud, Whitney made her way downstairs.

"Hi!" Standing on her doorstep was a pair of clowns. No, those weren't clowns, that was Tom and Mimi.

"Oh." Trying to summon enough energy to be gracious, Whitney opened the door. "The kids are asleep."

"We'll be quiet," Mimi promised as she and Tom prowled into the living room. "Wow! I like this place." She indicated the curving open staircase. "It's gorgeous."

"It's awful." Whitney indicated the child gates at both ends of the steps. "I never thought about toddlers when we bought it. "Coffee?"

The mimes nodded, so she went to fetch it. After all, she hadn't seen Tom and Mimi since they'd moved to Hollywood, although she and Mimi still talked on the phone occasionally.

The clowns followed her into the kitchen. "We've got a regular spot on *The Karl Kauer Show* now! Thanks for the introduction, Whitney," Mimi said.

She waved her hand airily. "The least I could do. I'm glad it worked out."

"You know, Carol's going to have a guest spot next week," Tom added, taking a stool at the breakfast bar and moving a high chair out of the way.

"Good." Might as well make the best of things; obviously, there would be no nap today, Whitney mused as she pulled out a jar of chocolate chip cookies. "Help yourselves." She tried to resist joining them, well aware that her waistline wasn't what it used to be, but she was too tired to deny herself.

The mimes kept her amused, but they served to remind Whitney of how constricted her life had become.

Everyone else seemed to be blooming. Carol's son Jimmy was married now, and her daughter Gini was in college. Sarah, Michael and Kip were spending the summer in England, where Sarah was working on a novel set during the Regency period. Gavin and Maria had expanded to a chain of three restaurants featuring home-style cooking, while Lina and her husband Arkady had just bought a home on the Riviera.

Whitney reached under the counter for a tissue and blew her nose. She'd awakened with a sore throat this morning, and it looked as though she was picking up the twins' cold.

She wondered what all those news photographers would think if they could see her now. Her wedding had been ballyhooed across the country, in spite of her attempts to keep a lid on things. It had been a traditional church wedding, except for the fact that Whitney insisted on having Sarah and Maria as co-matrons of honor, an innovation that Jonas accepted with good grace. The next week, Whitney's shining face beneath the white bridal hat had graced the cover of *People* magazine. She wondered idly what the public would think now if they saw her red-nosed and bleary-eyed, and had to smile at the thought.

"Be sure and watch us!" Mimi finished describing their role on the show as neighbors of Karl's.

"I guess we should go," Tom added. "We're down here for a party this afternoon, raising money for cancer research. I'm surprised you're not involved with it, Whitney. Didn't you used to do this kind of thing?"

"I used to do a lot of things," she agreed. "Thanks for stopping by."

Although it had been fun to see them, Whitney was relieved when the mimes left. Maybe she could still sneak in a half hour's rest....

"Bottle!" squalled Hannah from upstairs. The cry was quickly picked up by Hank's almost identical soprano.

It could be worse, Whitney told herself as she trudged over to the refrigerator. They could have chicken pox instead of colds.

But somehow she was sure that would happen one of these days, too.

"WHAT DO YOU MEAN, you don't want it?" Whitney glared at Hannah, who was pushing away the plate full of chop suey. The last time she sent out for Chinese food, the twins had adored it.

"Yuck." Hank made a face and reached to dump his plate onto the floor. Whitney set an Olympic record in leaning across and grabbing, and just managed to beat him to the punch.

She gazed longingly at the clock. Jonas should be home soon, and at least his presence would distract the twins for a while.

"Cracker," said Hannah.

"Cracker! Cracker!" Hank sent up a chorus and began rocking his high chair.

"You guys are not getting away with crackers for dinner again," she pronounced, then decided it wasn't worth a fight. "Okay. But you've got to eat something else with it."

Wearily, she slogged over to the counter and began spreading crackers with peanut butter and applesauce. At least the kids ate these, although they managed to smear peanut butter and applesauce all over the kitchen in the process.

After delivering the crackers, Whitney sat down again and tried to meditate herself into serenity, but it simply wasn't working. She thought back to the baby products show where they'd been pursuing Carol, to the mother with triplets. What had she said? That there were days when she would have run off with King Kong?

Well, I wouldn't quite do that, Whitney decided, *but then, I've only got two.*

"All done!" pronounced Hannah.

Whitney examined the wreckage on their plates and decided they'd eaten enough to keep a flea alive, or a toddler. It hadn't been long ago that they'd wolfed down everything she fed them, but lately they'd gotten to be picky eaters. And they now refused to let her spoon-feed them anything, so they could only eat what those grubby little mitts could manipulate.

She rinsed off two washcloths and made a few passes over their hands and faces. "All right." She lifted them both down, wondering how they'd managed to get so heavy when they ate so little.

Hank ran over to the refrigerator and pounded on it, shrieking at full volume, which meant he wanted a bottle of milk.

Before Whitney could respond, the front door clicked open. Shouting "Daddy! Daddy," the twins pelted into the living room.

Leaning against the refrigerator, Whitney listened to Jonas's deep voice saying, "Well, who have we got here? Is that Hannah? Hank, what happened to your nose? Oh, there it is!"

In spite of her exhaustion, she smiled. Jonas was a wonderful father. She would never forget the look of pure joy on his face the first time he saw the twins, all red and wrinkled as they'd been. And she suspected he'd even surprised himself, the way he'd turned into an expert at diaper-changing and bottle-warming.

"Hi." He emerged into the kitchen, a toddler clutching each hand. "How are you holding up?"

"Whoever invented colds must have been a sadist." Whitney gestured toward the table. "Hope you don't mind takeout."

"Smells terrific." Jonas released the children and began fixing two glasses of iced tea. "Wait till you hear—"

Hank was banging on the refrigerator and shrieking again. Whitney got out two bottles of milk and led the toddlers into the den, where she turned on a tape of *Sesame Street*. That usually was worth five or ten minutes of peace, at least.

"Hear what?" she asked as she joined Jonas at the table.

"That new public relations firm Mona found has come up with a terrific promotion!" Jonas's glowing eyes lighted up the kitchen. Although he'd just turned forty, he looked younger than ever. "You're going to love it."

Late-afternoon sunlight streaming through the window traced the planes of his face. He'd softened somewhat over the past three years, or perhaps that was because he'd gained a few needed pounds from Whitney's cooking. She'd actually turned out to be a fairly good cook, when she had time.

Suddenly hungry, Whitney downed a mouthful of Chinese food before responding. "Tell me!"

"Well, you know we're focusing on Mona's project." Their no-longer-new chief executive had hit upon the novel idea of introducing a Brite Kids line, featuring cola bottles shaped like cartoon characters. "So naturally they suggested an ad campaign featuring children."

"Mmm-hmm." Whitney ploughed through her food, well aware that the twins would be dashing back in at any moment.

"The theme's going to be, 'Brite kids have twice the fun.'"

"Sounds good," she mumbled through her egg roll.

"You haven't heard the best part." In his excitement, Jonas had barely touched his food. "They proposed a series of commercials starring none other than Whitney, Hannah and Hank Ameling!"

"Huh?" The names did sound familiar. Then realization dawned. "You mean, they want *me* to be in the commercials? And the twins?"

"It's perfect." Jonas didn't seem to notice her shock. "The public already knows who you are, and the magazines have been begging for interviews since you had the twins. It's about time you came out of retirement, don't you think?"

"Yes, but—" Whitney didn't know where to begin. "I've got to be at least fifteen pounds too heavy for TV."

"So you'll lose it," Jonas said. "I figure we could shoot right here on the beach—you know, the carefree family having a picnic with Brite Kids cola, that sort of thing."

"You're joking," Whitney said hopefully. "Is this April Fool's Day?"

"It's August," he reminded her. "Whitney, you of all people ought to recognize a brilliant public relations gimmick."

Torn between laughter and tears, she dropped her wooden chopsticks into the rice. "Jonas, it's preposterous." From the other room, she heard the beginnings of a quarrel. No doubt the twins both wanted to play with the same toy at the same time, as usual. Even when she bought two identical toys, they would fight over one of them. "Maybe I'd better—"

His hand on her arm stopped her. "They'll work it out. Whitney, why is it preposterous?"

She sank back onto her chair. "Because I'm not super-woman, that's why!" The strain of a near-sleepless night and a long day showed in her voice, but she didn't care. "Jonas, do you have any idea what my life is like now? I'm about as glamorous as a mud puddle!"

"Are you kidding? You've never looked more beautiful." He grinned. "Whitney, we weren't planning to stuff you into a sequined gown to wear on the beach, you know."

"Jonas, I don't have the energy!" She hated to douse his enthusiasm, but she had to get through to him. "I can barely drag myself around by the end of the day. How do you think I'm going to take care of the house and the twins and star in a series of commercials? I'd have to be out of my mind even to try!"

Jonas's face settled into what Whitney privately thought of as his Logic Lines, and she knew that something perfectly reasonable and intensely infuriating was about to issue from his lips.

"Why didn't you say so before?" He reached across the table and caught her hands. "Whitney, we have lots of options. We can hire a housekeeper—"

"I don't want some stranger bringing up my kids!"

"Don't give me that. You refused to have a cleaning lady even when you were single," he pointed out. "You just feel guilty, as if you'd be exploiting somebody by having them do your housework."

"And wouldn't I?" But Whitney realized her voice didn't have quite the conviction she would once have mustered.

"If there's something demeaning about housework, that means there's something degrading about being a house-wife, and neither you nor I believe that," he pointed out.

So calm, so sensible. She wanted to dump a plate of stir-fried pork over his head.

"Besides which, if you were willing to consider moving to Sonoma, Lupe's an old friend, certainly not a stranger!"

"No!" True, the few weeks they spent on the farm every now and then were a tremendous relief, but Whitney didn't want to live there full-time. "Anyway, having a maid, that sounds so snobbish. Not for a man, I suppose, but—well, I don't want people to think I've turned into a yuppie!"

He just sat there looking at her, which forced Whitney to think over what she'd said. *And darn it,* she was beginning to think he might be right.

"I guess I'm not the Counterculture Kid any more, huh?" From the den came the reassuring click of blocks being stacked. "Oh, Jonas, I thought I'd given up that silly self-image I had, of being a breezy young girl who could handle anything. But I just traded it in for being the all-capable Earth Mother, and I guess I'm not that, either."

"Is there anything wrong with being normal?" he asked gently.

"I just—" A great crash stopped her. "Oh, no!"

"Stay there." Jonas vanished into the den. "Hank, no! You know you're not allowed to push the furniture around!"

A wail followed, and then the sound of Jonas trundling the twins upstairs. From where she sat, Whitney could picture everything that ensued from Jonas's monologue and the children's chatter as he diapered the toddlers and put them into their pajamas, then sat reading to them from *Peter Rabbit*.

At last the tinkling of the night-night music box wafted downstairs, and was followed by Jonas himself.

Back in the kitchen, he washed his hands and dried them on a paper towel. "Now," he said. "You've got to stop taking the whole burden on yourself, Whitney. You need a life outside this house."

"I don't want my kids raised by someone else!"

"Not even me?" he asked. "Don't forget, I'm part of this team, too."

"Well, sure, but..." Resting her chin on her palm, Whitney wondered how she'd ever managed to win over this marvelous man. At the same time, it occurred to her that, for all her insistence on being his equal, she'd never really given up the image of him as being older and wiser.

Well, he *was* older and maybe a little bit wiser, but he was also her husband. And he was right. She had been trying to take on too much when it wasn't really necessary.

For the first time in hours, Whitney smiled. "You know what?"

He began making coffee. "No, but I'd love to."

"I just realized I've been protecting myself." Whitney automatically began scraping his plate onto hers and stacking them. "I mean, I gave up a lot of the madcap heiress stuff and carved out this new territory. Wife and mother. And I didn't want to let you inside, because I was afraid somehow you'd take over. I never wanted to get swallowed up by you, Jonas."

"It works the other way," he pointed out lightly. "It was the whale that swallowed Jonas."

"I'm not *that* fat!"

"Actually, you're not fat at all." He measured sugar into their cups. "I like you this way."

"That's just it," Whitney admitted. "You're a lot more flexible than you used to be. You do seem to accept me the way I am. If you want to spend more time around the house, that's fine with me."

"Let's forget the coffee." Jonas reached over and flicked off the coffee maker. "I think I'd like to enjoy my husbandly privileges."

"I think I'd like that, too," she said.

It was amazing, Whitney reflected later as they lay in each other's arms, that he could still inflame her the way he used to. Of course, their relationship had gone through changes, and she hadn't always felt responsive during her pregnancy and immediately afterward, but Jonas had understood. And now there were times when she felt even lustier than she had before.

That might be, she admitted to herself, because she could let go freely now. Their lives really had merged, these past few years. She hadn't lost her identity or her individuality. In fact, in some ways, she'd just begun to find herself.

"I love you," Jonas murmured sleepily.

"Me, too." She lay there for a while, listening to his regular breathing. "Hey—are you asleep?"

"I don't think so."

"I've been thinking about what you said." Whitney reached over and massaged his neck. "Making the commercials ought to be fun. And I wouldn't mind giving some interviews. Maybe I could do something for the image of homemakers. I mean, they really get a raw break, people saying things like, 'Oh, you're just a housewife?' and 'You mean you don't work?' as if they sat around all day! And what about the moms who have to go out and work, and then come home and do all the cleaning?"

"Mmph," muttered Jonas.

"Don't you think that's a good idea?" Whitney pressed. "You know how I'm always sticking up for causes. Well, here's one I can really get involved with!"

"Aren't you forgetting something?"

"What?"

"Well, when I offered to help more with the kids, I didn't mean I wanted to take on *all* the dirty work," Jonas pointed out.

"Oh, that." Whitney plumped up her pillow. "We'll have to hire a housekeeper, of course."

"Of course." Jonas began to chuckle.

It took Whitney only a moment to catch the irony of standing up for housewives while hiring a maid herself

"But I mean, I know what they're going through! It's a good cause, Jonas."

"You're special, Whitney," he said.

She burrowed under the covers and rubbed her toes against Jonas's. "You, too."

"Even if you are crazy."

"It's what you married me for," she said.

For once he didn't argue.

Harlequin American Romance

CAPERS AND RAINBOWS
by Jacqueline Diamond

Don't miss the book in which Whitney Greystone first burst upon the scene as a flighty heiress who took over her family-owned Brite Cola company and ran into trouble with its CEO, Jonas Ameling.

Find out how Whitney led her former fiancé, Michael McCord, and Sarah Farentino, the woman who later became his wife, on a merry chase up and down the California coast. Their fun-filled story is told in #218 *Unlikely Partners*.

Harlequin American Romance

COMING NEXT MONTH

#273 TAYLOR HOUSE: CLARISSA'S WISH
by Leigh Anne Williams

Clarissa Taylor Cartwright was determined to rebuild the family home. But architect Barnaby Rhodes's terms were unusual. Make Clarissa fall in love with him. Don't miss the final book in the TAYLOR HOUSE trilogy.

#274 A FINE MADNESS by Barbara Bretton

Billionaire Max Steel's Florida island was so secure that even he couldn't come and go as he pleased. While Kelly plotted to rescue him, he and an island of PAX operatives plotted a riskier mission. A mission that was destined to make heroes of Kelly and Max—if it didn't kill them first.

#275 GIFTS OF THE SPIRIT by Anne McAllister

Chase Whitelaw wanted a wife and family—but he wasn't prepared to give Joanna another chance to fill the role. Five years ago she had left him at the altar; now she wanted back in his life. But this time, was *he* ready?

#276 WISH UPON A STAR by Emma Merritt

Along with her three children, Rachel March was finally making it on her own—until Lucas Brand demonstrated his devastating tenderness and Rachel realized she was up against a master. How could she resist the irresistible—and more importantly, did she even want to anymore?

**There was no hope in that time and place
But there would be another lifetime . . .**

---

*The warrior died at her feet, his blood running out of the cave
entrance and mingling with the waterfall. With his last breath
he cursed the woman. Told her that her spirit would remain
chained in the cave forever until a child was created and born
there.*

So goes the ancient legend of the Chained Lady and the curse
that bound her throughout the ages—until destiny brought
Diana Prentice and Colby Savagar together under the influence
of forces beyond their understanding. Suddenly each was
haunted by dreams that linked past and present, while their
waking hours were fraught with danger. Only when Colby,
Diana's modern-day warrior, learned to love could those dark
forces be vanquished. Only then could Diana set the Chained
Lady free. . . .

Next month, Harlequin Temptation and the intrepid Jayne
Ann Krentz bring you Harlequin's first true sequel—

DREAMS, Parts 1 and 2

Look for this two-part epic tale, the

Temptation

"Editors' Choice."

Harlequin Temptation dares to be different!

Once in a while, we Temptation editors spot a romance that's truly innovative. To make sure *you* don't miss any one of these outstanding selections, we'll mark them for you.

EDITOR'S CHOICE

When the "Editors' Choice" fold-back appears on a Temptation cover, you'll know we've found that extra-special page-turner!

THE

Temptation

EDITORS

ATTRACTIVE, SPACE SAVING BOOK RACK

Display your most prized novels on this handsome and sturdy book rack. The hand-rubbed walnut finish will blend into your library decor with quiet elegance, providing a practical organizer for your favorite hard-or soft-covered books.

Only $9.95

Approximately 16" x 8" when assembled

Assembles in seconds!

To order, rush your name, address and zip code, along with a check or money order for $10.70* ($9.95 plus 75¢ postage and handling) payable to *Harlequin Reader Service*:

Harlequin Reader Service
Book Rack Offer
901 Fuhrmann Blvd.
P.O. Box 1396
Buffalo, NY 14269-1396

Offer not available in Canada.

*New York and Iowa residents add appropriate sales tax.

BKR-1A